THE DEATH PANEL

THE
DEATH
PANEL

MURDER, MAYHEM, AND MADNESS

EDITED BY CHERYL MULLENAX

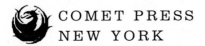

COMET PRESS
NEW YORK

THE DEATH PANEL

A COMET PRESS BOOK

The stories in this anthology are works of fiction. People, places, events, and situations are the products of the author's imagination or are used fictitiously. Any resemblance to an actual persons, living or dead, events, or locales is purely coincidental.

The Death Panel copyright © Comet Press, 2009
"Lipstick Swastika" copyright © Randy Chandler, 2009
"Blood Sacrifices & The Catatonic Kid" copyright © Tom Piccirilli, 2009
"What Makes an Angel Cry" copyright © Kelly M. Hudson, 2009
"The Neighbor" copyright © Brandon Ford, 2009
"The Name Game" copyright © Scott Nicholson, 2009
"Fly by Night" copyright © Tim Curran, 2009
"Detail" copyright © Fred Venturini, 2008
"Parental Guidance" copyright © Simon Wood, 2009
"Rindelstein's Monsters" copyright © David Tallerman, 2009
"The Hooker in the Backseat" copyright © Erik Williams, 2009
"The Mouth" copyright © John Everson, 2000
"Nine Cops Killed For A Goldfish Cracker" copyright © David James Keaton, 2009
"Board The House Up" copyright © Zach Sherwood, 2009

"The Mouth" was originally published in Delirium Magazine, January 2000

ISBN: 978-0-9820979-9-1

Comet Press website address: www.cometpress.us

FIRST COMET PRESS TRADE PAPERBACK EDITION, NOVEMBER 2009

CONTENTS

LIPSTICK SWASTIKA

Randy Chandler

Miami, 1950

Twilight Towers. 4D.

TRENCH STOOD IN THE CORRIDOR and eyeballed the lipstick swastika on the door. He reached for a grenade that wasn't there, his madcap impulse to open the door and blow up a lost nest of Nazis. Instead, he knocked on the door and then waited with hands jammed in the pockets of his pleated trousers.

The bolt clacked back and the door opened inward to reveal a buxom blonde in her early thirties, Veronica Lake hairdo and striking blue eyes. A white silk dressing gown that would've looked slinky on someone with a slenderer figure.

"Hotel security," Trench said. Then he aimed a finger at the red swastika and said, "You know anything about that?"

The woman looked at the lipsticked graffito and frowned. She muttered a curse in German, then turned her flashing eyes on him. "I want that removed. Immediately!"

He gave her a little nod. "Any idea who did it?"

"No. The world is infested with fools and malcontents."

"True enough," he said, noting the deep frown lines bracketing her mouth. "You *are* German, right?"

"Naturally. But that doesn't make me a war criminal."

"War criminal," he echoed. "That's a funny thing to say."

"Funny?" Her lips curled and thinned. "*Funny?*"

"Yeah. Nobody said anything about a war criminal. Except you."

She seemed to compose herself, crossed her arms over her chest and said, "You are the hotel detective, yes? The dick, as you say?" She pronounced it *deek*.

Trench nodded.

"Then do your job," she said, her accent thickening with emotion. "Find the person who did this and see that it is not to happen again."

She stepped back and slammed the door. It sounded like a gun-shot.

TRENCH SAT ALONE at a table in The Twilight Tavern, nursing an iced glass of ginger ale and thinking about halfway marks. He figured his life was half over, barring fatal disease or a violent end, and here he was in the middle of a century that had already seen two world wars and was ticking toward the next one, what with the Commies in China and Russia raising Red hell and things in Korea just about ready to boil over. At the moment he was halfway through his shift as house dick for Twilight Towers, which he sometimes thought of as the Halfway Hotel because it was about that far from being one of Miami's finest.

The Twilight Tavern was next door to the hotel, and Trench was also responsible for the safety and security of its patrons, most of them being guests of the hotel. He figured a house dick was half a step up from a run-of-the-mill bouncer—not that it mattered. Again with the halfway marks.

He sipped his drink and watched platinum-haired Lola's long fingers stroke the ivories as she coaxed dreamy tinkles from the Steinway. He couldn't look too long at her, not when she was dolled up in that tight sequined evening dress with the low-scooped neckline. A sight like that hit him where he didn't want to be hit, not since he'd come upon that stinking Sicilian field littered with dead German and Italian soldiers so bloated with rot that they sported ghoulish erections. Until he could scrub that obscene picture from his memory, he would be no good to a woman in an intimate way. That sex-and-death combo played hell with romance, zombie cocks standing at eternal attention while his was alive and as limp as a soft-boiled noodle.

He let his peepers drift off lovely Lola. They slid along the bar, pausing a moment to watch a cigarette bobbing on the lips of a chunky bald man talking to a slender woman too young to be his wife, then on they slid, finally coming to rest on the German woman from 4D. She was seated at a table with a handsome young man with slicked-back black hair and a scimitar-shaped scar along the left side of his jaw.

Since finding the swastika lipsticked on her door last night, he'd been keeping closer tabs on the fourth floor in hopes of catching the artist if she—or he—came back for another crack at a vandalistic masterpiece. He'd also checked the guestbook and learned that the German lady had registered as Greta Goff from Peoria, Illinois. You didn't grow an accent that thick in Peoria.

Trench lit a smoke and cocked an ear and tried to catch a snatch of conversation from Greta Goff and her dapper beau, but thanks to Lola's piano playing all he could hear was the occasional bust of the fräulein's honking laughter. From this distance she looked good but Trench had seen her up close, without the paint, and he knew her good looks were in harsh decline. A few minutes later the man got up and headed for the men's room. Trench decided to follow him, flash his house-dick buzzer and brace him for the skinny on his date, but then out of nowhere a small woman in a dark raincoat and black beret was bearing down on Greta Goff, approaching her from behind, and Trench froze, knowing something about her was all wrong. Maybe it was the odd look on her ferret-like face or the way she had her right hand buried in the pocket of the raincoat.

Trench was up and moving, crossing the floor in long strides and reaching out to grab the petite woman's hand as it came out of the pocket with a small-caliber gun. "No," he said softly as he wrapped his other arm around the woman's waspish waist and firmly guided her away from her obvious target. Greta Goff lit a cigarette, oblivious to what was happening behind her.

The small woman's body was stiff with tension but she didn't resist as Trench led her to his table. He took the pistol out of her hand and dropped it in his coat pocket. He planted her in a chair and sat opposite her. She looked at him with wide eyes, as if she'd just come out of a dream and wasn't sure where she was or how she'd got there.

"I'm the hotel detective," he said. "You wanna tell me what that was all about?"

She shot a glance at Greta Goff and said, "The Beautiful Butcher of Auschwitz."

Her accent was European but Trench couldn't precisely place it. She appeared to be in her middle thirties, may have been pretty at one time, but now worry lines marred her face and her eyes were a bit sunken from having seen too much of the world's horrors.

"You were there?" he asked.

She nodded. Her shoulders slumped and random raindrops ran down them. "She murdered my sister. And many others."

"You're sure she's the one?"

"I am sure. Her hair is longer and she has put on the pounds but I am sure. She beat me near to death with a riding crop." She looked at the woman in question. "There is no doubt. That is Gerda von Falk. Murderess!"

"Keep it down."

She nodded and dropped her eyes. "She and Irma Grese were in charge of the female prisoners. They liked to cut off the breasts of the prettier ones. They were Doctor Mengele's whores. Irma Grese was hanged as a war criminal but Gerda von Falk slipped out of Poland. And now, as you see, she is here for the good life. I saw her on the street two days ago and followed her to the hotel."

"And you're going to throw your life away as her executioner?"

"I have no life." She clutched at her small bosom. "No soul. I am like the golem."

Trench waved the waitress over and ordered a double shot of whiskey. He noticed a small man in a dark suit sitting alone at the bar, shooting furtive glances their way.

"Why not call the FBI and let them take her?" he asked.

"Why would they believe me? I am a Polish Jew. I am not yet a citizen here. I have no proof."

"So you were going to shoot her and wait to be arrested?"

"No. I would kill her, then flee."

"That guy over there at the bar with you?"

"My cousin. I live with his family."

"He was your get-away guy."

She nodded.

"Why did you draw that swastika on her door? Didn't you think it would scare her off before you could do her in?"

"I wanted her to know she is not free, I wanted she should taste the fear." She shrugged. "I don't know. Maybe I wanted her to run so I would not have to shoot her."

Trench nodded in the direction of the blond German. "She's not exactly shaking in her boots."

The waitress delivered the double-shot. Trench set it in front of the would-be assassin and said, "Drink that. A toast to your freedom."

"You are not going to arrest me?"

"I should turn you over to the police," he said, "but I won't if you promise you'll forget about killing her. Let me take care of her."

She made a sour face and downed the double-shot. "What will you do?"

"I've got a couple of ideas." He pulled an ink pen from his pocket and slid a cocktail napkin in front of her. "Write down a phone number where I can call you. I'll let you know how it turns out."

She wrote down a number and her first name: Anna.

Trench said, "I'll give back your gun when it's over."

TRENCH WALKED BACK to the hotel and called his friend Morgan at the *Miami Herald*. Morgan was a fact checker and sometimes pulled duty on the paper's night desk. He'd lost an arm at Anzio and worked extra hard to prove he was as productive as any man with two arms.

"I may have a scoop for you," Trench said when Morgan answered.

"What? Did Hemingway get caught stealing hotel towels again?"

"See what you can dig up on the Beautiful Butcher of Auschwitz. Gerda von Falk. If you can find a picture of her, I'll buy you a steak dinner."

"That Beautiful Butcher moniker rings a bell. No, no, that's not right, she was the Beautiful Beast and they hanged that Kraut cooze."

"No, that was the other one. They were like a tag team. The one I want got away. And I think she's a guest here at the Twilight, under another name."

"Holy mackerel, Kingfish! I'll get right on it."

"Good. I don't want this chick to fly the coop before I know for sure."

"What'll you do if it's her?"

"Wring her fucking neck."

Ten minutes later Trench was in room 4D, searching the German woman's belongings. He'd told the kid on the front desk to call the room if the woman showed her face in the lobby. He went through the two suitcases after picking the locks with his penknife and a paperclip. The first one contained nothing but clothing and makeup, but with the second suitcase he hit paydirt: three passports with the same woman's photo but with different names, and a loaded Luger. The passports were damned good forgeries with three different names—none of them Gerda von Falk. Wrapped in black panties was a pristine Luftwaffe dagger, and the feel of silk and steel sent a thrilling current through his crotch.

He put the items back where he'd found them and shut the suitcase. As he was about to leave the room, something under the bed caught his eye. He bent down and picked up a black-leather riding crop and smacked it against his open palm, wondering if it was a souvenir of her Nazi past, a prop for sadistic sex games, or both. He put it back and left the room.

When he returned to the lobby, the night clerk handed him a phone message from Morgan. Trench returned the call. Morgan said he had found one photograph of Gerda von Falk. "It's not a very good shot," Morgan explained. "It's a partial profile and the lighting is bad, but it's all we've got."

"Meet me at the Rod & Reel Grille at eight and I'll treat you to a steak and eggs. And don't forget that photo."

"DON'T SPILL COFFEE on it," Morgan said, "I have to return it to the morgue."

Looking up from the page of newsprint with the photo on it, Trench said, "The morgue?"

"The storage room where we keep all the back issues. Reason I found it so quick's because I remembered the story, the-ones-that-got-away angle."

Trench looked a few seconds more at the photo of the blonde in a Nazi uniform and then said, "I'm pretty sure that's her. I wouldn't bet my life on it, but I'd sure as hell bet hers."

Morgan grinned and said, "Not for nothing do they call you the Twilight Detective."

TRENCH WAS IN THE OFFICE behind the front desk waiting for the FBI agent to come back on the horn when the desk clerk stuck his head in and said, "The lady in 4D just phoned down and said she's checking out a day early. Today. Right now."

Trench motioned the clerk over and handed him the phone. "When he comes back, tell him to get here right away if he wants to nail this Nazi cooze."

Trench took the elevator to the fourth floor and knocked on 4D's door.

The blonde opened the door and gave him a big-eyed stare. She was wearing the same silky gown, but this time her bags were packed, ready to go.

Trench said, "The FBI wants to talk to you, Miss von Falk. Have a seat and we'll wait for them."

Her face showed nothing. Then she smiled and pulled the straps off her shoulders and let the top of the gown fall to her waist, exposing her voluminous breasts. Trench looked at them and froze, feeling as if he were looking down the barrels of a couple of howitzers.

Too late, he realized his mistake. But before he could tear his eyes off her tits, she shot a beefy fist into his face and rocked him with a hard right to his left eye. Then she grabbed his shoulders and kneed his nuts. He went to his knees, nauseated. With a move that would've made a female wrestler proud, she seized him in a headlock and wrangled him into the room, shutting the door with her hip.

He grabbed one of her muscular legs and yanked it upward as he straightened his spine and threw himself backward. They both hit the floor but the woman rebounded quickly, springing to her feet and spinning to kick his face with the ball of her bare foot. Then she grabbed a suitcase and swung it with both hands, the heavy blow ringing his skull like one of hell's lost bells.

He heard suitcase latches snap open and looked up at her through a red haze of dull pain to see her tits and the Luger all pointing at him. Her lips cut a cruel smile. He smiled back, meaning it.

It was nuts but he had a ferocious hard-on. For the first time since he'd seen that field full of dead soldiers with bloated boners, he felt real lust for a woman and had the hard evidence to prove it. He'd taken a few beatings since the war—most recently from Iron Skillet Scarlotti's goon squad—but never with this crazy result. It had taken a sadistic bare-breasted Nazi broad to raise his cock from the realm of the dead.

Trench figured he'd reached one of those turning points people talked about. A freak twist sure to take him to some very dark places if this buxom bitch didn't kill him first. Maybe he felt he deserved punishment for all the Krauts he'd killed or maybe just for surviving the war when so many others hadn't. He knew this wasn't the time to figure it out.

"Hold on," he said. "Look what you've done to me."

He rolled onto his back so she could see the erection tenting his trousers. She cocked a brow.

"I'll make a deal with you," he said. "You take care of this and I'll call off the Feds."

She laughed. It was a dirty laugh coming up from the diaphragm and shaking her breasts.

"I'm not joking," he said. "I told the desk clerk to talk to them while I came up here to stop you. Let me use your phone and I'll call 'em off. Then you and me can settle up. Whaddaya say?"

"What are you saying to me, *take care of this?*" She pointed the pistol at his crotch.

"Make it go away and I'll make sure you get away. Unpack your riding crop. And don't shoot off that cannon or you'll queer our deal and the Feds will nab you."

He stood, picked up the phone and called down to the desk. "Kid, did you talk to that Fédérale?"

"Yeah, but I think he thought I was some crackpot. He finally said he'd send somebody out."

"Call him back and tell him we were wrong about the lady and that she's already checked out."

"But . . ."

"Do it." Trench cradled the phone, unfastened his trousers and dropped them. His cock popped out of the slit in his underwear and pointed at the woman still pointing her pistol at him. He said, "Not exactly a Mexican standoff, but you can see I'm serious about this. Call it a hard bargain."

SHE TORE OFF HIS SHIRT and undershirt, then handcuffed him to the bedpost and worked him over good with the riding crop, each stinging lick pumping up his lust to the point where he could no longer distinguish pain from pleasure. Finally, she peeled her slinky gown off her hips, straddled him and took him inside with practiced ease. She rode him hard, whipping his hip with the crop to urge him on. Her gun was within easy reach on the edge of the bed, and it crossed Trench's mind that she could finish him off with it when the fun was done, but that only added to his twisted excitement.

When the big moment came, Trench felt as if the planet had flung him into the stratosphere, where he hung blissfully suspended, briefly free of worldly concerns and cleansed of wartime sins. Then gravity yanked him back down into the gooey thick of things and the Nazi vixen astride him whipped him mercilessly as she spouted spirited curses in her native tongue.

He stayed hard and she rode him harder, her pelvis and tummy gyrating like a belly dancer's. She whacked his face with the leather crop and all he could do was clench his eyes and grit his teeth. She shouted "Heil Hitler!" Then her eyes rolled up in her head and she brayed like a dying donkey. She went rigid all over as if an iron rod had been jammed up her ass, then she fell forward, breasts flattening on Trench's chest, passion spent.

He thought he should be feeling some kind of post-bang remorse now for having trafficked with the enemy to satisfy his twisted desire, but what he actually felt was grateful relief that his family jewels and scepter were no longer defunct. He wasn't much worried that he was now at the dubious mercy of a sadistic woman notorious for her gleeful practice of genocide. Maybe he was a little worried that he *wasn't* worried. But he was still hard inside her and he was already thinking of an encore performance.

But then the woman sat up, picked up the Luger and a pillow to muffle the shot and put the gun against his head. She smiled, clamped her pussy on his prick and pulled the trigger.

Laughing, she tossed the pillow away and looked at the smoking bullet hole in the mattress next to his head.

"What the hell did you do that for?" Trench shouted.

"I wanted to see if you would shit yourself like a scurvy Jew."

He drew blood from his tongue to keep from unleashing a long stream of hard-bitten G.I. profanity upon this nutso Axis Sally in the flesh. Instead, he said through clenched teeth, "Well I didn't, did I."

She laughed, clucking like the Queen Kong of hens. Then she got up, walked across the room and dug a deck of cigarettes from her purse and lit one, tossing the mussed tresses of that Veronica Lake hairdo with a heavy air of melodrama as she blew smoke at the ceiling. She sat on the bed and crossed one knee over the other, pursing her lips and blowing on the cigarette's ember. She spit a strand of tobacco off the tip of her tongue and took another drag.

"What shall I do with you?" she asked, blowing smoke in his face.

"Get these cuffs off me and I'll get you out of here. That FBI guy might be curious enough to come nosing around anyway."

She looked at the faded ink of the American flag on his left shoulder. "What did you do in the war?"

"Killed Nazis."

She made a clucking sound with her tongue. *"Die jungen Blumen des Vaterlands."*

"How's that?"

"The young Flowers of the Fatherland." She reached over and stroked his half-mast penis with one hand and blew on her butt's ember again, making it glow red-hot.

Trench began to sweat. He squirmed. The cuffs rattled against the bedpost.

"Let me see what you're made of, Yank." She touched the ember to the root of his cock, the tender spot just above the scrotum. He gritted his teeth and tried not to flinch as the cigarette sizzled his flesh. Amazing as it was, his dick remained rigid.

"Not bad," said the Beautiful Butcher of Auschwitz. She took another drag off the butt, then dropped it on the carpet. "Now I will make my mark on you so that you will not forget me."

She opened a suitcase and dug out the Luftwaffe dagger. Smiling as she unsheathed it, she sat on the edge of the bed, smoothed the hairs on his chest with her empty fingers and then set to work with the dagger, cutting a line in the flesh above his left nipple. Trench sucked wind through clenched teeth. He didn't try to fight the knife. The pain was sweet and he figured he had it coming for fraternizing with this sadistic Nazi cunt.

Couple of minutes later, Trench had a bloody swastika etched in his chest. And a cold-blooded hard-on that refused to flag.

Gerda von Falk chuckled and pressed the dagger's point against the underbelly of his penis. "Your little soldier remains at attention for me, his commander. But I must go now and leave him to his sad little outpost."

"Get these cuffs off and I'll carry your bags."

She lit a cigarette, then said, "I do not think you are as dutiful to me as your little ramrod trooper with the purple helmet. I think perhaps I should leave you as you are as I go to make my getaway."

"I'm going with you," he said, "wherever you're going. I'm done being a house dick."

"You see?" She pointed with the two fingers clamped on her cigarette at the bloody swastika on his chest. "I have marked you and you are mine. Like a Jew, yes?"

"Yeah, yeah, I see. Take me with you." As soon as he said this, he realized it was something a woman might say. *What the hell's wrong with me?* But he knew the answer. Something *had* been wrong with him but this witch had worked her evil magic and now he was cured. Did he actually want to go with her or was he just playing out the string to make sure she didn't leave him cuffed to the bed for the housekeeper to find? He wasn't sure. Not yet.

With an unreadable expression on her face, she keyed the cuffs open and he was free. Completely free. It was the freedom of not having a plan, of not knowing what you were going to do until it was done. Trench was amazed at how liberating this was. He could make things happen or he could let them happen. Either way, he was alive, and that was reassuring. He was more than a walking corpse with a hard-on. He was still in the game, and no matter how twisted it got, the game was only for the living.

She tossed him a towel. He blotted blood from his stinging new swastika while she got dressed. Ten minutes later he was carrying her two suitcases as they stepped off the elevator and into the lobby. He ignored the puzzled looks his battered face drew from the desk clerk and patrons. He kept his eyes glued on his blond companion's back as he followed her outside and into the hotel parking lot. He was subservient to her; it was right that he should walk behind her. And it offered a nice view of her undulating ass cheeks.

The car was an old Packard and she said he could drive. He put the suitcases in the backseat.

"Where to?"

"West. To California." The way she pronounced the state's name, it conjured mental images of forbidden forms of fornication.

They smoked in silence and soon they were outside the city, the Floridian flatlands drawing them toward the promise of landscapes less monotonous.

"I think you are a secret Jew," she said as she tossed her cig's butt out the window.

"How's that?"

"Maybe you don't have the Jewish blood but you are weak, submissive. Like the Jewish vermin we exterminated. No fight in you. You cower and piss yourselves like docile dogs."

He balled his fist and threw a crazy roundhouse left against the side of her head. Her head bounced off the passenger door, and the car swerved and just missed dropping a wheel into the roadside ditch. He hit her again to make sure she was out like a refrigerator light with the door shut.

That was when he knew he'd reached the end of his tether. He felt it and understood. It felt like a rubber band was attached to his belly, an invisible umbilical band that had let him get just this far and was now ready to snap him back to reality, back to his Twilight life.

Her eyes were half open, glazed and unseeing. Trench got the cuffs out of a suitcase and hooked her to the metal frame under the seat. Then he drove ten miles to a hick town with one traffic light and bought a garden hose and a roll of duct tape from a hardware store. Whenever the Kraut opened her eyes, he socked her jaw and put out her lights again. After the third punch, she didn't open them anymore.

Ten minutes later he was driving along a dirt road into a shadowy backwoods jungle. He pulled over at a small clearing. Black dirt salted with white sand. Lush vegetation surrounding. The woman's head bobbed. She moaned. Fluttered an eyelid.

Trench shut off the motor, got out and set to work with his hardware-store purchases. He stuck one end of the garden hose into the exhaust pipe and secured it with duct tape, making sure the seal was good. Then he ran the other end of the hose through the narrowly opened rear-door window of the Land Cruiser. He used duct tape to make the window as airtight as possible, then he slid behind the wheel and cranked the engine.

The woman looked at him with heavy-lidded eyes. She mumbled something in German.

Trench grabbed her purse and rummaged through it until he found her tube of bright red lipstick. He scooted next to her and drew a swastika on her forehead and then, as an afterthought, he drew another one on her mouth so that the four angled arms of the hated symbol surrounded her pouty lips.

Already the exhaust fumes were filling the car, burning his eyes and making him cough. He slid out and shut the door. He looked up at the thunderheads piling up in the east and said, "Jesus? Tell me not to do this."

Thunder rumbled, sounding too much like distant artillery.

Gerda von Falk was coming to now, coming to the realization that the end of her life was at hand. She rattled the cuffs and began shouting, first German, then in English. Thunder hammered the earth and sky, coming on like well-placed artillery rounds.

"Speak now, Lord, or to hell with her," Trench said to the sky. "And you know I don't speak thunder."

He watched the light leave the sky. He listened hard. Looked for signs and wonders.

Nothing.

He looked at Gerda von Falk sitting in a glassy cube of smoky exhaust. "God forgive us both," he said. Then he started for the highway.

Half a mile down the dirt road, he stopped, turned around and went back to the car. He knew he had to see it through as witness, knew he was bound by the executioner's unwritten code. He owed it to all those dead Jews and gypsies and to all the innocents mutilated and mangled by the mad Nazi doctor and his murderous bitches.

She was coming undone fast, suffocating in the devil's cloud of unmaking. She'd yanked against the cuffs so hard that her wrist was ripped raw and bleeding, her shoulder dislocated. Her blouse had popped buttons and her bra was full of vomit. A thick string of puke hung from her lips, which were going blue. She gasped for air like a decked grouper. She went fish-eyed as her brain no doubt began to die in a haywire shower of panicked thoughts and maybe even fear of divine retribution. She would be pissing and shitting herself by now.

Trench lit a smoke and watched her die. He ached in a hundred places and that was good. It was right that he should. It was the way of the world. You bought your ticket with suffering, and dead or alive you took the ride. He didn't know where *he* would end up but he knew it didn't much matter.

He was doing the Lord's work or the devil's. As things now stood, it didn't make a hell of a lot of difference which. Either way he was damned.

In halos of lightning, storm-cloud angels played hell on heavenly kettledrums. Then came the roaring downpour and the Nazi bitch was gone for good.

Trench walked away in the rain.

BLOOD SACRIFICES & THE CATATONIC KID

Tom Piccirilli

TWO MOVES FROM MATE Barry the chronic masturbator started pawing at the white bishop like he was choking his chicken and said, "Heya, hey, look there—" I turned in time to see the Catatonic Kid get up off his coma couch and cut Harding's throat with a shiv made from a shard of ceramic ashtray.

Harding the orderly stood 6'3 and went two-thirty of mostly muscle. He didn't go down easy. Arterial spray shot around the intensely white walls of the ward as Mary the Nictophobe started losing her shit. She screamed and sort of danced in place and couldn't even get herself out of the path of Harding's spurting carotid.

I didn't mind watching him go down. He was a rude, rotten son of a bitch who liked to intimidate and humiliate the patients. He had a habit of opening mail and stealing cash or candy bars or whatever appealed to him at the moment. Now he was scrambling on the floor trying to clamp one hand across his slashed throat. But he was so taken by the wondrous and terrifying sight of his own pouring blood that he kept pulling his hand away and staring at the frothing red puddling in his palm.

Harding checked around the room looking for mercy. Our eyes met and he saw I wasn't going to help. I mouthed, *Fuck you, prick.* He glanced up at Barry and, even as he bled out, an expression of disgust crimped Harding's features as he got a look at the unholy sight of what Barry was currently doing with a black rook.

The rest of the nuts, freaks, depressives, hysterics, deficients, and paranoids didn't seem to notice and just kept up with their muttering, hand-wringing, floor-licking, and carrot-waxing. Mary had crumpled trying to rub the blood out of her eyes.

The Catatonic Kid riffled Harding's pockets and snatched his wallet. He unclipped the huge key ring from Harding's belt, drew out Harding's smaller set of car keys from the orderly's back pocket, and even pulled the dripping watch from Harding's wrist. I thought that was going a little far.

Harding croaked, "Please—" and the Kid kicked him in the face.

Harding tried to lever himself to his feet one last time and toppled across the ping pong table. It collapsed under his weight and he lay unmoving atop the crushed net.

The Kid had been in a non-responsive fugue state for the three months we'd been here. He came in the same day I did and both of us were placed into the same group therapy. They tried to snap him out of his unresponsive state by pretending that he wasn't in one. They talked to him, asked questions, waited for answers. I thought the doctors were some ripe stupid assholes.

They finally wised up and dumped the Kid in the community lounge where he'd lay on his coma couch and stare at the ceiling. The other nuts kept clear of him. The doctors and nurses came in and flashed a light in his eyes every so often, tossed pills down his throat, and fed him. He'd eat slowly, hardly ever blinking. They'd wipe his chin and let him lie back down, and the rest of us would pass him by like he was a piece of furniture.

He'd been faking the entire time and I admired the amount of willpower it had taken. Not just to pretend, but to pretend for so long and then still manage to make it all the way back. I knew guys in prison who'd tried to fake insanity so they could get out of solitary or into the hospital wing. Some of them faked it so well for so long they just went crazy.

The Kid knew which key got him out of the ward. He'd been watching, aware, careful. He moved with a certain predator canniness, swift but cautious, with a restrained sense of power. During the nights he must've been exercising, keeping himself fit and sharp.

I followed along behind him, silent in my little baby booty slippers. When he got to the next security station, where Jenkins sat filling out his logbook and helping one of the nurses get medication ready for the patients, the Kid slid along the wall holding his shiv up like he was going to kill them both. I grabbed his wrist and pulled him into an alcove.

He tried to talk but his voice was inhuman, clogged with months of dust. I said, "Not through the front. There's a three-man team at the gate, two in a booth and one patrolling in a truck, and the administrative offices are between you and the door. Besides, Jenkins is a nice guy, not like that fucker Harding."

I let go of his wrist. I could see him thinking about stabbing me with his shard of ashtray. His eyes were red with bridled excitement. He was on the move for the first time in weeks and he wanted to cut loose. The taste of murder was in his teeth. I waited for him to try it.

But he wasn't just cunning, he was smart. He checked the halls and gracefully eased toward the east exit. It opened up onto the back grounds, the landscaper's shed, and the staff parking lot.

I followed him to the door and watched him unlock it and push through. I stayed behind. It was too chancy to shoulder my way into his escape more than I already had. He turned around. I waited. He rushed back.

His voice was returning. He tried a few more words. They didn't sound like English. He spoke again and I recognized what he was saying. "Come on, old man. Let's go."

"Hey," I told him, "I'm here for voluntary committal. I'm depressed, not nuts. Choose one of the other loons for your big breakout."

"Now or you'll get the same thing that bastard Harding did."

"What do you want me for?"

"I might need help along the way."

"How do you know I'll be any help?"

"Because I'll stab you in the heart if you're not."

I had been threatened with a lot of things in my time, but never a shiv made from a ceramic ashtray. I recognized the ashtray too. It was Barry's. I couldn't help picturing him working the clay, squeezing it, getting his hands slippery, and—Christ, I shook my head, I didn't want to think about it. He'd made it for his mother. On visitor's day she'd shown up with the family priest and tried a kind of impromptu exorcism to drive away what she called his "naughty touch demons." They'd given it a real go. The priest calling down the power of the holy spirit, Barry's mother wailing on about the power of Jesus, and Barry turning red and twitching, trying his damnedest to keep from tugging out his mushroom. The Kid must've filched the ashtray while everyone had been watching the show.

The Kid and I crept along the outer wall of the hospital. Jenkins and the nurse would be coming around in five minutes or so to hand out the meds. We didn't have long to get to Harding's car.

The Kid tried the remote unlock and an SUV tweeted. We rushed to it and the Kid tried to hop into the driver's seat. I told him, "Move over."

"What?"

"Let me drive."

"Why?"

It was a good question. I didn't have a good answer. I spun the smoothest lie I could. "Forty years without an accident or a speeding ticket."

"We've got to ram the gate and outrun the security trucks."

Point taken. "I live in town. I know this area. I can lose anyone who comes after us. Can you?"

I knew he couldn't. The Kid was new to the area. "If you fuck up," he said, "I'll kill you."

"I won't."

"Remember what I said."

I started it up and felt the thrum of the engine work into my chest, my hands, the back of my skull. There were only 22k miles on it. She'd been well taken care of. I put it in drive and grooved on the feel of my foot on the pedal. Driving with the slippers was almost like driving barefoot. I hadn't been behind the wheel in three months, the longest period of time since I was fourteen years old, nearly a half century ago. I circled the lot once before heading for the gate. I wished to Christ I'd had time to put on some clothes. The pjs and robe just weren't proper attire for a crash-out.

I centered myself, tamped down my rage, agitation, and impatience and let the cool take me over. The problem wasn't getting through the gate. An SUV had more than enough muscle to break through. I could outmaneuver the security detail in his truck.

The trouble was the state trooper station about three miles up the highway. They'd radio our escape and the staties would catch us in a roadblock or just chase us all to hell until they ran us down.

If we floored it in the other direction we'd wind up in a state park that ran out to a spit of land surrounded by the bay. It would be impossible to hide. The Kid would get nervous and try to take someone hostage. Or he'd make a grab for a boat at the nearby marina, and the water patrol would nab us before we got around the point.

"What are we waiting for?" the Kid said. He held his shiv to my throat.

"I'm working out a plan."

"Just go!"

"That's not a plan."

There was really only one choice. I eased down on the pedal and headed for the gate. No other visitors or employees were heading out, so it was shut. The guards didn't have guns but they did have tasers. They stood in their little booth talking and watching a little television. There was a direct phone line to the staties in there. I didn't gun it. I drove slowly while the Kid got more and more anxious. He liked the throat, it called to him. His eyes were fixed on my jugular. He liked to make a mess and splash blood.

The rage started to climb to the surface again and I pushed it back, not so easily this time. I took deep breaths and pulled up to the booth.

When the two guards showed their faces I smiled and said, "Get the fuck out now."

I put Harding's SUV in reverse, got up some ramming speed, and then floored it.

The guards hung in there until the last second. Maybe they were trying the staties, maybe they were calling in the rest of security from the perimeter and the hospital. They weren't going to have time. I sped towards them. The assholes inside finally realized I was serious. They both dove out the door. I spun the wheel at the last second and hit the booth broadside. It wasn't a paragon of architecture and went over like a kid's tree house. I straightened the SUV out and smashed into the gate. It was thicker than it looked but not by much. The front end of the truck buckled a bit, but we only lost one headlight and the hood stayed clamped down.

The locking mechanism on the gate screeched and the mangled fencing exploded as we went through. I twisted the wheel in order to keep from rolling over, overcorrected and we went up on two tires. I rode it like that for forty feet and we came down on all fours again in the middle of the road. I headed for the highway.

They would call the other security guards first. Then radio the cops. The cops would call in their own cars before informing the staties. It would take an extra four or five minutes. That was enough time to burn right past the trooper station. I got to triple digits and kept punching the engine.

"Jesus, you can drive," the Kid said.

"I've had a lot of experience."

"Yeah? Where?"

"All over."

"You said you knew this area."

"I do. I've lived out this way for a long time."

"Where's a good place to lay low?"

I grinned at him. "I know the perfect spot."

"Where?"

"My granddaughter's place."

"And where's she?"

"Away."

I got off the highway and onto the parkway, heading for the safe house. Things were rolling the right way now. I turned on the radio and clicked in an oldies station. I expected the Kid to give me shit but he kept quiet. We listened to a few crooners, Frankie and Dino, with me humming along.

I jockeyed among the thickening traffic. I took Sunset Highway through Port Jackson. I felt good for the first time in twelve weeks.

"So what are you so depressed about?" he asked.

"I've got issues."

"And what would they be?"

"I've been having trouble enjoying life lately."

"Are you fucking with me?"

"No."

"You sound as if you're fucking with me."

"I'm not."

"You're smiling and singing. I guess you're on the upswing."

"I think maybe I am."

"You're never as full of life as when you're on the edge of death."

"That's as clichéd as they come."

"Maybe," he said, "maybe, but it's true. Don't you feel your heart racing like it wants to bang out of your chest?"

"No."

He got in close. He whispered in my ear. "You're not afraid of me? Of what you just saw back there?"

"No."

"Not afraid of dying either. The way you took out that security shack, we almost rolled, but you kept your head. You didn't panic. Not even when I was this close to cutting your throat."

"No."

He snorted. "You are a lunatic."

"That's a matter of opinion. Tell me something. Why did you take the watch?"

"What?"

"Harding's watch. Why'd you snag it?"

"It's a nice watch."

"But you can't even read the time, his dried blood covers the crystal."

"Who the hell wants to know what time it is?"

He let out a barking laugh. The entire time his voice had been getting stronger. He sounded confident, effectual, his words and laughter resonating. I laughed along with him. He was going to start recognizing sites soon. I circled Port Jackson and went by the supermarket, the high school, the bank, the homeless shelter, the police station, the post office, the jewelry store.

The Kid said, "Where are we?"

"Port Jackson."

"Slow down."

I slowed down. I hung a left and cut into a housing development.

"Go back," he said.

"Go back?"

"Around the block and onto the main road again."

"Why?"

"You do what I tell you, right?"

"Okay."

I drove around the block and let him get his bearings. He nodded to himself. His face broke into a self-satisfied grin. He flipped the oldies station and put on something loud and obnoxious and unbearable. It was just as well. The rage was welling up in me. He was going to cut me soon. It would be a small cut, just to get my attention. Just to prove that he had the capacity, that he was capable. I glanced at my face in the rearview mirror. I'd been cut and beaten before, plenty of times. One more scar wouldn't mean much.

"Thank you," he said.

"For what?"

"Taking me where I needed to go."

"Where's that?"

"Never mind." He looked at me and grinned. It was a warm and amiable smile, the kind that young girls would fall for. "How far is it to your granddaughter's place?"

"A couple miles. We're almost there."

"We have to stop somewhere first."

"Where?" I asked.

"The post office."

"Kid, we're dressed in hospital pajamas, robes, and slippers. Shouldn't we keep a lower profile?"

"Pull over."

"What?"

"Pull the fuck over."

I pulled over. I turned in my seat and said, "Kid, you should listen to me here. If you—"

He reached out and slashed me on the forehead with his little shiv. It was so sharp that I barely even felt it, but the blood immediately began to pour into my eyes. The cut was small but there are a lot of blood vessels close to the skin on your head and any wound will bleed like a bastard.

That's what he'd been counting on. He thought the blood would rattle me. It was an old trick. It was a bad bet. He already knew I kept calm under pressure, but it hadn't mattered. He fell back to type. The Kid was growing edgy. The months of inactivity had worn down his composure. He was getting excited.

I tore the pocket off my pajama top, folded the cloth and held it to the cut. I tied it there with the belt of my robe. I looked at him through the blood dripping off my eyelashes. He was self-satisfied, his eyes alive and bright. Blood had leaked down my chin and smeared across the front of my shirt.

He said, "When I tell you to do something, you do it. You understand me?"

"Sure."

"Let's go."

With the wadded tail of my robe I wiped the blood off my face as best I could and drove over to the post office. He said, "Come on."

"You want me to come with you?"

"Quickly. We're in and out in under a minute. And I don't trust you."

"Take the keys. I'll wait."

"You're still arguing. Should I cut you again?"

"No."

"You'll come with me. Now."

I went with him. We walked in the front door. The employees and the folks buying stamps and mailing letters gasped and squeaked and backed away. I didn't look like a depressive who'd voluntarily committed himself. I looked like a maniac who'd probably killed somebody. The Kid pulled a key out of his pocket and walked confidently towards a PO box. He unlocked it and pulled out a satchel. He couldn't contain himself and let out a giggle.

I thought again of his innate willpower. To swallow the key before he went into the hatch, and then to shit it out and hide it on his person for months, lying there on his coma couch dreaming of the day when he'd get back here.

I glanced up at the cameras in the corners. My face was obscured by the bandage and the belt and the blood. The Kid turned and shoved me out the door. We got back in the SUV and I drove down towards the small house that Emily had rented right on the beach. It was a six month lease, paid up front. She used to lay out in a bikini and sun herself while I jogged along the shoreline.

"What's in the satchel?" I asked.

"None of your fucking business, old man."

The wind was up and the ocean road was obscured with sand and sawgrass. I had to drive over a couple of drifts. The sand spun out from our tires. I pulled into the cracked driveway. The Kid said, "This is it?"

"Yeah."

"It's a total shithole! You let your granddaughter live in a junker like this?"

"It's a bungalow, tucked away on a private beach. A good cool off spot. The cops will drop their search in a couple of weeks. They'll figure we made it out of state."

"Where's your grandkid again?"

"Away."

"She lives here alone."

"Yeah."

I climbed out and opened the garage door. Then I pulled in and parked. He was going to go for my throat soon. We walked into the bungalow through the inside garage door and the Kid said, "Thanks for the ride, old man, but—"

I spun on him reaching out with the shiv to slash me the same way he'd done Harding. I caught his wrist and wrenched it to the left. The snap was loud in the empty house. The opening note of his scream was even louder. I let it ring and ring, a nice tremolo. He dropped the shiv and I punched him in the Adam's apple. He gagged and went to his knees, tears leaking from his eyes. He huffed air. In agony he turned his eyes up toward me and I gripped the back of his head and drove my knee into his face. He flopped onto his back, out cold.

I checked the satchel. All the jewelry was there. It was worth just under a million on the market. Any good fence would take eighty percent off the top. There was no way to clean jewelry except get it out of the country or sell it to private collectors. That's why a professional crew almost never took down a jewelry shop. The return just wasn't worth it. But our team had been small and tight and the payoff was good enough to give it a go.

I showered and shaved and got my own clothes out of the closet. The cut on my forehead wasn't all that bad, it wouldn't even scar. I cleaned it with peroxide and put a tiny band-aid on.

I sat on the couch and looked at the Kid. His nose was pulped, his face mottled, and he was still sucking air through his teeth. He'd been smart and sharp and paranoid, but not paranoid enough. The jewelry score could've been a pretty sweet deal if only he hadn't gotten greedy.

I knew the Kid wouldn't recognize me.

We hadn't been formally introduced. He'd been chosen last minute by Cole as a replacement for Wellington who'd been picked up for flooring it through a yellow light, the prick. He'd had a shootout with the cops and been iced.

I wanted to call the score off, but funds were too low. Emily talked me into rolling the dice. Cole knew somebody who knew somebody who knew the Kid, who was fresh to the coast. Hershaw okayed the replacement.

We still should've moved the plan back a week or two and gotten a feel for the Kid. But there was no time. I'd picked him up and he'd climbed into the car and sat behind me. I'd caught his eyes once in the rearview. I hadn't suspected anything hinky. I'd done my job and driven to the shop and planned on getting us back to the safehouse without incident, where we'd wait a couple of weeks together until the heat was off. Emily and I would lounge around another month or two after that until the end of summer and then split.

I pulled up to the shop and Cole, Hershaw, and the Kid had gotten out. The three of them had entered the place while I kept an eye out for the cops.

My Blackberry rang almost immediately. It was Emily. She wasn't supposed to call. I answered and realized she was sending me video. I watched as the Kid's face filled the screen as he approached her. I could see Cole and Hershaw dead on the floor behind him. The Kid had popped them both in the back of the head with a pipsqueak .22. Up close it was an almost silent kill, I knew.

She had set her own Blackberry aside on the counter and it kept sending footage. I watched him reach out toward her and listened to her squeal in pain. That was him cutting Emily's forehead to get her attention and keep her from hitting any alarm. Then he asked about the jewels. She tried to explain that she was in on the score but he got antsy and slashed her throat. He was fast.

There was nothing I could do but drive away.

If I'd stayed, he would've popped me too. That was his plan all along.

I didn't carry a gun. No driver did.

Someone had hit an alarm. I pulled into the supermarket lot across the square and watched the door. He bolted through two minutes later, still on schedule. He looked around for the car and did a tiny dance of anguish. The police station was less than a minute away. They were already coming.

He'd been smart. He'd planned ahead for contingencies. He'd already taken out a PO box. He ran into the post office and hid the satchel of jewelry and then swallowed the key in case he got picked up. But he had no wheels. There was nowhere to run. He couldn't be caught on the street.

I had to give it to him, he stayed cool. He knew how to adapt and improvise. He took off his jacket and tore a hole in his t-shirt and kicked off his shoes on the way to the homeless shelter across the street. He stepped in the front door just as the cops came around the corner. It all seemed to have been perfectly rehearsed. I kept watch.

I found out the Kid played the crazy card and threw himself on the ground and pretended to be nuts. They shipped him off. I voluntarily committed myself the same day.

And I watched the Comatose Kid.

And I waited.

He rolled over on the floor, grunting in pain. "Aooww."

"You hear me, Kid?"

"Ooowww."

"I'll take that as a yes. Look at me."

He opened his eyes and touched his face and moaned again. "My nose—"

"Don't worry about it," I said. "I was your wheelman."

"What?"

"Your driver. I was your driver. Remember now?"

"You broke my nose."

I sighed. "Focus, Kid. You were a last minute replacement. But we only met in the car. You sat behind me. You killed Cole and Hershaw. You killed the girl."

He cleared his throat. He tried to sit up and couldn't quite do it. "I didn't need partners."

"If you'd followed the plan, you wouldn't have been stuck pretending to be in a coma for three months."

"I didn't mind it."

"And you call me a lunatic. You popped your partners. You cut the girl. You cut her and then you killed her because you like feeling a knife chewing through cartilage."

"I did what I had to do."

"The girl was our inside player. She was the one who got us the alarm codes. She was my granddaughter."

"I didn't know."

"It wouldn't have mattered. You would've done her anyway. And me, if she hadn't sent me the video feed."

"That's why you drove off."

"Yeah."

"And you committed yourself? And waited? In the hospital?"

"Yeah."

"But. But you could've taken me at any time. Why? Why did you wait?"

"I had to make sure you had the key on you," I said. "I wanted the score. I'm a thief."

I kicked him in the face, then slung him over my shoulder and walked out the back door. He didn't have much struggle left in him but he squirmed around and mewled a bit. I marched down the path through the dunes out to the beach. I tossed him down. Emily's chaise lounge was still where it was the last time she'd laid on it, but it was almost completely covered by sand now. I dug it out and there was a pretty sizeable hole left over. I buried the Kid in it and smoothed the sand out and placed the lounge over the spot. I sat down for a while watching the waves roll in.

WHAT MAKES AN ANGEL CRY

Kelly M. Hudson

THEY SAY WHEN YOU SLEEP with a succubus it takes seven years off the back end of your life. I don't know if that's true, but I do know that they're nothing but trouble, and they have a bad habit of turning up when you least expect it.

So when Delilah slunk into my bar and slid over to the counter, smiling pretty and sly, I wasn't so much surprised as I was pissed.

"What do you want?" I said.

"Vodka, on the rocks," she said. Succubi loved vodka. I don't know why. She was eyeing me the entire time; I could feel that hellfire gaze slithering over every inch of my body. She put the mojo on me and I knew it because each spot her eye stared at tingled with excitement. She lingered around my crotch and the buzz was burning me up, but I stayed focused and let my anger lead me through it.

"Now," I said. I made her drink and slid it over to her. "What do you really want?"

"Oh, come on, Billy," she said. She took a sip of vodka, her crimson, pillow lips kissing the glass and leaving perfect lipstick prints. She was gorgeous; there was no doubt about it. Delilah was an old school kind of woman, all hips and curves and cushions up top and behind that promised such comfort that you'd give your soul for a taste. Or seven years of your life. She had black hair when I was with her before and she'd changed it to platinum blonde, but I knew her the second I saw her. There was no fooling me. I knew my old lovers like the back of my own hand.

"Don't be so mean," she said, her cute, pert nose dipping as she spoke. "Can't a girl catch up with a former flame?" She tried to lock eyes with me, get me to stare into those deep brown chasms where a man could drown and thank God for the pleasure while he was dying.

I looked around the bar to break off the stare. It wasn't full, but we were doing some brisk business. I owned a local bar, what folks referred to as a "neighborhood bar," and I wasn't getting rich, but I had a steady clientele and income. I liked it and I didn't want anything to mess it up for me.

Every person was ogling Delilah like starved men staring through a restaurant window. The few women that dotted the place glared, too, drawn in by her beauty. Succubi were like that; it didn't matter if you were man, woman, child, or a goddamn dog. One of them walks into a room and everyone pays attention. It was like that then and I wasn't happy about it.

"You know, they got bars for your types," I said.

"Don't be a jerk," she said. She took another drink and threw her head back and laughed. "I saw your sign at the door. 'No Demons Allowed.' That's kind of racist of you, isn't it?"

"My bar, my rules."

"Then why does Tommy get to hang out here?" she said, her brown eyes, decorated with the longest, darkest lashes you've ever seen, flicking to the corner where Tommy sat, nursing a gin and tonic. Tommy was a demon, sure, but he was also my friend. And a good guy, too. As much as demons can be good.

"You're not here on some social cause," I said. "You want something, so spit it out."

Delilah met my eyes and I have to confess, when she gazed at me I nearly fell to my knees and wept. She still had that kind of hold on me and despite the five years that had passed since we'd last seen each other—five long, miserable years where I promised myself every day that I was over her, that I was through and had moved on—I knew I was still in love with the bitch. Goddamn her.

"Maybe we could go somewhere a little more private," she said, her finger circling the rim of the glass.

"You'd like that, huh?" I went from wanting to bend her over to wanting to jam an ice pick between those pretty eyes of hers. It was like that between us; the classic love/hate thing. And I guessed it always would be that way.

"Not as much as you would," she said. A wicked smile split her face and I went right back to thinking of bending her over again.

"Where's Butcher?" I said. Butcher was her personal assistant, driver, and bodyguard. He was a demon, too, and one of the meanest I'd ever met in my life. His love for his mistress was untouchable, and when Delilah left me long ago and I went after her, Butcher stood in my way. He beat me something pretty good.

Now, you need to understand something here. I haven't owned and run a bar my entire life. I was a boxer once, up to a year before I met Delilah. I wasn't great but I wasn't bad either; won a few, lost some, and I was tough in the ring; like a pit bull when it got its jaws locked on something, I wouldn't quit until I won or was beaten to a pulp. But I didn't really have a future in it; I wasn't going to be a champ and I certainly wasn't going to rise above the amateur circuit I was on. So one day, after having my ass handed to me by a guy nearly half my age, I got out of the business.

I'd saved some money through the whole slog, and after a loan from a neighborhood shark, I got this bar up and running here in Brooklyn. It was a quiet life, and I liked it just fine, being on the fading end of my thirties, gathering gray hair like a migrant worker picks strawberries, and generally having nowhere to go and no place to be.

All that ended when the Big Event happened and my life, like the life of all New Yorkers, changed forever. How to explain the Big Event? It's kinda like teaching a sighted person Braille; you can learn it but you never really get it, not like a blind guy.

One day, the sky above New York City split open and these things fell through the gap. They were thousands of little balls of light, and they floated down from the rift like giant tufts of cotton, swaying gently and coming to rest all over the boroughs. When they landed, the balls of light transformed, taking the outward appearance of entities from a lot of the world religions, becoming demons, angels, gods, and goddesses, with a lot of their attending abilities. And they ghettoized themselves; the demons and Satan took to Brooklyn, the angels took Queens, Allah and his gang got the Bronx, Kabala and whatever the Jews followed started up their operations on Long Island, the Hindus got Staten Island (yeah, I never understood that, either), and Manhattan, well it was sort of a neutral ground, a melting pot, where all the different groups could mix, along with local gods and spirits, indigenous to their neighborhood. Then the rift closed and that was it.

New York had an influx of some hundred thousand or so new resident aliens, and these folks were aliens for real. Or maybe they weren't. Maybe they really were the gods and goddesses that the world knew and loved and maybe even hated. Nobody knew for sure. Lots of theories got tossed around like abused wives. My favorite was that the lights were from another dimension and that when they arrived, they reached into the minds of the residents and took on the forms that could most readily explain their powers and abilities. And also something we'd all be comfortable with.

Anyway, the government had to have their say, like they always do. They drove tanks right down the middle of Manhattan, determined to uproot the illegal immigrants. The only thing was, the beings fought back, and four square blocks of Upper West Side Manhattan got leveled. Now, maybe if the fight had happened in Harlem and it got burned up, nobody would have given a shit. But this was the Upper Crust we were talking about here, and everyone knows that when it comes to the Upper West Side, a homeless guy can't wipe a booger on the sidewalk without SWAT getting called in on the case. So the rich spoke and the government backed off and the aliens settled in, Gods and Goddesses amongst the world of men.

New Yorkers responded like they always did. They bitched and moaned and then shrugged their shoulders and got on with their lives. The entities that came through that hole and made a new life here in New York stayed in New York. For some reason, they never spread out to anywhere else in the world. Some say it was because they were afraid, but I think that they're all stuck here, waiting, hoping that one day that rift will open again and they'll go back to where they came from. Hell, for all I know, they're all a bunch of criminals and they were sentenced to do hard time here on earth. They wouldn't be the first to show up in America with that kind of rep.

In Brooklyn, Boss Satan and his boys set up a whole new mafia-like organization and pretty soon, they were running everything. As to the other boroughs, I can't really say. I got problems enough of my own to pay any attention to those other folks.

Problems like an ex-lover that was a demon turning up on my doorstep.

Delilah sighed and told me that Butcher was outside, watching the limo. "I can call him in if you want," she said.

"No, thanks," I said.

Just then, a scream cut through the tension between us like a car antenna whipping down a highway. I jumped in place, dropping the glass I was holding and Delilah spun, spitting out her drink and calling out for Butcher.

The front doors slammed open and in staggered Butcher, all six foot eight of him. He'd been wearing his typical driver's uniform, a black suit with white button-down shirt and cap. He loved that stupid cap. Butcher was meticulous about his appearance. He polished his shoes every day and dry cleaned his clothes. But when he lurched into my bar that day, there wasn't an inch of him that was clean of anything.

Butcher had been cut open, his chest raw and bleeding. Flaps of his breast skin hung to the side, flopping around as he stumbled forward, held on by the tiniest, strained pieces of flesh. His jacket was gone and the white shirt he'd been wearing was red now, like it had been stitched that way, and his pants were shredded into tatters that matched the slashes on his legs. Blood poured out of seemingly everywhere. He was holding his guts in his hands and they were steaming in the air like a hot plate of spaghetti at a homeless shelter. Did I mention he was screaming? God, it was awful. I felt like at any moment my ears were going to burst and my eyes were going to pop from my head.

Then he fell to his knees, his baby blue eyes locking on Delilah's, a single tear running down his cheek. His mouth opened and shut, a bloody bubble forming between his lips as he tried to speak but couldn't find the voice. Finally, he pitched forward and died, his intestines spilling across my floor, a fart of foam and blood.

Delilah fell to his side, very careful not to get wet or stained with his blood, and touched the back of Butcher's head. He'd been cut open there, too, a chunk of his skull pried away to reveal his glistening, gray brain. She looked up at me, tears in her eyes.

"This is why I'm here," she said.

Boss Satan's men came along and cleaned up the mess. They were the real law out here, so there was no need to call the cops. This was a demon matter, anyway, and it was best they dealt with it.

Delilah hid up in my apartment above the bar and her involvement was never mentioned. One of the demons, a burly fellow that would have passed as a pro wrestler if he wanted that kind of job, asked me pointedly about Delilah. Everyone knew that Butcher was her driver.

"Butcher told me he was coming by to talk to me," I lied. "He told me Delilah wanted to see me and I told him to go get fucked,"

Pro Wrestler gave me a funny look.

"Hey, I fooled around with her once, and that was enough for me," I said, holding my hands up to show my innocence. "You're a demon. Maybe you can handle those succubi better than a human can, but I tell you the truth: those broads are ten times worse than a regular woman."

Pro Wrestler laughed. It was our own private joke between man and demon. Here's something else for you to know: demons, hell, all the creatures that came through the rift that day, they all looked human. If you weren't paying any attention, you couldn't tell them apart from anybody else. But they all had a funny smell to them—a slight undercurrent of cinnamon—and you could see, just by looking at them for more than a few seconds, that there was something different about them.

"What's with the 'No Demons' sign outside," the other demon said. He was smaller than the Wrestler, but he was still bigger than me. He had the body of a dock worker and the brow of an ape man. "You prejudiced?" "Hey," I said. "I got that cleared by Boss Satan. You got a problem, take it to him."

Dock Worker didn't like it and he grumbled under his breath about it to let me know. But there wasn't anything he could do. Boss Satan ran things. And he understood, better than his underlings, that humans and demons needed their own places to mingle without the others getting involved. Besides, he had a regular string of succubi whorehouses and sinful gambling spots that kept everyone mixed and happy. A bar here or there that catered to one clientele over another was no big deal and was, in the end, just good business.

"Don't leave town," Dock Worker said.

"Where do I have to go?" I said, spreading my empty hands even further apart.

It took a couple of hours, but they got the place cleaned up so good it was almost like nothing happened. I closed shop and went upstairs.

Delilah threw herself on me as soon as I stepped through the door. I'd like to tell you I pushed her away, told her to go back to hell, or some other clever line. But I didn't. As soon as that familiar body slid into mine, it was over. We locked together, like we always used to do, like the last two puzzle pieces out of a box that finally revealed the masterpiece being assembled. We weren't a masterpiece, though. We were raw, uninhibited sex. Her groin met mine through our clothes and a heat rose between us terrible enough to scorch old Boss Satan's eyebrows right off. Before I knew it, she had me out of my shirt and was working my chest with her hands and mouth and then my pants were off and she was naked, too, and we were on the floor, pushing against each other, sweating and groaning and going to places I never thought were possible.

I guess I lost another seven years off the back end of my life.

When it was over, we lay on the floor, our bodies a sheen of sweat like we'd been wrestling in oil for a captive audience. I was trying to catch my breath but it was like grasping the wind in the palm of your hand; it was there one moment, gone the next.

She snuggled up next to me, that vixen of fire and brimstone. I hated myself right away for what I'd done and cursed my body for betraying me. It didn't listen. It had its own needs and was quite happy right about then. I decided to ruin the fun.

"Why did you come to me?" I said. "And who killed Butcher?"

She sighed and rubbed her nose against my chest. "I want to sleep," she said.

"No," I said. "I want some answers."

Delilah bolted straight up, anger on her face. She slapped my chest with an open palm, raising a welt. I yelled at her and then she laughed and pulled away. That's how she was. Pleasure one minute, pain the next. She was a demon, after all.

She leaned over to the pile of her clothing and fished through the rumpled garments. Finally, she found a pack of smokes and a lighter. She took one out and plopped it between those two pillows she called lips and lit it up. Delilah took a long drag, letting the smoke sit in her lungs for a minute and twirl. She blew out a plume and looked over at me.

"Someone's been killing all my ex-lovers," she said. "And he's coming after me next."

"You came to me for protection?" I said.

Delilah laughed. It was bitter and rich, like a spoiled cranberry. I have to say, the bark of her snicker cut my heart in two. It was so snide, so arrogant.

"You couldn't help me," she said. "I came to warn you. That's all."

I sat up and slid my pants back on. "Consider the warning given, then."

"Oh, you want me to go?"

"I think it's best."

"So you get a piece of ass and then you kick me out on the street, huh?" she said. She was hurt, I could tell, but she was playing it cool. "What if I don't have anywhere else to go?"

"That's your problem," I said. I got up and walked barefoot across the living room to grab a bottle of whisky. I didn't normally drink much anymore, but I figured this was a special occasion. I got it out of the cabinet, took the cap off, and swallowed a swig.

I looked around. My place was okay, a bit small, but hell, in New York, that was the same story everyone told. I had a good life going. It was quiet and kept to itself, like I'd always hoped for. And now she'd come along, back into my world, sure to ruin everything.

Delilah stared at me as I moved about the place. She smoked her cigarette and watched, not saying a word. Finally, I got tired of being looked at like I was in a zoo exhibit, so I sat on the couch and sighed.

"Why are you still here?" I said.

She thought on it a moment and then spoke between puffs. "Don't you ever wonder why we broke up, Billy?"

"Not really," I said. "You're a demon. And a bitch. I'm human. And a bastard."

"You'd think we'd fit well together, wouldn't you?"

I shrugged.

"We had some good times, didn't we?"

I kept quiet.

"And it wasn't just the sex. We had some laughs, too. But you were always my favorite human when it came to fucking. Did I ever tell you?"

"Cut the crap. I'm tired and I've had a long day. So I'd like to go to bed, if you don't mind."

"You were the best," she said, ignoring me completely. "Still are. But things happen, don't they? People and creatures change. That's why we moved on. You went your way, I went mine."

I took another drink of whisky. At this rate, I was going to be drunk in another five minutes. It was probably for the best.

"Some people, they can't understand that, though, can they?"

"What are you going on about? If you've got something to say, then spit it out," I said.

Delilah stared at me. She wasn't mad, she was just looking. Her brown eyes peered through the swirls of curling smoke that drifted from the tip of her cigarette and circled her head like a wreath.

"I never stopped loving you," she said.

The door exploded open and crashed to the floor. A big blonde guy, the same size as Dock Worker, flew through the opening. He was pale, almost white, thick with muscles, and brimming with power. He had green eyes that burned with hatred, boring in on Delilah with disgust and anger. In his left hand he held a short sword, polished and gleaming in the low light of the room.

"Eddie!" Delilah said. She threw her arms up over her face and screamed.

Eddie stomped into the room, his beautiful face an ugly mask of resentment.

"Fucking bitch!" Eddie said. He swung the sword, the flat side of it slapping Delilah upside her head and sending her tumbling across the room.

I jumped up, dropped the bottle of whisky, and rushed the guy, but I never stood a chance. He was too quick, too strong, and too full of wrath. He swiped me to the side with one brush of his right hand and it was like somebody had taken a concrete block and punched me with it. I fell and crashed into the cabinet, hitting my head pretty hard.

What happened next I saw through a haze.

Eddie pointed at me and screamed at Delilah.

"Is he another one? You're unbelievable!"

"Please," Delilah said. She held her hands up. Blood stained the side of her head where he'd whacked her with the sword, turning her blonde hair crimson. It trickled down over her ear and dripped onto her naked shoulder.

"There is no more please," Eddie said. "There is no more anything, ever again."

He chopped her head off.

It was that quick. Eddie swung the blade and it sliced through her neck and bones and Delilah's head plopped off with a loud pop and then fell to the floor. It landed on the crown of her head and spun in place, upside down next to where her body flopped.

I wanted to scream but, just like Butcher, I couldn't find my voice. I watched through tears and disorientation as Eddie, not satisfied with merely killing Delilah, set about destroying her body.

He used his sword to cut her breasts off, carving each one free and then poking it with the point, skewering them both. He held them up in the air, looking at them, a delighted smile on his face. He swung the sword and the two globs of fat slid off and smacked the wall behind Delilah.

Next, he sliced down her sternum, exposing her intestines and stomach, nudging the contents with the end of his sword like a kid poking a dead rat lying on the side of the street. He studied her organs, his head tilting to the side, that queer smile growing larger by the second.

Finally, he reached her groin. Eddie took the sword and sliced around her vagina, pushing and grunting until he'd carved it out, a small rectangle of bloody pubic hair and glistening meat. He pushed the chunk around on the floor with his sword and then kicked at it with his boots. Eddie bent down and jammed the sword inside of Delilah, twirling it around and twisting it until he jerked it back suddenly. Her uterus popped out with a sick, wet gush of black fluids and blood. He held it up by the end of his sword and sniffed it before wiping it onto my floor.

All this while, he never touched her. He let his sword do all the work.

And all this while, I watched, my senses coming back to me. I pieced it all together, and came up with a desperate plan.

"You're an angel," I said. I sat up and blinked, feeling the last of my bearings returning.

Eddie spun and glared at me. He was crouched down, lost in his reverie when I interrupted him. Now he was angry again, his stare pinning me to the wall.

"You're next," he said. He stood up and swung the sword a couple of times. It whipped and cursed the air.

I got to my feet and stood my ground, even though I was trembling and more scared than I'd ever been in my life. Angels. They were a real bitch. I'd only run into a couple in my time, both when I went to Queens on some errand, and I found them to be real self-righteous pricks. They thought everything they did was mandated by God and that they could do no wrong. They were always so sure, so certain, that they wore on my nerves whenever I saw one on TV or bumped into one.

They weren't so hot, though, that they came to Brooklyn.

That would be a violation between the two families and would be untenable. You see, God was a gangster, too, and he had his own crew of angels and they ran Queens. For a quick minute, back when the Big Event had just happened and each camp was staking out their area, a turf war almost broke out between Boss Satan's group and God's. A truce ensued, but it was tenuous at best. If an angel got caught running around over here, it would mean trouble.

"Let me guess," I said. "She broke your heart."

"You know nothing."

"Well, cry me a river. You think she didn't break my heart?" "You're just a human. You don't matter."

"Or a bunch of others? Was killing her really the best idea?"

"You are ignorant to the truth," he said.

"Maybe" I said. "What's an angel doing sleeping with a demon, any-way? Won't that piss off your boss?"

"Shut up," he said. He stepped towards me.

"That's it, isn't it? You slept together. For her it was a fling, something new to do. She'd never slept with an angel before, so it was a kick for her. But you, you poor sap, you fell in love, didn't you?"

"She . . ." Tears filled his eyes. What makes an angel cry? Apparently, a broken heart. They were just like anybody else. "She was special to me. And when I told her, she laughed at me."

"She's a demon," I said. "It's what they do."

"But that's not all," Eddie said. "She threatened to tell on me. She said she'd go to God and rat me out."

"Damn."

"Yes. And they would have killed me, if they found out. They would pluck the feathers from my wings and banish me from heaven for all eternity," Eddie said. Angels referred to Queens as Heaven. It was news to the folks that lived in Queens, let me tell you.

"You don't have wings," I said.

He glared. "It was a metaphor."

"Sorry," I said. "So what did she want? Money?"

Eddie looked at the floor.

"It's always money, isn't it?" I said. "So you decided to kill everyone who knew her, just on the off chance she'd told them."

He nodded. "That's why you have to die, too."

It was my turn to nod. I looked at the bottle of whisky sitting on the couch where I'd left it. The cap was still on. I looked at Eddie then at the bottle. He nodded. I walked over and picked it up, took the cap off, and took a long drink. It might have been my last taste of the good stuff, so I figured I should enjoy it. When I finished, I smacked my lips together, put the cap back on, and held the bottle out for Eddie. He shook his head.

"You sure?" I said. "It may be your last chance."

"What's that supposed to mean?"

"It means that in a minute, you and I are about to have a little boxing match," I said.

Eddie laughed. "Why would I do that? Why wouldn't I just cut off your head and be done with it?"

"Because," I said. "You want to beat me at something."

"How so?"

"Before you lopped her head off, Delilah told me that I was the greatest lover she ever had. That would mean you come in, at best, second place," I said.

Eddie's pretty face turned a violent red. He growled and I knew I had to tread careful here, but I was banking on his pride getting the better of him. All angels have a real big and bad problem with pride. If I could appeal to it, then I had a chance. If he saw through it, I was done.

"That's not true," Eddie said. "She told me I was the finest."

I looked at her dead, devastated body and shook my head. "I guess we'll never know," I said. "But you're an angel, you know the truth when you hear it. You look into my eyes and tell me: Am I lying?"

He stared at me, transfixing me with his gaze. He searched my words and he knew I was telling him the truth. Angels can do that. They can separate lies from fiction like a homeless guy sorting cans out of a dumpster.

I saw the anger flicker on his face and I knew I had him. He nodded slowly and turned, jamming the tip of his sword into the wall so that it hung there. I didn't know a lot about angels and their swords, just stuff I'd picked up through rumors and drunken ramblings. I did know that they had the finest, sharpest blades on the planet, and that they were blessed by God so that no impure hands—meaning, nobody but an angel's—could handle them. Their swords could destroy the unclean and the sinful with ease; Delilah and Butcher were cases in point. But I wasn't interested in the sword, except that he didn't use it on me. No, I was more interested in Delilah's dead body.

I put up my dukes and smiled, circling towards the door, to the vicinity of her corpse.

"I have to warn you," I said. "I was one hell of a boxer back in my day."

Eddie grinned right back at me; a smug smile that bled arrogance. "Your skills will not save you today."

"Maybe," I said. Delilah was right behind me. It was now or never.

I spun and dropped, sticking my fingers into her bloody uterus. I quickly wrapped it around my right fist like I was taping my hands for the gloves. Eddie stopped moving and stared at me, puzzled. I looked at him and smiled.

I squeezed the uterus tight around my hand, wrapping it in layers so it would stay and not come off on contact. Then I stood up and took a step back, towards where Delilah's head lay.

Eddie lunged forward. Angels, like all the creatures that came through the rift, looked and sounded human, but they were stronger than us, faster than us, and deadlier than us. I barely blinked and he was across the room, his fist flying. It slammed my left shoulder and knocked me back against the wall. I fell, my breath gone, and sprawled on the floor.

I couldn't let him get so close again.

He circled me, dancing in rhythm. He would have made a good boxer, I have to admit. He was agile, quick, and knew what he was doing. If I hadn't been trained, I couldn't have avoided that punch to the extent that I did, and it would have been my head smashed into the wall, not my body.

I struggled to get up onto my knees. He could have finished me right then, but instead he chose to hot dog it. I'd really gotten to him, stabbed his pride. He wanted this to last. Maybe I'd pushed him too far.

"Not done yet, are you?" I said, climbing to my feet. My shoulder was numb and I could hardly raise my left fist to give myself some protection. I don't know when my smart mouth decided to enter the fight, but it was there now, so I decided to roll with it.

"I am just starting," Eddie said.

"Come get some."

I laughed. He growled. He took a step forward and I spit straight into his eye. Eddie screamed and leapt at me again. This time, I was ready.

I stepped back, had time to flash a grin, and then cold-cocked the bastard. I caught him with an uppercut so clean, so sweet, it would have knocked out any of the people I'd fought in the past. Eddie was an angel, though, so he could take a lot more punishment.

What he couldn't take, what I'd hoped to be proven true, was the touch of Delilah's dead uterus. When the bloody tissue scraped his chin, it tore his flesh off, scorching it in a brilliant blaze of green and red. And as my fist continued, grazing his left cheek, the uterus burned his flesh off there, too. Eddie fell back, howling in agony.

I'd wiped off that smug grin from his face.

How do you make an angel cry? I wasn't sure, and when I was lying on the floor, watching Eddie take apart my ex, I tried to apply logic to the situation. Demons couldn't stand the touch of something holy or pure; it burned and killed them. It stood to reason that an angel, therefore, couldn't stand the touch of something unholy and impure. And I couldn't think of anything more unholy and impure than the dead uterus of a demon whore. So I came up with the idea and bet my life on it. I'd gambled right.

I couldn't let up now that I had him shocked and on the ropes. He could go for his sword, or he could get so angry that he came at me, full force, no longer playing around and toying with me.

So I moved into him, punching him over and over again with my uterus-wrapped fist, leaving behind bloody, blistering splatters. I gave him no chance to back away, to beg off, to push or punch me away. I struck him, again and again, wherever I could. My first blow took a chunk out of his right forearm when he brought it up to block me. My next carved a burn deep into his chest. Eddie screamed in pain. His eyes were wide and bright and so very full of fear.

I was having the time of my life.

I punched him in the mouth, his lips sizzling under my fist and his teeth blasting into the back of his throat. Eddie gagged and spat, real panic on his face now. I hit him again, above his left eye, taking his eyebrow and a good lump of his forehead with me.

It couldn't last forever, though. Eddie finally got his bearing and shoved me hard in my chest. I stumbled back and tripped over Delilah's dead body and landed right next to her head, still sitting upside down, her eyes staring at nothing.

Eddie stood a few feet from me, breathing hard. He had the wildest, most hateful look in his eyes. The skin on his forehead had melted and slid down, making his left eye appear hooded. Despite my own pain, this made me smile. Regardless of the outcome, his pretty face was ruined forever.

That was enough to send him over the edge. Eddie screamed and dove for me.

I bent down, stuck my hand inside Delilah's dead mouth, grabbed the lower jaw, and scooped the head up. I swung it around, bashing the side of Eddie's head as he flew at me, shattering Delilah's skull. It exploded in a mist of blood, bone, and brains.

Eddie screamed again. This time, though, it was a mix of desperation, fear, and blind agony. The bits of Delilah's head that came off from the blow and stuck to his head acted like an acid, boiling and burning Eddie's skin. Blisters popped up all over, rupturing and pouring out thick, yellow pus. He stumbled and fell against the couch, his screech so loud and so high-pitched I thought it might shatter the windows.

I stood and watched, fascinated and repulsed, as the blood of a dead demon whore melted parts of his face. My hand trembled as I held the only part of Delilah's head that was left, her lower jawbone. It gleamed in the overhead light, the few remaining teeth not scattered on the floor or imbedded in Eddie's skull rattled in their sockets. I wasn't sure what to do, so I let my instinct take over.

Eddie fell from the couch onto his back, one visible eye glaring at me, full of loathing. I stepped over him and squatted on his chest as he continued to writhe in pain, the left side of his face gone, revealing a shining white skull underneath. The right side of his head was caved in, burbling and stewing, a cauldron of melted flesh and broken bone.

"It's too bad, Eddie," I said. "You should have left well-enough alone."

I rammed the jawbone through his throat, pinning him to the floor. Eddie gagged and struggled up against me, but most of his strength was long gone now. He was a shell of his former self, but still, he bucked and clawed and nearly tore one of my ears off.

That's when my own anger took over, and the next few minutes are a blur to me. I remembered punching his face, over and over again, with my uterus-wrapped fist. Smashing, bashing, crunching, I drove hook after hook after jab until there was nothing left of Eddie's head but a red smear across my floor. What had been bone and eyes and sinuses and brains mixed together, becoming a paste under my hammering fist.

I didn't stop until I couldn't breathe anymore and my heart threatened to burst in my chest.

I fell off of Eddie, exhausted. I lay next to his body and wept. I had two dead, headless bodies in my apartment. Two creatures that were supposedly supernatural, or at the very least from another world; one that I killed and the other that was murdered. It was so unreal, I didn't know how to react, so I cried until I was all out of tears, and when that was done, I got up and found the bottle of whiskey and finished it.

Then I made the call.

PRO WRESTLER and Dock Worker stood over the remains of Delilah and Eddie and shook their heads, in sync, over and over again.

"An angel," Pro Wrestler said.

"And a demon," Dock Worker finished.

They both looked up at me.

"You killed an angel," Pro Wrestler said. I nodded.

"We better call the boss," Dock Worker said.

BOSS SATAN SHOWED UP half an hour later. He had an array of demons at his beck and call. Three large guys, bigger than Pro Wrestler and Dock Worker, flanked his sides, wearing black business suits and black sunglasses. All were bald and none spoke; they just stood around, looking tough.

In the middle was Boss Satan himself. I'd met him once, years ago when we set up the deal with my bar, but he didn't remember me. Why should he? I was just another stupid, ugly human that worked his streets. He was the same as I remembered, though: tall, skinny but stout, the body of an Olympic swimmer and the grace of a ballerina. When he walked it was more like a performance than a simple act of moving from one point to another. He sweated grace and oozed charm. He was probably the most handsome man I'd ever seen, with a perfectly tanned face, cleft in his chin, dark brown hair styled in the latest fashion, and blue eyes, icy and hot at the same time. And his smile, well, it could charm the pants off the Pope.

Boss Satan stood over the mess on my apartment floor, nodding his head.

"Yep, it's an angel alright," he said. He looked up at me. If I'd been more sober, I probably would have shit my pants. "What did you say this was all about?"

I pointed at Delilah's dead body and then Eddie's. "He slept with her and she broke it off. She threatened to blackmail him and he killed her and tried to kill me."

"But you killed him instead?"

I said nothing.

Boss Satan studied me for a long moment, a look of whimsy jitterbugging across his brow.

"I'll be," he finally said. "How did you do it?"

"Oh," I said. "You know us humans. We have our ways."

Pro Wrestler and Dock Worker, both lower echelon minions of Boss Satan, had been standing in the corner, watching things. Dock Worker stepped forward.

"Watch your mouth," he said. "Realize who you're talking to."

I smiled.

Boss Satan grinned right back at me. He nodded his head and snapped his fingers. "It's cool. I can dig it," he said. "Me and you, we'll have ourselves a little talk, once you sober up."

"Sure," I said.

Boss Satan looked at Pro Wrestler and Dock Worker. "You two, clean up this mess. Bring me both bodies," he said. "And get this man another bottle of whiskey. He's earned it tonight."

And with a wink, Boss Satan was out the door and gone, like he'd never been there in the first place.

I WATCHED THEM clean for a while before I finally passed out, the whiskey doing its work. I woke up a day later, my mouth rotten to the taste and every muscle in my body aching so bad I thought I must have come back as a zombie.

I got up and looked around. There was nothing left of the incident; they'd wiped the place clean. The only thing still around was Eddie's sword, still stuck in the wall. I guessed it would stay there because the demons couldn't touch it and neither could I.

I walked over to my window and looked out. The sun was rising in the distance, painting the streets with a red-orange glow that made the city look like a giant Popsicle. I stood there for a while, thinking about things, what had happened and what was going to happen. I thought about Delilah and how I'd treated her. I wished I'd been nicer to her, despite her demonic nature, and I wish I'd had more time with her. And I thought of Eddie, and the kind of jealousy that can make even an angel kill. And I thought about how lucky I was to be alive.

A tear ran down my cheek as I ruminated. I watched Brooklyn wake up and come to life, the citizens taking to the streets like ants marching off to war as the sun rose and the Popsicle sky melted and turned the prettiest blue I'd ever seen.

I shrugged my shoulders and went downstairs to open the bar up.

THE NEIGHBOR

Brandon Ford

THAT WAS A SCREAM. That was *definitely* a scream.

Nora dropped the dish into the soapy water and peeled away the rubber gloves cutting off the blood circulation from her elbow down to the tips of her fingers. A few short paces from the kitchen sink and she was in the living room, where Lander lay passed out in his recliner, some post game wrap-up on the TV in front of him. Nora switched it off and listened with intent, her sharp ear picking up nothing but the sound of Lander snoring.

"Shut *up*, you fat piece-uh crap!" she scolded in a loud, raspy whisper, giving his bald head a hard backhand. He, in turn, gave no response whatsoever. Just kept right on snoring.

Nora groaned, rolled her eyes, and pushed open the screen door. She stepped out of the trailer and into the summer night. All around her, a multitude of crickets performed a moonlit serenade. Breath held, she inched away from the shoebox she called home. Flip-flops on her feet, she felt the long stems of wet, unmowed grass with every step. Felt the mosquitoes already feasting on her exposed thighs. Under the light of the moon, she tiptoed around neighboring mobile homes, hoping and praying she'd hear that scream again.

When she felt something soft and wet poke her from behind, she gasped, covered her mouth, and spun around. Startled, but relieved at the same time, she found an old German shepherd who'd chosen to spend the last weeks of summer begging for table scraps all over this quaint little trailer park. She'd given him something here and there, so he knew she was friendly. But now wasn't the time and so she shooed him off. He scurried away, both anxious and hurt.

For a long time, she stalked about, like a predator waiting for just the right time to strike.

Where could it have come from?

How desperately she wanted to know. That shrill, frantic bellow hypnotized her, possessed her, rang inside her over and over again and all she wanted was to hear it one more time. Just once, so she could follow the sound. Track the source. Maybe even see . . . something.

But all she heard were the voices echoing from multiple TV sets. Voices chattering on and on all around her. And the occasional electrified *snap* of a buzzing bug zapper.

It was useless. She wasn't going to hear it again. Defeated, she padded home, head hanging low. Falling into a torn and rusted folding chair, she lit a cigarette, and stared up at the twinkling stars.

HOT DAMN, this one sure was cute! Sure *was* . . .

Arnie couldn't believe his eyes. Couldn't believe his *luck.* He was on his way back from the bar, feeling good and buzzed after more than a few beers, and there she was. Just standing there in the middle of the road. Not a car in sight.

As he slowed down and the lights of his pickup lit her face, he damn near collapsed with relief. When she leaned into the passenger side window and he saw her fresh little freckled face, he knew how young she was. Not a day over fifteen. On that he'd bet the farm.

For a mile or two, he listened to her sob story. It was all so terribly clichéd, really. Parents didn't understand her. Wouldn't let her have a life. Wouldn't let her have any friends. Wouldn't let her do *anything.* She couldn't take living under their roof another night, not with all the rules they insisted she abide by. Naw, she wouldn't take it any longer. She had dreams—*big* dreams—and was on her way out west to make 'em come true.

When Arnie asked why she hadn't bothered to pack a bag or at least have enough sense to dress in a few layers, she didn't know *what* the hell to say. Didn't have a damn clue. And so she just flashed him this big, stupid, wide-eyed smile, shrugged her shoulders, and turned to face the passing wilderness.

Falling deep into thought, Arnie dreamed of all the things he'd do to that pretty pink flesh of hers. So soft and smooth . . . He was gonna have himself a fuck of a lotta fun tonight. Yessir.

He reached for the six-pack lying on the floor by her feet, plucked one of the longneck bottles from the flimsy cardboard case, and twisted the cap off with his teeth. After chugging half the twelve ounces, he caught her eyeing him funny.

"Don't you know how dangerous it is to drink and drive?" she said and shifted uneasily in her seat.

That was enough to give him one pause.

If Arnie was a game-player, he might've appeased her. If he was a patient man, he might've tossed the bottle out the window, apologized, and told her there was no need to worry. He would've done all he could to put her at ease, tell her all she wanted to hear, and simply laugh on the inside as he bided his time.

But Arnie *wasn't* into games. He *wasn't* a patient man. And he *wasn't* fond of driving under the speed limit. So, when he jammed on the brakes, that pretty little piece shot out of her seat like a rocket, hit the windshield face-first, and put one hell of a crater in the thick sheet of smooth glass.

Not to worry. He'd drive on into work tomorrow, tell the boys at the garage that he stopped for a deer in the road and forgot his toolbox was in the front seat. The boss would probably cut him a sweet deal on a new windshield. He just had to make sure he cleaned all the blood off.

But later for that. Now was the time to have some fun.

What the windshield did to her face was a shame, really. She was no-where near as cute as she was when she first climbed aboard the pickup. Features all flat and dented. Like someone grabbed a frying pan and just took to wailing on her. And *man,* was she bloody.

Later, when he was carrying her out of the truck and over to the trailer, he felt his pants tighten. Cowboy at heart, he had to stop himself from letting loose with a few joyous hoots and maybe a heel-click or two.

Inside the trailer, he dropped her onto the kitchen table—the kind that doubled as a bed, can you believe it?—and went on over to lock the door. He'd just had all the blinds shut tight when she came to life with one hell of a shriek that stabbed into his eardrum like an ice pick. Thanks to all that beer, his bladder was full and weak and he quite literally pissed himself where he stood. He couldn't believe it. He hadn't pissed himself since pre-school. But there was no time to have a good laugh about it. He had to act *fast.*

And so he reached for the hammer lying beside the busted microwave he'd been meaning to fix for the past three weeks.

WHACK!

The round end met her skull, crashed in deep, and that was all she wrote.

He was a little disappointed she wouldn't be alive for this. A little disappointed, too, that he hadn't thought to use the hook end. But what the hell. He couldn't complain. He really couldn't. Her face was all fucked up, sure. She had no pulse, fine. And there was a hammer sticking out of her skull, okay. But she still had tits and a cunt.

Right?

Yeah, he'd be okay. She'd still be a bit of fun. But he couldn't help wondering if anyone had heard that scream. Well, besides the few stray dogs that roamed the trailer park incessantly.

"Party time, cupcake," he sang through an animated grin.

He unlaced his boots, kicked them aside, and, with roving eyes, once again made sure the blinds were shut tight. As he peeled away his paint-stained, piss-soaked jeans, he felt the warmth of his own fluids against his skin and contemplated a shower—a ritual he hadn't performed for several days—before he made good use of Little Miss Sunshine over there. Hands on hips, teeth chewing his bottom lip, he silently considered, then finally decided *fuck it. Why the hell do I need to impress* her?

And so he peeled away the yellowed and skid-marked briefs, tossed them atop a glowing lampshade, and scooted on over to her.

EXHALING THE SMOKE, Nora flicked aside the butt of her fourth cigarette, uncrossed her legs, and let out a sigh. She hadn't heard a thing—well, nothing out of the ordinary, at least. It was business as usual amid these solemn and lonely grounds and so she stood, picked the bunching fabric from her buttcrack, and stepped back inside the trailer just as a nearby bug zapper claimed the life of another mosquito.

When the screen door slammed, Lander came to life again, bursting into consciousness with a start big enough to knock the empty beer cans from his lap. Eyes wide, he looked from left to right before focusing on Nora.

"Where'd ya go?" he said and yawned.

"Nowhere." Nora padded down the short, slim hall to their poor excuse for a bedroom, lifting the camisole covered in sweat over her shoulders before falling atop the mattress. Her bare breasts were still full and high, even without the aid of a bra. She allowed herself a moment to admire them, knowing she was doing just fine for 36.

Thumbs slid beneath the waistband of her cotton shorts and they slid down her smooth legs. It was too hot to sleep any other way but bare-assed. Lander, the loathsome sack of meat, wouldn't spring for a new air conditioner, or even get the old one fixed. And it was impossible to sleep with the windows open without being woken several times during the night by the couple in the trailer next to theirs. They screwed like bunnies and were very, very vocal, too.

Already, Nora was beginning to sweat.

The TV switched off and the recliner gave several loud and rusted squeals as Lander shifted, then pulled himself up—all 400 pounds of him. He grunted, groaned, and farted as he staggered toward the bedroom.

Nora quickly rolled over onto her side and folded her arms to cover her breasts. Closed eyes facing the window, she cringed at the sound of Lander's heavy footfalls and his boisterous mouth-breathing.

"Don't try giving me that shit," he said, standing before the bed. "I know you ain't 'sleep yet."

She exhaled. "Lander, I'm tired."

"Whatchu tired from? You ain't got no damn job."

"And your fat ass is on disability, so don't act like you've been working the damn coal mines all day."

He laughed. Belched. He'd always told her how much it turned him on when she was feisty like that. He *loved* it when she took him down a peg with one of her many quick comebacks. She knew she should've just kept her damn mouth shut, but being passive never was part of her character.

It sounded like he was getting undressed. At the sound of his unbuckled belt, Nora died just a little more inside.

When he planted his fat, probably naked ass on the end of the mattress, Nora felt her body rise at least two feet. Grimy hands felt her all over. He even pushed her arms away to give her breasts a good squeeze.

"Lander, I told you I'm tired."

"Oh, come on now."

"Come on nothing. I wanna sleep." There was heat behind her words and her eyes pinched at her mistake.

He moved in closer and his stiffness prodded the small of her back. "Come *on,* baby. You're drivin' me crazy."

"Lander, stop."

"You have to give me one good reason why I should."

"Because I'll chew your sack off if you don't."

Again, he poked her with his erect manhood. "Promise?"

Nora opened her eyes. Through the Venetian blinds, she saw a crescent moon surrounded by gray clouds in the blackness of the night sky. It was a challenge, but she forced herself to think before she spoke. Lips parted, she took in a breath, and in her sweetest, calmest voice, she said, "Not tonight, honey. Please? I'm real tired."

And just like that, the little bit of pressure against her back disappeared and the mattress shifted as Lander rolled over and settled on his back.

Victory.

Nora closed her eyes and for the first time in days, she smiled.

CHUGGING A COLD BEER, Arnie lay sweaty and spent. Beside him, torn and bloody, lay the still remains of . . . whatever the hell her name was. With a belch and a scratch, he stood, tossed the empty bottle into the garbage, and pulled for his soiled briefs. Their foul stench immediately repelled him and he tossed them into the garbage, too.

"I hope you know I need my hammer back," he said.

With a swift, open-legged leap, he landed atop the padded seating, feet on either side of her. He wiggled both arms and bounced against the springs, like a boxer preparing for a heavyweight championship. Right foot firmly planted between her breasts, he reached down with both hands, fastened a tight grip around the hammer's smooth wooden handle, and pulled with all his strengths. Eyes closed, jaw tensed, he grunted and strained. This was harder than he thought it would be.

Pausing to regain his composure, he took in a few deep breaths, wiped the sweat from his brow, and tried again. Muscles so tensed and tight it hurt, he put all of himself in that second attempt, sweat pouring down his chest and over his mountain of gut in buckets.

With a sharp *pop,* not unlike that of a champagne cork, the hammer came free in his hands. In triumph, he laughed and admired his stained and bloody trophy. So proud and relieved, but only for an instant, for when he lowered his gaze, he found a fountain of red spilling from the open wound.

"Ooh, *shit*!"

It was a fright big enough to make him cry out. He leapt backward onto the linoleum and tossed aside the treasured tool he simply couldn't part with. Heart pounding, he turned to face every angle, unsure of what exactly he was looking for.

A plug of some kind would be just perfect. He tore through cabinets, shuffled through drawers, sliding along the flowing river of blood every step of the way. There was nothing—nothing he could use to stop this and already he'd reached the edge of sanity. Just when he was certain he'd be swimming in it, he tore an empty beer bottle from the overflowing garbage can and shoved the mouth end into the volcanic eruption. In an instant the bottle filled, but the fountain stopped.

When it was all over and Arnie was certain he could breathe easily, he belly-laughed. How could he not? It was the craziest thing he'd ever seen in his whole damn life.

And now here he stood, his body, his floor, his *kitchen* quite literally covered in blood. The trailer looked like a fucking *slaughterhouse.* It was gonna be a bitch to clean this. He sighed.

"Damn, woman," he spat, giving her left tit a slap. "You's more trouble than you's worth."

He turned on his heels, preparing to spend the rest of the night scrubbing and mopping this shithole until it sparkled.

A sparkling shithole. That made him smile.

He started for the sink, but his left foot went out from under him. Against the linoleum, he landed flat on his back, head smacking the tile as it landed.

And there he slept until the sun came up.

IT WAS JUST PAST TEN when Nora woke, sticky with both her sweat and Lander's. His warm and dripping gut was nearly flat against her back, his hot breath in her ear, his poor excuse for an erection between her legs.

Disgusted, she shoved him aside and climbed out of bed and made a mad dash for the bathroom. She took a cold shower that both cleansed and refreshed her.

Dressed in only an oversized t-shirt and flip-flops, she stepped outside and fell into a folding chair. The humidity this morning was just about god-awful. It hurt just to breathe. Hand over eyes squinting through the burning sun, she examined her surroundings. The trailer park stood eerily quiet and calm. Only the faint rumble and roar of a generator somewhere out of view.

A cup of coffee would've been nice about then, but she didn't want to risk waking Lander. Instead, she decided to enjoy the peace and solitude while she could and figured he'd make a fresh pot whenever he decided to peel his fat ass out of bed.

Not far from where she sat, Nora heard what sounded like a slamming door. Then what could've been a bag of rocks hitting the dirt. Remembering the scream she'd heard the night before, she stood and flicked the cigarette. Careful not to make a sound, she kicked off her flip-flops and tiptoed around the trailer, never minding the dirt clinging to the damp soles of her bare feet.

She was less than fifty feet from home when she heard the low grumbling of a deep, hoarse male voice. Eyes wide with focus, she poked her head around a corner and saw a very large man dragging something—something wrapped in a blue tarp—from the front door of a nearby trailer. He muttered a few choice words of obscenity and pulled with all his strengths. Grunting, he lifted the bag of goodies into the back of a pickup. As Nora felt her heart race with excitement, she watched him climb inside the driver's seat and peel away.

With a smirk, she stepped out of hiding and tentatively approached the trailer. There was so much going through her mind as she took each step one at a time, turning over her left shoulder every so often to see if anyone was watching. So many thoughts that all seemed to blend together, creating one distorted mass of imagery. Thoughts of what—or who—could've been wrapped in that tarp. Thoughts of the stranger dragging it off and who *he* may have been. Thoughts of Lander. Thoughts of the new life she'd been hoping for for quite some time.

She didn't know why, but she tried the door. Locked, of course. If it had been open, she wondered if she would've had the nerve to step inside—and what she may have found when she did.

Two steps from the door, she stood on the tips of her toes to peer inside the window, which she noticed had been left open. As a matter of fact, it looked like *all* of the windows in the trailer had been left open—all covered by rusted screens, too. Peering from left to right, she didn't find anything out of the ordinary. But the aroma of ammonia and bleach was overwhelming. Beneath that was the resonance of something lemon-scented. Probably some other cleaning product. The smell was so strong it burned her lungs. As though the entire trailer had been hosed down with Clorox. She had to turn away.

An involuntary giggle escaped her and it was because she *knew*. Arching an eyebrow, she lowered her gaze to the trail of dirt leading to where his pickup was once parked. The trail he'd made only moments prior when he'd dragged that tightly wrapped package from the trailer. Again, her heart raced. She hadn't felt this way in years. What she needed right now was a cigarette. Turning to skip her way home, she stopped when she felt the moisture beneath her right foot. Her eyes fell on the small pool of red.

"Careful now," she sang to herself, knowing it must've leaked out of the tarp on the way to the truck. "Careful, careful."

Using her hand, she knelt down to slide a mountain of dirt atop his little slip-up, figuring it was the least she could do. And with that, she headed home.

"You're only playin'" two chords, ya know," he said, just before taking another sip from his beer bottle. Two chords—*the same two chords* she'd been playing since he picked her up—were slowly but surely driving him insane. E-minor and A-major, the easiest of all acoustic guitar chords. He learned that ages ago, when he first picked up the instrument.

Finally, she stopped. Smiled. But didn't put the instrument down. The head stretched mere centimeters from his own and each time the truck passed over a bump, the pointed end grazed his cheek or poked his ear. That, along with her constant strumming, had almost pushed him over the edge.

He was on his way home from the bar when he saw her hitching. Quite a surprise that he'd come across another so soon. As he watched her climb aboard the cabin, guitar and all, he thought of the last. The last, as she lay wrapped in a tarp, rotting in a cornfield. And how much he enjoyed her cold, dead flesh—definitely more than he thought he would've.

This one was rather petite. Not as pretty as the last. Plain. Kinda bookish. Glasses. Slightly hooked nose. Thin lips. Small tits. Even still, he invited her inside. It was probably the half-dozen beers he'd had that night that made him so optimistic about this one. Probably the half-dozen beers that, too, killed his patience.

"Where ya from?" he said. Another bump and the guitar head poked him right in the cheekbone. Hurt, too. Another inch and it could've taken out his eye.

"Dallas," she said, eyes straight ahead. She didn't seem to notice the close call. Didn't appear to notice all the other times the instrument jabbed him, either.

"Where ya headin'?"

"Nashville. On my way to visit the fam."

He winced at her use of the phrase "the fam," noticing the twang in her voice for the first time.

Using only her fingers, she began to strum once more—strum the same damn chords. While Arnie thought of jamming the brakes, sending her through the glass the same way he had the last. But he feared the guitar might break her flight. And he'd just gotten the windshield fixed this morning. He'd have to figure another way.

"Where are *you* from?" she said.

Her voice was soft and sweet, kind and gentle, her question completely innocent. But even still, it gave him a start. He wasn't expecting she'd take a personal interest. Who would've thought she gave a shit?

"I'm from right here," he said, flashing her a big ole toothy grin before downing the last gulp of beer in the bottle. Left arm swung through the open window as he tossed the empty into the black night. Watching it spin and sail towards the clouds above, he regretted the motion, realizing only too late that he could've used it on her.

A few quick strums of A-major before she spoke again. "How'd you trash your windshield?"

This gave him another start. Leaning towards the six-pack at her feet, he froze mid-reach. "What's that?"

"The windshield. How'd you break it?"

"I . . . hit a deer."

"Is that right?"

"That's right."

"Don't see many deer out this way."

"I see plenty."

"Do you?"

"I do. How'd you know about the windshield?" Beer in-hand, he eyed the tiptop job the boys at the garage did just that morning, feeling a twisting knot form in his stomach.

Turning towards him almost flirtatiously, her eyes sparkled. "I'm psychic," she said.

He twisted the cap off the bottle. Offered a dubious smirk. "Really."

"Uh-huh."

He didn't like that. Didn't like it one bit. As he drank, she gave him an innocent smile while he gave her the side-eye.

And then she let out a high-pitched squeak of a laugh. "I'm just funnin' ya, teddy bear!" she cried, giving his shoulder a playful nudge. "I saw the invoice." She motioned toward the folded piece of yellow paper resting on the dashboard with a simple lift of her chin. When the smile faded, she gave him a wink and went back to practicing her chords.

The same two chords.

The same fucking two chords.

And inside, he seethed.

Another bump and another cheek-poke.

"Oh, for Christ's *sake.*" Patience lost completely, he floored the brake and the truck came to a jarring stop. The guitar slipped from her lap and just as she turned to face him, he slapped her over the head with the half-full bottle in his right hand. Slapped her *hard.* Slapped her to just shut her the fuck *up* already.

The bottle broke and drops of silver and gold rained down upon them both. For an instant, her eyes sprang open wide, then closed as she fell forward. Gripping her by the shoulder, he stopped her before she hit the dash. Lips pursed, eyes focused, he grasped her head in both hands, held on tight, and twisted. One final jolt of tension shot through her body before she went limp completely.

Ready to roll, Arnie allowed himself only a few breaths and a short moment to regain his bearings before he cracked another beer and peeled away.

ANOTHER NIGHT, another ball game.

Lander sat snoring in front of the television while Nora paced the trailer. She'd spent the day chain-smoking and watching the window while Lander merely lazed about. Several times he'd asked her what she was looking for and "nothing" was not an answer he was willing to accept. So, Nora told him her sister might be paying them a visit. That seemed to suit Lander just fine. He enjoyed leering at Nora's younger, but equally attractive sister quite a bit and when he learned she was on her way, he smiled, eased back in his seat, and shoved a hand behind the waistband of his pants.

For Nora, the day was long and endless. She couldn't tear herself away from the window. Couldn't relax long enough to enjoy the peace when Lander actually left her alone. Couldn't stop the wheels inside her head from turning.

"Babe?" Lander called, then paused to clear the phlegm from his throat. "Hey, babe?"

Worn and irritable, Nora turned from the window and faced him. "What is it."

"Grab me another beer?"

She crushed her cigarette in an ashtray and made her way over to the fridge. When the door swung open and the coolness inside swathed her, she heard the sound of a roaring engine and of heavy tires crushing dirt. Mouth agape, eyes darting from one side of the room to the other, she listened closely and smiled when she was certain of what she heard.

With an anxious and impatient hand, she reached inside, grasped a sweaty bottle, and slammed the door shut. "Here, last one," she cried, already out of breath as she dropped the bottle into her husband's lap and raced for the door.

Stepping out into the humidity of a scorching August night, she tiptoed away from the trailer, still managing to hear Lander mutter something about her being crazier than a shit-house rat, an expression she never quite understood.

The same way she had that morning, she crept her way through the park, pausing every few paces to glimpse over her shoulder or listen with intent. When she saw the truck pull up and park outside the trailer, she took in what would be the last breath she'd allow herself to take until she was certain he was in for the night. Squinting, peeking, hidden from view, she watched until the driver's side door creaked open and out he stepped. In his arms, cradled and comforted like a little baby, he held a young girl—a young girl most probably would assume was sleeping. But Nora knew better.

Rushing and unbalanced, he unlocked the door and rushed inside. Before Nora had the time to wonder why he'd left the truck open and unattended, he came racing outside and back into the driver's seat. There was a moment or two of fumbling inside before he resurfaced, carrying a six-pack and an acoustic guitar.

Brow tight, eyes glazed over, Nora watched as he locked the truck and did a little spin on the dirt before heading back inside. Over to the windows would've been her first move, if only he hadn't closed all the blinds. She could hear them rattle where she stood.

A sharp scraping rung loud in her ears and she realized only then that she'd been clawing at the rusted trailer she'd been hiding behind. Flecks of brown were now embedded beneath her fingernails and though she tried, they were impossible to remove.

"Damn," she huffed, defeated.

She folded both arms, threw her back against the wall, and wished she'd brought her cigarettes.

ARNIE COULDN'T *believe* he'd gotten it in past the sixth fret. And he wasn't finished. No, sir. Putting all of his weight behind the guitar, he opened her legs just a bit wider, and pushed with everything he had in him. He could hear and feel parts of her shifting and tearing inside. Things breaking and crumbling beneath the force of the guitar neck. What a sight it would be if he pushed hard enough and *deep* enough to pop her head clean off. *That* would sure as shit be a Kodak moment.

He let out his trademark laugh—the laugh he was known for all his life—and prepared himself for the hardest, meanest thrust of all.

But stopped when he caught sight of her lady bits.

How the hell was he supposed to get his nut *now*?

She was torn up something *awful* down there. He'd be slipping and sliding out of that mess all night.

And just like that his joy dissipated. Sure, fun was fun, but what was the point of it all without the main event?

Finger-picking six strings soaked with various fluids, he gave himself a moment's rest. A minute to decide what would come next—what and how.

And then he remembered something.

A fantasy he'd had for quite a while. Something he'd wanted to do, but hadn't yet had the opportunity.

He decided that *now* was the time. Yessir. Now was the time, this was the place, and it was gonna be *good*. Man, oh *man*, was it gonna be good.

He clapped both hands with delight, then drummed them against the smooth surface of the guitar and gave the strings a few quick strums. With a skip and a twirl, he trotted on over to the kitchen counter, pulled open the drawer top left, and plucked a butter knife from the clutter of steel. Sauntering back over to her, he whistled a damn fine rendition of *Jimmy Crack Corn*.

When her head was in the perfect position, he dug the butter knife in. With full force, he pushed it deep, the entrance by the crease of her left eye. A little twist here, a little pull there, and the eye came loose, still dangling by its stem. Scissors handy, he snipped it free and laughed when unfamiliar fluids started to leak. They were good and slimy. Would make one hell of a lube. Yessir.

With pleasure and glee, he tossed the eyeball into the air and caught it, considering removing its mate so he could juggle the slippery orbs. Wouldn't *that* be a sight?

But maybe later. Now, there was some business to attend to.

"Yee-haw!" he hollered and tossed the eye over his shoulder. With a *clunk,* it landed in a glass of water by the sink and floated.

He pulled off his sweaty and malodorous t-shirt and tossed it aside. Rubbed his nipples in anticipation. Both eyes fixed on the gaping, leaking, oozing hole, he unfastened his belt. Reaching inside his pants and—

There came a knock on the door.

Startled, he didn't know what to do. And so he did nothing, standing there stiff with a hand in his pants, face blank. He considered just waiting it out, but they knocked again, harder and faster. Five times in rapid succession.

"Damnit," he grumbled, buttoning his pants and throwing the shirt back over his shoulders.

He breathed in and opened the door, but only a *very* slim crack. His nighttime playmate lay only a few feet behind him.

When his eyes adjusted to the darkness outside, he grinned, liking what he saw.

"Hi there," she said. "I'm Nora. I live just a few trailers down. So sorry to disturb you, but I was wondering if I could have just a minute or two of your time? I'm having a problem and I think you might be able to help."

Less than enthused, his features dropped and instantly, his hesitancy became visible.

"This'll only take a second, I promise," she said, not giving him the opportunity to say no just yet.

He sighed. "Hang on a sec." He slammed the door and reached for his keys. Wondered what he was going to do with *her*. A touch of sadness fell over him and he thought of all the things he *could* do with her—all the things he was *about* to do with her—had he not been bothered.

But he'd get to that. What mattered now was hiding her. When he saw the light switch, he chuckled to himself and flicked it. Darkness. She was gone—or at least it appeared as such.

When he opened the door, he once again found this strange woman—Nora, he thought she said her name was—waiting for him oh so patiently. His eyes shot up and down her slender figure, positive she wasn't wearing a bra beneath that oversized t-shirt.

"Right this way." She led him through the near-pitch darkness and around a bend, the chirp of crickets all around them and the smell of burning charcoal resonating. The sights, sounds, and smells of summer were everywhere.

They approached a trailer not far from his own. Through the windows, he noticed only a faint flashing light of bluish gray. Probably the TV.

Extending an arm, she pulled open the door and waited for him to enter first. If he was a trusting man, he may have walked on in. But he wasn't. He didn't know her and he didn't know where this door would lead.

He shifted all of his weight onto his right foot and looked her in the eye. "After you."

She didn't argue, which was a good sign. She gave him a look that could've only been described as sheer apathy, and stepped inside.

Guard up, he followed her and turned to glance over his shoulder as the door swung shut. Inside, he found a quaint living space not unlike his own. The extraordinarily burly gentleman slumped and sleeping in a stained, torn armchair gave him one pause. Arnie halted step. The man, snoring peacefully in front of a baseball game, sat surrounded by empty cans. An eyesore of a human being, he took up most of the limited living space.

Arnie cleared his throat. "Who's *this*?" he said, motioning toward their sleeping host.

"My husband."

Blank, Arnie nodded. "Uh-huh . . ." A punchline would've been nice.

"I brought you here tonight because I was hoping you'd work your magic on him."

He laughed. "'Scuse me?"

"Well, I know what you do. I mean, I've seen . . . I mean, I . . ." She paused. "Okay, look. Just tell me what you need, all right? If you need knives, I've got knives. If you need tools, I think there's a set collecting dust around here somewhere. If you need money, that may be an issue, but I can make you happy in ways that money can't, if you know what I mean."

"Whoa, whoa, whoa, slow down," he said, both hands raised. "What the hell are you talkin' 'bout?" His head was spinning.

She rolled her eyes and suddenly seemed rather exhausted. "I'm guessing you weren't the brightest in your class, were you," she said, almost under her breath. "I'm saying I'd like for you to kill my husband." Then she exhaled. "Please."

Eyes bulging wide, he looked around nervously. Innocently. "What makes you think I'm the person for something like that?"

"Oh, come on now. Let's not play games."

"*I'm* not the one playin' games here, honey."

"I thought I was rather straightforward in my request."

"Are you nuts? What if this guy wakes up?"

"He won't wake up for hours. Trust me."

"*Trust you?* Right."

"So? Are you gonna do this or not?"

"I still don't understand why you chose *me*."

Eyebrows raised, she smiled wide and looked around. Like she knew something. "Let's just say I've seen things."

"*What* things."

Hands on hips, she eyed the ceiling, as though she were searching her memory. "Well," she said, "I've seen a certain middle-aged gentleman in a certain local trailer park recently unload something very large. Something wrapped up tight in a blue tarp. Something that left behind a small puddle of deep red. I've also seen said gentleman bring home a young woman earlier this evening—a young woman I'm willing to bet is in the very early stages of decomposition as we speak."

He burned inside, growing hotter with every word she spoke. He didn't know what to say or do next and judging by the way she studied him, he was growing redder by the second.

"Look," she said, her tone returning to casual, "I don't care about either of them. I don't care about *them* and I don't care about any of the others, although I'm sure there's plenty. Just do this for me and we never have to see each other again. I'll even take care of the body. Deal?"

He blinked. Thought hard. "Why don't you just do it yourself?"

"Not all of us can muster the nerve to do something like this."

He didn't like this. But he *really* didn't like leaving her dissatisfied, especially with her knowing what she knew. And what she wanted really wouldn't take much. The guy looked half-dead already.

"Is he drugged or something?" Arnie asked, eyeing him curiously.

"He's self-medicated."

He nodded, as though he understood.

Hours passed, or so it would seem. He stood, silently questioning. Weighing. Contemplating. Gaining his nerve. The two-tined meat fork lying on the kitchen counter was the first thing he saw when he glanced away from them. The points were long and looked razor sharp. Bits of food had hardened along the slim, smooth shaft, as though it had been cooked with recently. Still uncertain, he reached for it with an unsteady left hand and grasped it by the handle. "Cool if I use this?" he asked, holding it up.

"Have at it," she said, gesturing with both hands.

She stood, turned the television up all the way—presumably to cover the screams of the poor bastard she was so desperate to get rid of—and moved a few paces to the opposite side of the trailer. She stopped outside the bathroom door and watched, both hands joined at her waist.

Arnie took one final look at her, figured *what the hell*, and then acted.

Clutching the giant fork by the handle, he rushed forth, storming straight ahead and grunted as he gave a powerful thrust. The double spikes impaled the sleeping sloth at the throat and continued straight through, entering the padded back of the recliner, and stopping there.

When Arnie pulled away, it was like it didn't happen. The guy didn't move a muscle. Not one. Didn't flinch, didn't blink, didn't stir. Arnie wondered if his death was instantaneous. Wondered if the life of this sweaty, slovenly beast was gone the very second the cold steel penetrated him.

Now feeling the rush of his heart and savoring the adrenaline, Arnie laughed. Gave his own thigh a good, hard slap. At ease, he stood tall, believing it was all over.

But it wasn't.

Because the poor, nameless bastard started to twitch . . .

. . . and jerk . . .

. . . and cough . . .

. . . and gurgle . . .

. . . and blood shot from his mouth by the gallon.

He tried to move, to stand, but he was pinned to the back of his seat by the giant fork jutting out of his throat. Eyes wide and filled with terror, jaw hanging, he kicked both legs wildly and used his hands to clutch his own throat, as though he were choking. And then his entire body shook violently and if Arnie didn't know better, he would've thought he were witnessing a prison death by execution.

The efforts of this man were great and strong enough to free him from his blood-soaked seat. To Arnie's surprise, this very large, uncontrollable man was up and on his feet, thrashing about, both arms flailing as he suffered through what had to have been an insufferable agony.

Windows shattered. Dishes broke. Pots and pans shot through the air. Everything around them was tossed about. It was chaos. Pure bedlam. Arnie ducked, taking cover by lifting both arms above his head.

And then it all stopped when he fell back into his chair, gave a few more coughs and gurgles, and died.

Arnie panted, hoping that it was really all over. He kept both eyes on the recliner, knowing that if this madness saw a second course, he wanted to be ready for it.

He heard a click. The roar of the television faded. When he turned, Nora was standing before the set. In all the mayhem, he'd forgotten she was there—forgot she was the one who requested this, even.

"Wow," she said, turning to face all corners of the room—or rather what was left of it.

Arnie said nothing. There was nothing *to* say. He just needed a moment to collect himself.

It startled him back into the world in which he lived when she got down on her knees before him. When he saw her arched brow and the look in her eyes, he knew exactly what she was doing.

"Hold on a second," he said, placing his hands on top of hers when she tugged at his belt.

"What's the matter?"

"Nothing. It's just that . . . See, well . . . There's something I just recently learned. Something about myself."

She didn't take her eyes off of his. "What."

He smiled. "I like 'em without a pulse."

Before he reached down and held her head in both his hands, he saw the exact *moment* she understood—saw it in her eyes as they bulged wide. And then he twisted.

Pop!

As he ducked behind neighboring trailers on his way home, Nora's cold body in both arms, he remembered the empty eye socket that would be waiting for him when he walked through the door. Smiling, he thought of what he'd be doing on this night for the very first time. That smile grew bigger and wider when he realized there'd be something else he'd be doing for the very first time.

A threeway.

THE NAME GAME

Scott Nicholson

WHEN MONROE AWOKE, he felt as if he'd been dropped headfirst from the Statue of Liberty's torch.

He moaned and rolled over into a stack of moldy cardboard and newspapers. The avenue tasted of Queens, smog stung to the ground by the long rains of the week before. A car horn bleated, amplified by the brick canyons so that the noise rattled Monroe's eardrums. He tried to peel back his eyelids so that the brilliant green in his vision could be scrubbed away by the orange crash of daylight.

Damn this city, he thought, each word a hammer blow. And since he was bothering to think, he figured he might as well try to remember. That was a little harder. He was on his knees, supporting himself against the slick skin of a Dumpster, by the time he got past the previous two seconds and on into the last few hours.

It was morning. The aroma of bagels and coffee drifted from some back door along the alley, fighting with the stench of gutter garbage before mingling into a deeper smell of rot. And if this was morning, then Monroe was—

Late.

He was supposed to catch a pre-dawn flight, to be out of town before another sorry New York sun rose. No, *he* wasn't supposed to catch the flight. He remembered harder, and more painfully. *Robert Wells* was supposed to catch that flight.

Robert Daniel Wells, his new identity, a boring tourism official from Muncie. The Feds had set it up that way. A tourism official could go places, sleep in a few motels, get lost in America's excess. Los Angeles for a convention to pitch movie locations, then Oregon for a meeting of the Christmas Tree Growers Association, *zippp* down to, where was it? Oh, yeah, Flagstaff, Arizona, to sell Muncie to wealthy retirees. Good old

Indiana, that scenic destination, that mecca of the masses.

Dumb damned Feds. Like Joey Scattione couldn't figure that one out. With Joey's resources, Monroe was meat no matter what identity they gave him. What he needed was a new face, new bones, a new *brain*, because his brain was halfway down the back of his neck. He touched the welt on his head.

Ouch.

He struggled to his feet, took a step, and nearly tripped over a pile of rags. The pile stirred, a bottle rolled to the asphalt, and a bleary eye opened amid a dark crack of cloth.

"Suh—sorry," Monroe said. He waited a moment for the bum to acknowledge him, but the eye closed, extinguished like an ember dropped in mud.

His hand went to his back pocket. No surprise, his wallet was gone. It had contained nothing but cash, a few hundred bucks. No biggie. He hadn't dared carry his fake IDs in there.

Monroe took a couple more steps. Even if he missed the flight, he still had the ticket. They'd let him catch a later one. If he had a connector in St. Louis, maybe he'd slip out of the terminal and throw Robert Wells in the ditch somewhere, dig up some new papers. It could be done. Easier that way than screwing around and counting on the Feds.

That's why he'd went alone. With a spook escort, Joey's people would have spotted Monroe a mile away. Feds' shoes sparkled like skyscrapers, and they always looked as if they should be wearing sunglasses. Might as well carry a sandwich sign that said, "Hey, bad guys of the world! I'm a spook."

So Monroe had talked them into playing it his way. Take up the tourism official act, gawk at the skyscrapers, do the same kind of dumb things an Indiana bumpkin would do. Like try to catch a cab at four in the morning.

Whoever had clobbered him must have been an amateur. Certainly wasn't any of Joey's muscle. Joey would want Monroe whole, uninjured, wide awake, and ready for some slow face-to-face. Joey's people would show Monroe ten thousand ways to die, all at the same time, and none of them easy. Joey would want it all on videotape, since he couldn't be there in the flesh.

And the Feds, they weren't in for the double-cross. Not only were they too dumb, Monroe had given them the slip back at the hotel at around midnight. Sure, they probably would have a spook or two haunting the airports, but they wouldn't want to make a scene. Better to let Monroe get out of town and track him later.

Monroe neared the end of the alley, the traffic thick on the street in front of him. Pedestrians clogged the sidewalks, hustling off to make the nine o'clock ritual. He felt better already, though his pulse was playing "The War Of 1812" in his temples. Safety in numbers, and nowhere were numbers more numerous than on a Manhattan street.

He attempted to whistle, but his throat was too dry. He put on his indifferent grimace, the mask that New York wore, and slouched into the crowd. He fell in behind a woman walking her poodle. He nearly stepped on the poodle when it stopped to relieve itself. The woman pretended not to notice either Monroe or the steaming brown pile on the concrete.

Monroe reached inside his jacket, to the inner pocket. He stopped. The ticket was gone.

Someone had taken his papers. The social security card, the Indiana driver's license, the credit card made out to "Robert Wells," even a blood donor card. All the FBI's clever forgeries, along with four more bills, were now in the hands of some idiot mugger. Or mugger of idiots, whichever way you wanted to look at it.

Monroe had been so wrapped up in worrying about Joey Scattione that he hadn't considered falling victim to a less ruthless and much more random predator. His predicament hit him like a wrong-way cab. If he were forced to be Monroe Hartbarger, he wouldn't last a half a day in this city. Not with Joey's people on the hunt. And Monroe Hartbarger at the moment was broke, no way out, no standby plane ticket, no bulletproof vest. No gun.

"Out of the way, dude," growled a kid with a skateboard under his arm. The kid shoved past Monroe, greasy black hair shining in the lights from a nearby shop window. Monroe moved against the glass, out of the main crush of foot traffic. He glanced at the passing faces, on the lookout for Joey's people.

Calm down, take a breath. Think.

Thinking brought the headache roaring back. Goon must have used a tire iron.

He fumbled for a cigarette, then remembered that Robert Wells didn't smoke. But he wasn't Robert Wells anymore. He searched for the secret folds in his coat, the place where he'd kept his Monroe effects. Because he'd planned all along that, once he blew this town and shook the spooks, he'd return to being Monroe, at least until he could scrape together a new identity. He didn't have much faith in the Feds and their "witless protection program."

But the worse got worser. His fingers came away empty. The mugger had taken his Monroe stash, along with the extra fifty he'd tucked back for hard times. Monroe closed his eyes and leaned against the wall, inhaling car exhaust as if the carbon monoxide would dull his headache.

I'd rather be anywhere than right here, on Joey's turf, in Joey's town. Hell, I'd even take Muncie. At least in Muncie, the only thing I'd have to worry about would be dying of boredom. And I hear that takes YEARS . . .

Voices to his right pulled him back to the morning street. Two people were shouting, pointing into the shop window. In New York, two people talking on the street either meant a drug deal, a sex solicitation, or the beginning of a murder. But these seemed like ordinary folks, the kind who talked to windows instead of invisible demons.

Monroe looked into the storefront. It was a pawn shop, bars thick across the window, a bank of surveillance cameras eyeing the street like hookers on payday. A Sanyo television lit up the window, the flickering images reflected in the glass. It took Monroe a moment to register what he was seeing.

A shot of the East River, a harried-looking reporter trying vainly to control her hair in the breeze, a cutaway to emergency response and fire vehicles, then a wide shot of Kennedy Airport. Back to the river, a small orange speck in the water. Zoom in. A torn life jacket.

A computer graphic popped up in the corner of the screen, the station logo a leering eye. Underneath, in slanted red letters, "Flight 317 Crash."

Poor bastards, Monroe thought. *Imagine what kind of headache you get from dropping a mile-and-a-half from the sky.*

He was turning back to the street, his pity for the victims already fading, when the number "317" bounced back into his roaring head. He froze, got shoved by a balding man in a suit, yelled at by a package courier.

317. Hadn't that been *his* flight? The one that was supposed to whisk Robert Wells to a new life?

He went into the pawn shop. A bank of TVs filled one wall, half of them tuned to news coverage of the crash. The anchor had her hair in place now, must have snagged some hair spray during the cutaway. The computer graphic now read "Live!" under the station logo, in those same blood-red letters.

"We're at the scene of the crash of NationAir Flight 317, which plummeted shortly after takeoff from Kennedy Airport this morning—"

"What a mess, huh?" said a voice behind Monroe. He thought at first it was one of Joey's boys. But it was the pawn shop proprietor, a small man with glasses and a scar across one cheek. His nose looked like an unsuccessful prizefighter's.

"Yu—yeah," Monroe agreed.

"Took about a minute for it to hit the water," the shop owner said, leaning over a glass case of watches. "Just enough time for them to pray and crap their pants."

The man starting laughing, the laugh spasmed into a coughing fit. The news anchor's voice fought with the racket of the man's lungs.

"—no survivors have been found. The Boeing 747 was reported to be carrying a full contingent of 346 passengers, according to NationAir records. F.A.A. authorities are arriving on the scene—"

"It was one of them Aye-rab bombs, I bet," said the shopkeeper. "Don't see why the rest of us got to suffer 'cause the kikes and the ragheads can't get along."

"They said the plane was full," Monroe said, half to himself.

"Yep. You know how they are these days. Wedge 'em in with a crowbar. They interviewed the man who was first in line to go standby. Everybody showed, so he never got on. He was thanking God seven ways to Sunday."

No standby passengers. But what about the ticket belonging to Robert Wells? Someone must have used it. Someone—

Monroe stumbled toward the street, his head reeling.

"Hey, got a special today on handguns," the shopkeeper called after him. "No waiting."

But Monroe was already out the door. He walked fast, fell into the New York rhythm, blind to everything.

Someone must have used his ticket. Who?

The mugger.

The mugger must have checked in with the ticket, became "Robert

Wells" himself, and grabbed a seat across the country. Maybe the mugger wanted out of this town so desperately that he'd risk having the authorities waiting for him at LAX. And for his trouble, the idiot was probably now in a thousand pieces, feeding fish in Long Island Sound.

If so, the creep had gotten what he deserved. Monroe touched his sore head to remind himself that everybody had to go sometime. Everybody had to pay that one big debt. The trick was to put it off as long as possible.

As he turned the corner, another thought came to him. Unless the spooks had been watching, then they didn't know that Robert Wells a.k.a. Monroe never boarded the plane. They would get the list, see the name, go over the data on the terminal computer, and verify that indeed Robert Wells had met his end on Flight 317.

A perfect bow-tie on their witness protection program. Case closed. The Fed's star witness against Joey Scattione was now utterly and forever safe from the mobster's long reach. Even Scattione couldn't finger a man in the afterlife.

Monroe walked faster, excited, his pulse racing, red wires of pain shrieking through his temples. He realized that Scattione would also think him dead. Scattione was way sharper than the Feds, even though he'd been convicted on racketeering and drug charges. Thanks to Monroe, who'd been one of his best street lieutenants.

But Monroe knew a good deal when he saw one. When the net tightened and the Feds needed a pigeon, Monroe did even better than squawk: he'd sung like a deflowered canary. After, of course, eliciting a long sheet of promises, including permanent immunity and protection. And a new identity.

An identity that was dead.

What he needed right now was his old friend Sid.

Monroe turned into a bar, though it was scarcely ten o'clock. A man in drag who looked like he hadn't slept was slumped in one corner, holding a cigarette that was four inches of ash. Two cabbies were drinking off the effects of the third shift. The bartender kept his attention focused on the tiny black-and-white that hung in one corner. It was tuned to the same news coverage of the crash.

"Help you, buddy?" the bartender said, without turning.

"Scotch and water. A double."

"Poor bastards," the bartender said, still watching the television as he reached for the stock behind him. "We think we got it bad, but at least we ain't been handed our wings."

"Yeah," Monroe said. Catholic humor. Like everybody was an angel.

The man poured from the Johnny Walker bottle as if dispensing liquid gold. The ice cubes were rattled into the glass before Monroe could complain about the weak mix. Then Monroe remembered he had no money. He acted as if reaching for his wallet, then said, "Excuse me, where's the rest room?"

The man nodded toward the rear, eyes still fixed on the set, where the field anchor was now interviewing a witness. As Monroe headed for the dark bowels of the bar, he overheard the witness talking about airline food. The news team was groping, fumbling to keep momentum, the tragedy already sliding toward ancient history. The transvestite winked as Monroe passed, and up close Monroe couldn't tell if she were a man dressed as a woman or vice versa.

Sheesh, and I thought I had an identity problem.

But maybe the she-male was onto something. In the bathroom, Monroe studied his own face in the mirror, trying to picture himself in lipstick. He shuddered. Better to take on Joey Scattione than to pluck his eyebrows and duct-tape his gut.

He washed his hands and went out. The transvestite was waiting by the door. Monroe cleared his throat. "Say, you got change for a phone call?"

The transvestite sneered and produced some coins, then dumped them into Monroe's palm as if afraid to catch a disease. Monroe mumbled thanks and stopped by the pay phone. He dialed a well-remembered number. As the phone rang, he watched to see which gender of bathroom the transvestite chose.

Neither. The transvestite went out the back door. The line clicked as the connection was made. "Hello," came the welcome though nasal voice.

"Sid, hey, it's me. Monroe."

"Monroe? Like I know any Monroe?"

"Hartbarger. You know."

"Afraid not, friend."

"Jesus, Sid. Monroe Hartbarger. You sold me the damned name yourself, for crying out loud. Driver's license, Rotary Club membership, credit cards."

"I don't know any Hartbargers."

Monroe sighed. "It's Charlie Ehle."

"Charlie? Why the hell didn't you say so? You expect me to remember every job?"

"Yeah, yeah. Listen, I need another one. Like pronto."

"Rush jobs cost extra, my man. But for you, I can have you set up by five o'clock."

Monroe nodded into the phone. Sid always got chummy when he smelled green. For a document man, Sid had enough smarm to work every side of the fence: green cards, counter check scams, fake IDs, forgery, bogus lottery tickets, anything that involved paper or photographs. But Sid liked cash, lots of it, payable when services were rendered.

"Can't you do better than five? I'm kind of in a jam."

"Oh, the Scattione thing."

The Scattione thing. Damn those Feds. Monroe's testimony was delivered in closed court, the records sealed. Sure, Monroe expected stoolies in the judicial branch to leak to the Mafia. This was America, after all. But when even the criminal fringes such as Sid knew the score, that meant the clock was ticking down twice per second on Monroe's remaining life span.

"Fix me up, what do you say, pal? Just the basics."

Sid let out a slow whistle. "It don't pay to cross Scattione. But I guess you already know that, huh?"

"I can give you five grand."

That shut up the weasel. For a moment. Then the shrewd voice came across the wires. "How come the spooks didn't set you up? Figured you'd be a family man from Des Moines by now."

"We decided to part company," Monroe said. "You think I could hide from Scattione while some of them secret agent types were guarding me?"

"Suppose not. So, what are you in the mood for? Irish? Got some McGinnitys all ready to roll off the press."

"With my coloring? You got to be kidding." He glanced at the bartender, who was watching the news as if it were a boxing match. The transvestite entered through the back door, ignoring Monroe.

"Okay, okay, already. Where you at?"

"Just off Van Wyck."

"Meet me at Naomi's Deli on Greenway. Five o'clock."

"You need a recent photo?" Monroe asked out of habit. He knew Sid kept files on all his old customers. You never knew when blackmail might come in handy.

"No. And let's make it six grand. I got two kids to put through college." The phone clicked and then hummed. Monroe hung up and went back to the bar. He thought about asking the transvestite to pay for his drink, but that would be pushing it. Instead, he walked past the bar, hurried out the door, and was lost in the crowd before the bartender could react.

He walked for a while, ten blocks, until his feet were sore. He didn't know if Joey's people could find him more easily if he kept moving, or if he tried to hole up. Eventually, fatigue and the dull ache in his head sent him to a bench in one of those half-acre dirt patches that the city called a public park. The two trees clung stubbornly to their oxygen-starved leaves.

Someone had stuffed an afternoon edition, the *Daily News Express*, in the trash can. Monroe fished it out. More crash coverage filled the front page, photos of the obligatory grieving survivors, bits of wreckage, FAA talking suits. On page seven was a list of those believed to have been on board NationAir Flight 317.

Monroe ran his finger down near the bottom of the list. *Wells, Robert.*

So far, so good. Wells was officially presumed dead.

And Scattione, with his resources, would know that Monroe Hartbarger had become Wells. Scattione would get the word in his Sing Sing cell, his lips would veer to the right in churlish anger, and he'd pound his fist against the hard mattress. Nothing could tick Scattione off more than revenge denied. Monroe had to smile.

But not laugh.

He couldn't laugh until later, when Monroe Hartbarger was officially laid to rest, along with Charlie Ehle and the half-dozen other identities that Monroe had adopted over the years. Fingerprints were no problem, really. All he had to do was build up the kitty, turn a few deals, and grease a few palms. Everywhere a record was kept, there was a human recorder who had access to it. All Monroe needed was access to the recorder.

Monroe had learned that it wasn't a question of whether integrity could be bought and sold. It was only a question of price.

He managed to nap a couple of hours, keeping the newspaper over his face. Scattione had probably passed out a hundred photos. Monroe could change his name, but he was stuck with those same recognizable features. At least until he got to Cayman, where he knew a decent plastic surgeon. First things first, he needed to live long enough to get his new identity.

The walk downtown took longer than he expected. When he entered the deli, Sid gave him the once-over. Monroe's suit was rumpled, the knees dirty from being rolled by the mugger. He hadn't shaved, either.

"How the mighty have fallen," Sid said, as Monroe slid into the booth opposite him.

"I haven't fallen yet," Monroe said.

Sid was eating a Reuben, and though Monroe hadn't eaten all day, the smell of the sauerkraut curdled his stomach. Monroe checked the door. Sid wasn't known as a double-crosser. He couldn't afford to be, in his line of work. But, with Scattione in the mix, everything was subject to change.

Sid brought out a large envelope, put it beside his plate. "Hello, Mister Raymond Highwater," he said.

"Highwater? What sort of name is that? It's so phony, I won't make it to Jersey."

"I stole it out of the phone book. That's what you get when you ask for a rush job." A piece of corned beef was stuck between Sid's teeth.

"Listen, I got to ask you for a favor."

Sid patted the table. "Pay for the last one, then we can talk."

Monroe leaned over the table. A group of Hassidic Jews were across the room, two women were chatting over coffee, a college-aged kid, probably a film student from Columbia, was reading a magazine at the counter. None of them looked like Scattione's people. But in this city, the walls had ears, eyes, and sometimes a .45 automatic.

"I'm short at the moment," Monroe said. In the ensuing silence, he heard a bus honk outside, and somebody in the kitchen dropped a pan.

Sid stopped in mid-bite, took a slow chew, then began working his jaws like a ferret. "Short," he said, spraying rye crumbs across the table.

"Listen, I can make it good." Monroe's words came fast, like bullets from a clip. "You know me. I can have it for you tomorrow. And—what say we make it ten big ones? All I need is a little time as this Highwater guy."

Sid wiped at his mouth with a paper napkin. Then he put one hand on the envelope, and in a smooth motion, slid it back inside his jacket.

"Come on, Sid," Monroe said, checking the door again. "We've done business for years."

"Always cash on delivery."

Monroe tugged at his collar, sweat ringing his forehead. He knew the window of opportunity was small. Even though Scattione thought "Robert Wells" was dead, at least one person knew that Monroe was still breathing. Sid.

With a fake credit card, Monroe might still be able to get out of the city. All he needed was a name. He'd already died once today, he'd killed off a dozen other identities in his time, but he'd always been the one to deep-six himself. By choice. "I can deliver, Sid. I know you got skills, but it only takes you an hour to crank out a set of documents."

Sid shook his head. "It's not about the money. It's about pride and reputation."

Same with Scattione. What sort of rep could a Mafiaso have if the man who'd fingered him was walking around as free as sin?

"Nobody will know, Sid. I promise. I'll deliver, then you'll never see my ugly mug again. I'm thinking Cozumel, maybe Rio."

Sid sat back and pushed his plate away. The group of Hassidic Jews continued chattering. The college kid set down his magazine and ordered something. Monroe looked at the clock.

"Please, Sid."

Sid pursed his lips. Then he stood, dropped some bills on the table to cover the cost of the sandwich, and brought out the envelope. Except this one had come from a different pocket. He dropped the package in front of Monroe. "Joey pays twenty."

The bell rang as Sid went out the door. Monroe stooped, picked up the envelope, and tore it open. Who was he this time? Not that it mattered. He'd even be a damned McGinnity if he had to.

He stared at the driver's license.

It didn't make sense. It was his face, all right. But this license was gone, floating somewhere in the East River. He read the name slowly, his lips shaping the syllables.

Robert Daniel Wells.

He moved fast, got to the street, but Sid was gone.

Monroe glanced at the crowd, among the eyes that seemed to shine like search beacons. Which ones belonged to Joey's people?

He broke into a run. A laugh tore itself from his lungs, a spasm borne of fear and hysteria. He should have known that Joey's reach, even from a prison cell, was longer than the longest arm of the law. Monroe had been around long enough to know that Joey liked to play.

Like a cat with a cornered mouse, like a spider with a stuck fly.

Monroe ran on. He thought that maybe if he ran fast enough, someday he'd catch up to himself. But somedays never come, and Robert Wells had a debt to pay. Under any name.

FLY BY NIGHT

Tim Curran

1

WHEN DONNY CERRONE was pulling five years hard time for extortion conspiracy at the federal hole in Lewisburg, he got into a beef with a black drug runner named Willy Sikes. Just some bullshit over a lottery the cons were running and distribution of said profits. Typical thing cons banged heads about. Donny, working in the prison infirmary, told the doc there, said to him that if Sikes didn't cool his fucking heels, he was going to wake up one morning with his head shoved up his own ass. The doc, some Korean dude sitting on a stretch for trafficking OxyContin, thought that was funny. Said such a thing was not physically possible.

Donny figured he was right.

Years later, he found out different.

2

"THAT HIM? That the stiff?"

The guy doing the talking was Archie Mann, a ballbuster out of the State Police Organized Crime Bureau. He was a real regular over in Ducktown, Atlantic City's Italian neighborhood, though he was about as Italian as beans and rice. But he wanted the people to know he was there, that somebody in New Jersey gave a rat's ass about them, the shit they had to chew and swallow. Because Atlantic City was mobbed-up and always had been. Maybe it wasn't as bad as the old days when Nicky Scarfo was running things and bodies were dropping like rice at a wedding, but it still could have been better. So Mann liked to drop around, let the old wops see him, let them know he had his eyes open and his hands in on things.

And that's what brought him in on this, a dead man in a cold water walk-up. Just that stiff hanging there, looking like something a couple anatomy students had just gotten through hacking on.

Michael Perno stood by Mann, his face twisted-up like he'd ate something rancid that wouldn't stay down. But a lot of cops looked like that and more often than not, it didn't take a corpse to inspire it. It just was.

Looking at the body hanging there, the CSI techies in their white utilities measuring things and scribbling other things in their notebooks, Perno said, "Richard Rice, age thirty-two, got a sheet on him longer than a horse's pecker and not much better to look at . . . assault, attempted manslaughter, strong-arm robbery, all the goodies . . . a real fucking boy scout here. Around the block they called him Richie R. He's been out of Yardville maybe sixteen months, word has it he's been real tight with Donny Cerrone and his crew."

Mann nodded, looking at the stiff and thinking it was enough to put a guy off meat. Rice looked like something from an Italian zombie pukefest. "What do you make of this? What kind of chord is this striking with you?"

Perno shook his head, pulled his eyes away from the body which looked like about 250 pounds of raw hamburger. "It's not good, Archie, but I don't see LCN in this one. I mean, shit, this isn't La Cosa Nostra, no way. This is just fucked-up."

That pretty much said it.

Richard Rice, a.k.a. Richie R, had been—according to the Medical Examiner's cursory exam—beaten to the proverbial pulp, nearly decapitated, then disemboweled and hung up like a party pinata with his own intestines. That was real sweet, that bit. Took real imagination to come up with that one. But Mann had seen lots of crazy shit in his time. He told Perno about that Puerto Rican broad over in Vineland, how she'd been sharing the goods with some of her husband's friends, so he stuck the barrel of a Remington 12-gauge up her cootch and pulled the trigger. Said that had been an ugly one, all right. With the Remington hanging out of her, she looked like a corndog on a stick someone had taken a big bite out of.

Perno said, "This is just disgusting, Archie. This isn't a trunk job or a slice-and-dice, let's hide the body parts so no one can put Humpty Dumpty back together again . . . no, this ain't like that. This is . . . *what?*

Like whoever did Rice wanted people to see his work, say, lookit the shit I can do. I'm something, all right. Like maybe a serial killer, that sort of thing."

Mann nodded. "Yeah, still I wanna have a talk with my pal Donny. You say Rice was bouncing with Cerrone? Well, you never know, old Donny might be in on this, might have pissed somebody off."

"Whoever it is, Mike, you remind me not to piss 'em off."

Perno gave Mann what Cartland, the M.E., had given him, the sort of stuff that made you want to skip lunch. Rice had been worked on pretty good, smashed around so that the majority of his bones had been broken. His left lung was collapsed, neck shattered, skull fractured in three places, right arm snapped off at the elbow. "Like he was hit by a train, Archie."

"Yeah, a pissed-off train that kept coming back for more." Mann sighed. "What about all those lacerations . . . Jesus, looks like somebody was trying to peel him like an orange, then changed their mind."

Perno nodded, swallowed something down. "Cartland's saying some sort of knife, maybe a sword . . . something real sharp. The only thing that's bothering him is the angle of penetration at the entry wounds, more like sharp hooks than a blade."

Mann turned away. "You look at stiffs long enough, you start thinking they're looking back at you."

Perno understood. "I've saved the best for last."

"I knew you would."

Perno smiled, then decided this wasn't the sort of thing you smiled about. "As a joke, whoever did this took Rice's *heart* with him. Don't that beat all?"

Swallowing, something bad being born down in his belly, Mann had to admit that, yeah, it was really something.

3

DONNY CERRONE was shaking his head, saying, "Okay, you go figure this shit out, you're so smart. I'm telling you what I know is all. What do you want from me? Pull something better outta my ass . . . that make you happy?"

Archie Mann pulled off his cigarette. "I'm of the mind that there's nothing up your ass I'd want to see, Donny. So let's try something dif-

ferent here. I'll go real slow so I don't confuse you and your third grade
education . . . okay?"

"Sure, but take it easy on me, will ya?"

Mann smiled thinly. "I will. I'm all heart. That's what they say about
me."

"Is that what they say?"

"Sure, just like they say you're some kind of stand-up guy. You know
they say that about you?"

"No, that's gangster-talk, so I wouldn't know about that shit. I'm an
honest, hardworking businessman, ask anybody. People bring things
in here, I front 'em some cash, they don't come back, I sell the stuff. Hey,
Mann, you need a guitar? I got some nice guitars. No, that wouldn't be
your thing . . . you're a trumpet sort of guy, I bet. Like to blow your fucking horn all the time."

"You think so?" Mann said. "But when Jimmy Jack Furnari and some
of the Georgia Street Irregulars decide to cut your trash-talking head
off, Donny, I'll set that trumpet down and play my fucking violin. How's
that grab you?"

Cerrone didn't bother smiling. He just leaned on the counter and
let Mann have his fun. They played tag like this every month or so and it
got to be like old times after awhile. Cerrone was thinking he should've
ducked out for lunch ten minutes earlier and he could have missed
Mann altogether. That cheered him some until he remembered he was
still here. With Mann.

Donny Cerrone ran a pawnshop over on Mississippi Avenue called
the Whole Nine Yards, cute name, and regular as a woman's cycle and
about as wanted, Mann would stop by and ride his shit for free. Mann
was of the mind that Donny was connected up with some heavy players
out of Georgia Street, the sort of guys who liked spaghetti and made a
habit of dumping dead bodies in the trunks of cars. Those kinds of guys.
Thing was, Mann was right, not that Donny was going to admit as such.
He was in deep and Mann knew it, just couldn't prove it was all.

"I'm clean," Donny said. "And that's all there is to it."

"Yeah, you're clean, all right. Clean like a sewer."

Yeah, that Archie Mann was some kind of character. Like a tick that
burrowed under your skin and bled you dry drop by drop. That's the
kind of guy he was.

"Okay now, Donny, here we go." Mann pulled off his cigarette, flicked his ash on the counter. "You say you know a boy named Richie R? But you say you haven't seen him in about a week, he was doing some work for you? That what you're serving up today?"

"That's it, boss. You got it right the first time."

Mann nodded. "Well, not to piss in your punch, Donny, but I think I should let a hardworking honest businessman like you onto something . . . Richie R, he was a bad boy."

"No shit? And here I trusted him."

"Yup. Guy pulled state-time twice, federal time once. Been in half a dozen county lockups in his career as a dumbfuck white trash criminal."

"Damn. You're scaring me now, Mann. Come back here, lookit my balls, will ya? They're all shriveled-up and shit."

Mann laughed. "I love you, Donny, you know that? I would've thought a hood like Richie R would scare you . . . but then I remembered you'd done some time yourself. Where were you at? Let me see . . . oh, that's right, FSP Lewisburg. I remember now. People say there's lots of Mafia-types in there. You meet any?"

"Me? No, I worked in the chapel."

Cerrone knew they could go back and forth like this all day. Mann never got tired. That's the sort of guy he was. Pushing sixty, lots of snow on the roof, face seamed like a peach pit, but tough, Jesus, tough and randy and smart. The way cops were once before the steroids, lawsuits, and departmental therapists molded them into mass-produced skinheads.

Mann kept talking about Richie R and his career of crime, the bad things that happen to guys like him and those they associate with, pretty much running circles around what he really wanted to say. But that was Archie Mann all over, you had to give him room, let him run around a lot like something that was kept on a leash for too long. Sooner or later, he'd come back home and use the front door. Maybe piss on your leg or dry-hump your slacks, but he'd come home.

So Cerrone waited while he talked.

Now and again a customer would come through the door, jingling the bells, take one look at Mann standing there and go back out again. The sort of people Cerrone dealt with—thieves, junkies, small-time hoods needing to move some hot merch fast—they could smell a cop half a mile off. They made Archie Mann right away, decided they'd better come back. Maybe it was the bad suit or the worse haircut. But maybe it was the eyes . . . dead and fixed like the eyes of a stuffed toad. Eyes that always seemed to be saying, you can't show me worse shit than I've already seen.

Either way, Cerrone didn't need this right now. He was losing customers with a cop in his place. He had too many things going on, too many angles that needed working. The pawnshop was basically just a front for Cerrone, put him on paper as being legit. When you were a loanshark and a bookie, fenced stolen goods for a living, you had to have something legit to launder your income through. A fact of life.

Mann was telling Cerrone about this guy he knew, thought he should hear about it. "This guy . . . we'll call him *Donny*, just for the hell of it. He's not a bad guy for the most part, he just came up in the wrong neighborhood and started playing with the wrong sort of kids. You know the kids I mean . . . the kind that always end up in reform school and prison later, earners and players. That's the sort of people Donny got jammed up with. Pretty soon, he's just like them, got his hands dirty—"

"All right, all right, Mann, Jesus Christ. I don't have time for this shit. How many times we gonna stand here and dance this same tired fucking tune?"

"Maybe until you're straight with me."

"Straight about what?"

Mann just looked at him. "About what you do for a living."

Cerrone tried to laugh, but his throat felt too dry. "I run a pawnshop, Mann, I'm not John fucking Gotti here. Shit, I'm not saying I'm clean as a whistle. Sure, I run some book, put together a few card games."

"What about loansharking?"

"No, not me."

"Hijacking?"

Cerrone did laugh now, but it didn't come out sounding too good. "That's for the pros, I'm just a small-timer. I don't touch that stuff."

"No? Then what did you have a boy like Richie R around for? Because you know what? People I been talking with, they're saying Richie R was a hijacker: warehouses, semis, that sort of bit."

"Nothing like that," Cerrone told him. "I was using Richie for odds and ends. I use lots of guys like that. He was a runner, took bets on games, shit like that. No strong-arm stuff."

Mann just shook his head. "If you say so, Donny. I just hope what happened to Richie R don't happen to you. Because I got the feeling he pissed somebody off. Some real mean, psychotic sonofabitch."

Cerrone licked his lips. "They shoot him or what?"

"No, nothing like that." Mann told him all about it, how Richie R looked like something you saw hanging in a Chicago stockyard when they were done with him. "And you know what, Donny? Whoever did him took his fucking heart."

Then Mann left and Cerrone relaxed inch by inch. As much as he could after what he'd just been told. Thing was, he *had* been using Richie R for some heavy stuff, for muscle to take down some lucrative heists. But other than that, Mann was way off base. There was nothing they'd been doing that could have pissed anyone off . . . and particularly not like that.

This is what Cerrone was telling himself, but down at the pit of his belly, he was starting to get a real tense feeling.

4

DONNY CERRONE had an apartment over on North Georgia Avenue, about two blocks from the tenement he'd grown up in. He wasn't married, never dated anyone but hookers because once you paid them, they invariably left. So when he got home that night, there was nobody waiting for him. Not even a cat or dog. In fact, animals weren't even allowed in the building.

And that's why what he saw didn't make much sense.

Up there on the fifth floor, his door was scathed with what looked like claw-marks, as if a dog had been trying real hard to scratch its way in.

Cerrone stood there, that feeling in his belly again.

It don't mean nothing, he told himself. Some animal got in.

The fifth floor, though? Did it take the elevator? But Cerrone dismissed that. He studied the scratches, noticing with unease that they were not down low like the sort a dog would make, but up high on the door, from midline to the top and dug in real deep like somebody had been using a garden trowel . . . one that was *real* sharp. Some of those gashes were imbedded a half an inch or more. And in solid oak yet. Cerrone started wondering the sort of strength it would take to sink a blade in that deep and then pull it down at the same depth.

Like claws, he found himself thinking. *Like something very strong with big claws was ripping at the door.*

He started to tremble, the flesh on his forearms and at the back of his neck prickling. Making a funny moaning sound in his throat, he got his key in the lock and went through the door fast as he could. Then he shut it, locked it, even threw the deadbolt though his building was high-security with keyless entry, security guards, the whole bit. His fingers found the lights and it occurred to him at the last possible moment that there could have been somebody in there *waiting* for him.

But there was no one.

Just silence and Donny Cerrone, a forty-nine year old loanshark, bookie, and fence. A connected guy who'd done time and didn't know the meaning of fear. Not really. Not by this point. But there he was . . . shaking, scared white inside like some kid who'd just escaped the neighborhood haunted house.

Sure was funny what your mind could do to you, Cerrone found himself thinking as he poured a Chivas on the rocks and threw it down the hatch, refilling it just that quick. His hands were still shaking. There it was again, that awful, inescapable feeling in his belly, that tenseness touched by nausea: fear.

Christ, get a grip here.

So he did. He threw back the second Chivas and got a grip on a .38 Smith Airweight he kept in his bedroom. The feel of a gun relaxed him some. Standing there, he tried to sort it out. He had no reason to be afraid, none at all . . . yet, he was. These past few days it had been on him, the sense that there was danger and a far worse sense that he was being watched.

But there was never anyone there.

Nobody, nothing . . . just that feeling at the back of his neck that got so bad sometimes he thought he might scream.

That's enough.

Cerrone sat down, turned on the tube, started watching some lesbo act on the Playboy Channel. Couple broads, lots of legs and tongues. Jesus Christ, who was he to be afraid? He'd dealt with thugs and criminals and psychopaths of every stripe since he was a kid. He was in tight with Jimmy Jack Furnari, a capo in the Calabrian Mafia, the sort of guy, you pissed him off, he'd have a couple hitters do you with chainsaws in a warehouse. These were the sort of sharks he swam with, but if you knew the moves—and Donny Cerrone knew 'em, all right—you could dance away from their jaws every time. And after three decades of that and five years in a maximum security prison, Donny Cerrone did not frighten easy.

Yet, he *was* afraid.

Right then, thinking it over, it came on him again, that electric and somehow sour feeling of adrenaline down low in his guts. The sense that something really nasty had happened or was about to. Yeah, that was it. Like when his mother was in the hospital, shot through with cancer, and he sat around expecting the phone to ring, some half-ass intern saying, yeah, she went down, Mr. Cerrone, she took the leap. It was very much like that, the sense of expectancy in him jarring him with negative energy—

The phone rang.

Cerrone felt something kick in his chest like it wanted out. His breath wouldn't come. The .38 slid from his grip and thudded to the carpet. No, no, no, fucking no, it's not ringing, you're freaking out here, having some episode like when "Fat" Bobby Scolari said those little men were coming out of the walls and he started shooting up his apartment, killed the guy next door.

But Bobby had been a blowhead, spiking more coke than he was pushing on the streets.

The phone rang again and there was no denying it.

Cerrone picked up the .38 Airweight, like maybe he was going to bust a few into this caller that made him almost piss his pants. He set it back down, chuckled. Jesus, you gotta stop this shit.

He picked up the cordless. "Yeah?"

Static, lots of it. Droning, rising, falling. A bad connection. But Cerrone knew it wasn't that, nothing that simple. He waited, felt his heart squeeze like a fist. Felt a trickle of sweat run down his temple. Then a voice . . . ragged and raw like its owner had been chewing on shards of glass, swallowing them: *"I missed you tonight . . . but I won't miss you next time."*

Cerrone thought he might faint, but he kept it together. Found some streets inside him, some attitude. "Who the fuck is this?"

The connection wasn't broken. Just that droning static, the sound of lungs pulling in scraping breaths. *"Baby-killer,"* that awful voice said.

"I've prepared a place for you."

Click.

Cerrone wasn't easily intimidated, but that voice was terrible. Flat and evil and remorseless, it started filling his mind with reaching shadows and grinning white faces, the sort of things made a man want to sleep with the lights on. Nothing . . . nothing sane could have a voice like that. It reminded Cerrone of musty cellars and rotting crypts, moldering coffin linings. Stunned, dazed, the phone had fallen from his grip and he didn't even remember dropping it. He just stood there, not really knowing and not wanting to. Inside him, something had broken like eggs on a sidewalk and that's how he felt—yellow and runny and messy.

After a time, he found the sofa again or maybe it found him, all the while wondering just what sort of shit he'd stepped in this time.

5

BRIGHT AND EARLY the next morning, Archie Mann was over in lower Chelsea, wondering what was happening in this goddamn town. Mike Perno had called him again, said *you gotta see this shit, Archie,* and now Mann was seeing it and, being a cop, he was trying to label it and fit it in its proper box . . . but he just couldn't find the right one in his cluttered mind.

How did you explain this?

How did you label this one and file it away?

The street was a hive of activity—metro homicide people milling around, CSI techies, the M.E.'s ghouls, uniforms holding back the wave of spectators and newsies, and . . . get this . . . a couple cherry pickers from public works. Heavy trucks with extendable booms and buckets on the ends, the sort electricians used to service the high lines. The booms had double buckets on them and both were extended an easy thirty feet in the air. CSI people were in the buckets, examining what was lodged up in the crotch of two limbs on a massive elm tree.

"What kind of fucking joke is this?" Mann said out loud.

Perno didn't have any answers. "Somebody spotted the stiff up there this morning, thought it was some crazy bastard stuck up there . . ."

Perno said the investigating uniforms knew a corpse when they saw one, even when it was thirty-odd feet up in the air. They brought in homicide and cordoned off the area. Perno hadn't been up there, but he talked to one of his metro friends that had been . . . the stiff had been badly mutilated, bones broken, belly slit open, head almost cut off. Crazy thing was . . . if it could get crazier than this . . . there didn't seem to be any blood around, like maybe the John Doe had been murdered somewhere else and dropped there.

"From what?" Mann said. "A passing plane? A big Jesus hawk?"

Again, Perno had no answers. "I called you over because I knew you were going to want a look at this one. Maybe it has nothing to do with our friend Richie R, but I'm willing to bet it does."

Mann swallowed down a bad taste in his mouth. "How so?"

"The mutilations are similar to Richie R's for one thing," Perno said to him. "We pulled the guy's wallet out of his pocket and we ran his name—" Perno flipped open his notebook "—Carlo Arroyo, first generation Cuban-American. His parents got out of Cuba just before Castro. I didn't figure you'd care about that, but when I say that Arroyo was a known hijacker and strongarm thief, was in Lewisburg about the same time as Donny Cerrone . . . well, thought you might be interested."

"Shit," Mann said.

He took a breath and let it out real, real slow. Tenuous as all hell, that's what this was, but Mann trusted Perno's sense of intuition, his ability to string together things others might miss. You worked Intelligence as long as Perno had, you got real good at things like that. Mann lit a cigarette and stirred it all around in his mind. Okay. Injuries apparently concurrent with those of Richie R. That was a start. A known hijacker. That added fuel. Did time with Donny Cerrone. That lit a spark. No fire yet, but the tinder was there and the conditions were right . . . still, it was a hell of a reach.

"What're you thinking, Archie?" Perno asked him. "You got a feeling on this, don't you?"

Mann exhaled a column of smoke. "Sure, I get lots of feelings. Cops are like that . . . don't you ever watch the late show for chrissake? Problem is, mine are mostly gas or my prostate acting up."

Perno chuckled.

The CSI people were bringing the body down now. You could almost hear a hush fall over the crowd. Some vacuous-looking blonde with a nice set of ta-tas and a plastic sort of face she probably kept in a drawer was speaking into a mic and staring into a TV camera. Story at six.

The body was taken down carefully, loaded in a gurney, brought behind a barrier the cops had set up. The techies, led by the M.E. himself, descended on the fresh meat like turkey buzzards, elbowing their way in for the best parts.

Mann crushed his cigarette out under his shoe. "They tell me this guy ain't got a heart, I'm calling her quits and going down to Florida."

6

ABOUT TWO THAT AFTERNOON, Donny Cerrone was sitting at a basement bar about two blocks from his place on North Georgia. Just sitting there with a Chivas on the rocks in his hand. Thing was, he wasn't drinking it, just holding it. Feeling how cool it was. Sitting across from him was Jimmy Jack Furnari, just staring at him, giving him the sort of look that could have stripped varnish off a door, not saying a thing.

You had to love the guy.

He could be smooth as imported silk when it came to schmoozing with politicians or casino bigwigs, assorted celebrities and industrialists, but when he was around his people—made guys, high-ranking criminals, connected guys who got to see him, which were few—he didn't bother with any of that shit. He just sat there, staring holes through you with those black, narrowed eyes of his, that crooked toothy grin on his face like he was thinking about taking a bite out of your throat.

That was the real Jimmy Jack Furnari, Calabrian-Italian racketeer and out and out homicidal maniac if you didn't tell him what he wanted to hear. And that was the rub . . . Cerrone didn't know what Furnari wanted to hear on account he wasn't saying a damn thing.

Just staring.

And Cerrone had to wonder how many guys got that look right before Furnari had them put down like sick dogs.

The mob capo sat there, just watching him. He was wearing a white polo shirt and it made his thick, tattooed forearms look almost vibrant. Finally, he sighed, shook his head. "What is this shit, Donny?" he said. "What the fuck is this shit I'm hearing all over? What can you tell me about it?"

Cerrone knew what he was talking about. Even though not a word had been spoken on the subject, he knew all right. And he wasn't stu-

pid enough to pretend ignorance. You didn't do that with these Cal-
abrians. They were a hardcore bunch. Maybe you could joke with the
Sicilians . . . sometimes . . . but not their Calabrian brothers.

Cerrone shook his head. "I don't know, Mr. Furnari. There's something
fucked up here, but I just don't know what it is."

Furnari nodded, smiled thinly, but his eyes were simmering and
dark like pools of acid you might drop bodies into, watch the bones come
bobbing back up. "Let me see what I'm hearing here. Some shit . . . crazy
shit . . . about two boys, Richie R and some spic name of Arroyo, work
for you, got themselves clipped and in a real bad way. Am I right on this
shit?"

"Yeah, you're right."

"They work for you?"

"Yes."

"Now they dead . . . you don't know why?"

Cerrone told him very honestly that he didn't. That he'd been all over
this and he couldn't think of any reason why somebody would want to kill
the two men. Sure, they were tough boys, hijackers, ran some muscle for
Cerrone, but he'd never gotten them involved in anything that could have
pissed somebody off like this. Unless, well, they'd been bopping around
on their free time, doing some grabs from the wrong people.

Furnari nodded. "Sure, I see. Thing is . . . we been talking to people
here. You know the kind of people I mean? People who play rough, don't
like poaching on their turf? Them kind . . . but nobody saying shit here.
This is some kind of fucking mystery. So I want you to think real hard . . .
whoever these boys pissed off, don't matter who, I can straighten it out. I
just don't want a lot of trouble on this, I don't want it getting out of hand.
You hear what I'm saying, Donny? I don't want your people tracking shit
back to me."

Cerrone almost laughed at that, despite the threat behind Furnari's
words. Laughed because it was classic Jimmy Jack. He didn't care where
the shit fell or in which direction it sprayed, as long as none of it got on
him. Because if it did, if it did and you didn't get in the way and catch
it . . . you want it in the belly or the head? Your choice, friend. Of course,
it wasn't just Jimmy Jack, all made guys were like that. Cerrone had been
playing with these boys for a lot of years and they were all the same. Fuck
that men-of-respect shit you got in *The Godfather*, that was Hollywood

fantasy. The reality was that these Italians were greedy, violent animals that would slit your throat for a nickel.

"No, I don't think you have anything to worry about here, Mr. Furnari."

"You don't *think?*" He didn't exactly look satisfied with that. "I wanna know what these boys were into, Donny. I want to know what kind of fucking dirt they were scratching around in."

So Cerrone told him all there was to tell.

Rice and Arroyo, along with another tough named Pauly Wade, were basically smash-and-grab artists. When they took something down, they did it the hard way. Cerrone knew their reputation, used them to do some collecting for his loansharking operation and, now and again, some heavy takedowns where a guy had to have some real balls. Mostly over-the-road tractor-trailers, hijacking stuff. They'd taken down four rigs in the past month.

"But you got your cut on that, Mr. Furnari, I made sure of that. You know what I'm talking about here, right?"

Furnari nodded. He remembered. One hijacked rig had a load of furs, another cigarettes, and another top-of-the-line HDTV's. Cerrone had middled the swag on those, moved the merch through his contacts, turned some good numbers on it.

Furnari said, "I remember those three . . . but there was a fourth? I'm hazy on that one."

So Cerrone told him about it, how the whole thing went south, belly-up. Wade, Arroyo, and Rice had taken down a truck, conked the driver into dreamland, discovered that there wasn't a damn thing in back worth grabbing. Just soil or some shit for a tree nursery. Something like that. Nothing.

Furnari said, "Okay . . . this Wade is still above ground, you get on his ass, find out what they were up to. I don't like this shit. I'm smelling something here and it's bad, Donny. Real bad. But these are your people here, so clean your own house, Donny. Because you know what they say: a fish rots from the head down . . ."

7

CERRONE DIDN'T GO to the pawnshop that day. There was nothing that the hired help couldn't deal with. He drove around Atlantic City, watching all those streets and avenues pass by as he winged down Pacific in his sky blue Crown Vic—Pennsylvania, Carolina, Kentucky, Illinois, Indiana—thinking, and not for the first time, that living in this damn town was like living on a Monopoly board . . . though you had to look damn hard for that Get-Out-of-Jail-Free card. If you fucked up here, you pissed off some of the meat-eaters and leg-breakers that greased the wheels, you didn't pass Go, you went straight off the pier with a cinderblock chained to your leg.

Take Jimmy Jack Furnari for example. The feds had been taking one unsuccessful run after another at that guy for years and probably would still be wearing out their shoes if it weren't for budget cuts. But he was smart, crafty, dangerous as all hell. They knew he had his fingers in the unions, extortion, drug trafficking, illegal gambling, and cyberporn . . . they just couldn't prove it was all.

But Cerrone wasn't worried about Jimmy Jack.

For Jimmy Jack was a known quantity, but what had happened to Richie R and Carlo Arroyo was definitely on the unknown side of things. It all tied together somehow just as it tied in with those gouges in his door and that weird phone call he'd gotten last night. He hadn't slept much after that and he had a feeling he wouldn't be sleeping for some time to come.

Baby-killer . . . I've prepared a place for you.

Although it was a hot day, Cerrone found himself shivering. What did it mean and what in Christ's name kind of voice was that? Like the guy had been gargling with rusty nails and rock salt. A raw, bleeding sort of voice . . . eerie and wavering. What the hell did it all mean?

Cerrone pulled into the lot behind his building and there was Archie Mann waiting for him. Thick-necked old bull leaning up against a state-issue Lumina, a real piece of shit. Just like the guy who drove it.

"Okay," Cerrone said when he got out. "What now? I'm plotting the overthrow of fucking Paraguay? I'm counterfeiting Beanie Babies? What kind of shit did I do this time, Columbo?"

Mann just smiled thin as a paper cut, flicked the ash off his cigarette. "Hey, Donny, how's things? You look tired . . . you getting enough sleep? Eating right?"

"Sure, three squares a day. Watching the cholesterol and shit." He patted his expanding belly. "In the gym every morning."

Mann nodded. "Me, too." He pulled off his cigarette. "Reason I stop by, Donny, is I met this friend of yours."

"No shit? Well, you give him my respects. I'd like to stay and chat, but I gotta go cut my toenails and—"

Mann caught his arm as he passed. "Think you ought to stay and be sociable, Donny. Think that's what you ought to do."

"What is this? A fucking pinch?"

"Nothing like that. Just wanted to talk about that friend of yours, guy name of Carlo Arroyo, Hispanic fellow, though he could pass for a cracker easy enough. You know the guy?"

Cerrone just stood there, not knowing what to do with his hands. Not knowing how to stand. Not knowing what to do about that dread creeping up from his balls in slow, shivering waves.

"I see that you do," Mann said. He looked tired, too many lines on his face, lips pulled into a frown. "See, Donny, when I met this friend of yours, he was something like thirty feet up an elm over in Chelsea, treed like a fucking cat. You should've seen him when they brought him down, Donny . . . just a fucking mess. All busted-up and swollen, most of his bones broken, like something made of red, white, and gray pulp. Like maybe he'd taken a dive off a ten-story building, kissed the concrete, then some wise-ass, as a joke, scraped him up and dumped him way up in that tree."

Cerrone was trying to find something smart to say, but he was suddenly dumb all over. Dumb and numb, his guts filled with something greasy and shifting. "You don't say? What was this guy's name again?"

"I was thinking maybe you and your crew pissed off Jimmy Jack and his boys, but I'm not thinking that anymore. Not at all." Mann wasn't playing the game here, he was serious as a heart attack. He looked sad, worn-out, just flat used-up. "Donny, I'm not fucking around here . . . Arroyo, they cut his heart out, too. Cut it right the fuck out."

Cerrone swallowed, but his throat just wouldn't obey. Up his spine and down his arms there was gooseflesh now. His mouth was dry and his heart was hammering. "I don't know about this shit, Archie," he heard himself say. "I don't know what it's about, I just don't know what's going on here."

Mann seemed to believe that. "If I were you, Donny, I'd get the hell out of town," he said and meant it. "If you need a better reason, one that'll keep you up nights, I got one for you: Arroyo didn't have a drop of blood left in him, he was bled fucking white."

And then Cerrone was stumbling away, feeling dizzy and sick to his stomach, his entire world, the one he'd known all his life, unzipping around him and something out there, something dark and nameless, reaching out for him.

8

"JUST ANSWER the fucking question," Cerrone told Pauly Wade that evening. Feeling night coming down slick and dark like an oil-spill, swallowing the world in black rivers and murky lagoons, making something in his soul rot to carrion. "I ask and you answer . . . that ain't so goddamn hard is it, Pauly?"

Wade just shrugged.

You couldn't intimidate or muscle the guy, not Pauly Wade. He was full of muscles and concrete. A career criminal that had been in some of the worst hard time joints on the eastern seaboard, you just couldn't shake a guy like that. But at least they were alone now. Wade had sent Celia, his black girlfriend who was probably a casino hooker, out for an order of something called shrimp pizza . . . Jesus, *shrimp* pizza . . . and now Cerrone could talk to him, try to get something out of him.

"The last job I sent you boys on," Cerrone said to him. "You know the one I mean?"

Wade nodded, stroked his thick black mustache. "What about it? Was a bust. Shit, nothing there worth grabbing. A fucking waste . . . I shoulda capped that driver for taking up my time with something like that."

"Yeah, yeah . . . was there anything, I don't know, *unusual* about that bit? Something that stands out?"

Wade sat there, pulling off a bottle of malt liquor, staring out the window of his apartment which was above a clam shop and smelled like it, too. Then, slowly, he shook his head. "Like I said, a bust."

Cerrone turned away from him, looked at the wall, the ceiling, the furniture and home electronics, knowing it was all probably hot. He ran a trembling hand over his face, gripped his jaw with it. Jesus, there had to be something here. *Had* to be. They'd been over everything else, this was all that was left. And if Wade got whacked, well, there wouldn't be any answers left . . . just a lot of dying for no good goddamn reason.

"Okay, then, okay. Just go over that clusterfuck with me, step by step. You conked that driver, tied him up . . . then what?"

Wade shrugged. "The usual. We drove his truck out into the boonies, to that old warehouse out near Margate. You know the one. We pulled it inside, opened it up. Nothing in there, just those boxes."

"Boxes? You never said nothing about boxes? You said *dirt,* just a lot of dirt, that's what you told me."

"Yeah, the dirt was in the boxes . . . what you think? It was just piled in the back?"

"Boxes full of dirt?"

"Yeah, crates I guess you'd call 'em."

Cerrone was feeling something worming at the back of his mind, something he'd seen in an old movie once. "Crates . . . what do you mean? Like . . . like coffins full of dirt?"

Wade shook his head. "Not unless they was coffins for little kids. These weren't no bigger than suitcases. We broke them all open, cracked the lids open with crowbars, thought maybe there'd be something good inside, something special, you know? Nothing but dirt, though."

"Dirt? Little crates full of dirt?" Cerrone felt himself getting farther away from the truth here all the time or maybe he was getting closer and he just couldn't see it. "All right, tell me about the dirt."

Wade looked at him like he was crazy. "Just five, six inches of dirt in them. Stuff smelled pretty rank, rancid-stinking dirt and really black, moist. There were worms in it."

"Worms?"

"Yeah." Wade, a guy who was unmoved by just about anything, seemed uneasy or uncomfortable with the memory of those boxes of black earth. It was there on his face, just behind his eyes, then it was gone. "Worms . . . like maggots, you know? Big fucking maggots rooting around in there and that stink. It was pretty bad."

Cerrone felt his breath catch in his throat. It was filled with razors. Maggoty black dirt? The smell of putrescence, of death? What the hell did that mean? "Anything else?"

That look passed over Wade's face again, lit up like a shooting star and then died in his dire, gray eyes where there was nothing really alive and hadn't been for years. "I think . . . I think rats got into those boxes."

"Rats?"

"That's what we thought. Rats. Fucking rats." Wade sat there a moment, a disgusted look on his face like maybe the shrimp pizza was going to have to wait. "I don't know where you grew up, but I grew up in a shithole tenement in North Boston. Full of rats. My brother got bit lots of times. Me too. One time . . . one time my old lady found a nest of 'em under the cupboard, right? A big gray mama rat and her brood. My old man killed mama with a carving knife, flushed the babies down the toilet. But we seen 'em, all us kids . . . little pink, blind squirming things, curled-up limbs moving around . . . fucking creepy."

And it was. Cerrone was feeling it, too. "You found rats in those crates?"

But Wade shook his head. "No, just one little baby rat in each box . . . ain't that funny? They were big, but that's what they had to be, something like fetal rats . . . all pink and pulsing, kind of unformed, just squirming in that dirt with the maggots . . ."

Baby-killer . . . I've prepared a place for you.

Cerrone had to sit down, catch his breath. "You . . . you sure they were rats?"

Wade shrugged. "Had to be, right? It was a little dark in the warehouse, but they looked like rats . . . pink and squirming things. Ugly little bastards, eyes not open yet."

"So . . . you just dumped 'em out with the dirt?"

"Yeah, we dumped 'em out on the floor."

"And that was it?"

Wade grinned, his eyes shining and his teeth crooked. "Yeah, then we *stepped* on those ugly little pricks . . . Arroyo almost ran out of there because they squealed when you stepped on 'em. Awful sound, went right up your spine."

Cerrone was shaking again and there were things blooming in his mind, terrible sprouting growths like funeral lilies. He didn't ask Wade any more questions. The only one left he asked himself:

If those were babies . . . then what do they grow up to be?

9

MIDNIGHT.

A shattering of glass. A rending sound, something crashing and something else going to fragments. Donny Cerrone came awake and couldn't honestly say in that moment of racing adrenaline if he'd actually been asleep in the first place. Just sitting in that chair, watching the tube, mind full of crawling things and squirming pink things that would not let his eyes close.

And now this.

He came out of the chair, disoriented, foot slipping somehow on the teal shag, barking his knee on the coffee table. That brought some pain which cleared his head and he realized the .38 Smith Airweight was still in his hand. Eyes wide and throat pulled down to a pinhole, he scanned the gun around the room like some kind of half-assed TV cop. He just sat there, knees on the carpet, hearing his own breathing and feeling the graveyard stillness of the apartment. Except, okay, it wasn't still, not anymore. Maybe it was soundless since that crashing, but it was not still, not exactly, not *untenanted* . . . the atmosphere had been violated somehow.

Listen.

He was doing that, but it wasn't telling him much. He could hear his own body—breath in his lungs, blood rushing in his ears—but not much else. His mind raced from room to room, trying to find the point of trespass. Cerrone's apartment was big: living room, dining room, kitchen, two bedrooms, bathroom. Plenty of places. But that had been a window which meant either his bedroom or the dining room . . .

There.

He could hear footsteps now . . . gradual, creaking, as if their owner were trying to be stealthy. Which made no sense if you crashed in through a window.

The dining room. Whatever had come into his apartment in the dead of night was in the dining room. Cerrone could smell them and it made something in his stomach blanch . . . a filthy, dark smell of buried things and backed-up storm drains.

Cerrone licked his lips.

He wondered if he ran full out if he could make the front door, get out into the hallway before . . . before that thing took hold of him. He figured it wouldn't happen. Because whatever in the Christ it was, whatever brought its young to term in crates full of black, wormy earth like poison mushrooms, it was capable of incredible feats like tossing a guy thirty feet up into a tree or crashing through a fifth-story window at three a.m.

Cerrone figured this is where he either shat or got off the pot. Regardless, he had to do something. He had to meet this prick on its own ground and show it the size of his balls. Because he had a real crazy idea that things like that would matter to something like it, the sort of thing that inspired campfire stories.

But it wasn't so easy.

Didn't seem like there was much Cerrone could do but crouch there with the .38, all the things that made him a man and a player drained right out of him. There was something in his place and it was something insane, something impossible. Something that had come with a chill dankness one might associate with vaults and catacombs.

Cerrone stood up.

It had to be done. He had to go to it because it probably wouldn't come to him, something like that that was used to jumping out of the shadows at people. So Cerrone kept the .38 up, walked into the kitchen. The light was on. All the lights were on. He walked past the stainless steel face of the stove he never used, noticing that the tile near the window was starting to get yellow from the sunlight. And, yes, now he was smelling his visitor . . . a black sewer-smell of stagnation.

Of course, it would have to smell bad. Because whatever in the hell it is, it's vile from head to toe. The sort of nightmare that plants its children like seeds in maggoty soil.

Cerrone stepped into the dining room and there was glass all over the place . . . shards sprayed over the oak table like crushed ice. And standing there, just inside the window that was blowing in the hot, salty Atlantic City air, was a man. Or maybe something like one.

Cerrone swallowed.

Not, on second thought, it was *not* a man.

It had wings . . . or at least one of them, a great black and membranous wing shot through with pink vein networking that was attached to the underside of its left arm. As Cerrone saw this, saw that webbing of sticky diaphanous flesh over narrow spines of bone, the wing folded up. And it was a real good trick, because with those wings folded down like that, it looked like the guy just had some long dark coat on made of oily leather. The only thing that gave it away was that the bottom of the "coat" was jagged like the wing of a bat or the outer edge of an umbrella.

Cerrone stared, something inside of him rapidly drying up like a pond.

He looked at the thing.

It looked at him.

And he thought: *I don't stand a chance in hell.*

It stepped forward and Cerrone saw that beneath those spreading, enveloping wings it wore a black suit with a wine-colored tie and a gold watch chain of all things. On its head was a wide-brimmed black hat of the sort a Mormon might wear. A study in contrasts. And the face . . . well, Cerrone wasn't ready to call it a face. It was white as chalk or quicklime, flaking and fissured, elongated in shape, flattened-out, the lower jaw jutting forth giving it a vulpine look. Its nose was a skullish cavity and its eyes were wet and red and bulging like fresh cherries, completely without pupils.

When it spoke, its voice was aged and rasping. *"Mr. Cerrone . . . I said I would come and here I am."* It drew in a few sharp breaths, then exhaled with a cold stink of tombs.

Sure, it talked. It had talked on the phone, too, and maybe that was the most obscene thing about it . . . it looked like some bizarre bastard offspring between man and bat, yet it was intelligent and well-spoken. There was something very shocking about that—like being expelled from the womb. Donny knew there was simply no turning back now. Not after seeing this thing and hearing it speak.

"You're . . . you're not human," he finally said.

The thing laughed, cackled really, and it was an awful, mocking sound echoing out. *"Not quite,"* it said. *"But human or not, I do not kill children. I will not lower myself to killing children . . . can you say the same, Mr. Cerrone?"*

Cerrone couldn't say anything. He had a gun in his hand, he could feel it there, but the idea of shooting this thing . . . no, he was afraid of the idea. Afraid that if it didn't kill this monster, it might do something worse: piss it off.

And then Cerrone was talking, his brain functioning completely on auto and telling his mouth what to say. "I wasn't there . . . I wasn't in on that business . . . it was those three guys . . . they didn't know, Jesus, how could they know? They . . . they thought those things were rats . . ."

Those garish red eyes blinked, blinked again. Though that face was not remotely human, Cerrone could see the rage settling into it. The fissures deepening, that exaggerated skull beneath the flaking skin pressing forward like it wanted out. The thing exhaled with a groaning, growling sound, lips snarling back from yellow teeth that were long and thin like knitting needles. *"Vermin? Vermin? My children were vermin?"* It reached out towards Cerrone with a hand that was grotesque, exaggerated, the spindly fingers tapering into black talons that looked incredibly sharp . . . the tips needle-fine and probably capable of the very finest manipulation and dexterity. Then it drew back, closed the fingers into a fist and shook it. *"So your friends . . . killed my children, did they? Because they were vermin? Unfit to live?"*

Those red eyes were larger than ever, wide and moist and electric red, drilling holes right through Cerrone.

And all he could say was: "They didn't know."

The thing started forward, those eyes gleaming in gray-shadowed sockets. The teeth slid out again and then retreated. It stood there, breathing with a ragged, hollow sound. A voice in Cerrone's head kept telling him to shoot it, shoot that ugly motherfucker already. But he ignored it because, as horrible as that monster was, it was intelligent. And there was something about that wizened face that seemed almost, well, sympathetic.

"Your end will come, Mr. Cerrone," it promised him. *"But not today, not when you're expecting it. I've prepared a place for you and at an hour of my choosing, I will take you there."*

With that, it simply turned on its heel and dove out the window with a chill gust. Cerrone heard the flap of those great wings like the high shrouds of an old brig filling with air and that was all.

It was gone.

Cerrone dropped to his knees, feeling drunk and empty and just about out of his head. After a time, he said, *"Holy shit . . ."*

10

THE NEXT MORNING, wired and wasted from too much black coffee and Dexedrine, Cerrone was confronted by Archie Mann outside the pawnshop on Mississippi.

"You look like shit, Donny," he said.

Cerrone laughed. After what he'd been through, this guy couldn't have been more non-threatening if he had floppy shoes on and was riding a unicycle while he pumped a horn. "You *always* look like shit, Mann. Must be all the donuts and frustration that your life has been a fucking waste."

Mann just looked at him. "A little surly today, Donny?"

"Yeah, I didn't get much sleep."

"I bet you didn't." Mann lit a cigarette. "I thought I might drop by and tell you some good news."

"You're retiring?"

"No, not just yet. But your hijacking pal, Pauly Wade, is dead."

Cerrone felt the air bleed out of him. He leaned back against the brick façade of his shop. Dead? Is that what this prick said? Sure, sure. And why not? Pauly Wade had to be dead. *Probably why that ugly bastard didn't kill me last night, its belly was already full.* Cerrone sighed. "Dead, you say?"

"That's what I say. You have breakfast yet?"

"No, I don't do breakfast."

"Good, because I wouldn't want to ruin your appetite." He pulled off his cigarette, his hard cop's face unreadable. Either he was enjoying this or sick to his stomach . . . it was really hard to tell. "They found Pauly Wade over on the South Side up on top of some church they're putting a new roof on. Yeah, he was up there, busted-up and bloodless, Donny, kind of tangled up in a ball. You know why?"

Cerrone just waited for it like an inmate in the chair waiting for the first kiss of electricity. "No, but you're gonna tell me."

"This one's funny, Donny. It'll really have you laughing. He was tangled up because somebody, some wiseass, tried to shove his head up his own asshole. Almost did it, too. What do you think of that?"

"Fucking hilarious shit, Mann. You got any others?"

Mann tossed his cigarette. "One more. See, this whole bit is funny.

Because last night, I put a couple men on Wade. One down on the street watching the front door and one out in the alley watching the back. Funny thing is, thing that's gonna have you rolling, is that Wade never came out either of those doors . . . looks like he left through the window. Isn't that just a fucking knee-slapper, Donny?"

Cerrone turned away, his belly full of enough shit for one morning. "You're killing me, Mann, but I got a business to run."

"Donny? It doesn't matter to me at this point what you and those three hoods were up to. Doesn't matter one bit. But I think you're *next* and if you're smart, you'll let me put you somewhere where our friend can't get at you."

"I'll keep it in mind," Cerrone said, then shut the door in Mann's face.

11

THAT AFTERNOON, Archie Mann was in an alley just off Magellan and thinking that, Jesus, it was some kind of job, some kind of life he had here. Looking at corpses just about every day and never a simple shooting or stabbing or trunk job like in the old days. Now it was always this exotic shit that looked like it had been cooked up by some Hollywood FX guy.

Perno was there at his side, saying, "Celia Ann Bishop, twenty-three, prostitute. She had a thing going with Pauly Wade if her friends can be believed . . . and I'm guessing they can."

That was it then, that was what tore apart Mann's stomach in an eruption of ulcers. This had to happen and he'd been waiting for it ever since they found Wade's mangled corpse on top of that church and his girlfriend couldn't be located. Last night had been a twofer . . . Wade and his old lady. Now wasn't that fucking rich?

Celia Ann Bishop had been jammed down between the brick wall of a foundry and a green metal bank of transformers about the size of a small train car. There was less than fourteen inches of space in between them and yet she had been wedged in there, all the way down. Her ass was touching the ground, her legs sticking straight up, both her arms missing. She was crushed and flattened like a boulder had been dropped on her. Looking in there at her, Mann thought she looked like she'd been caught in a downpour last night and the sky had been pissing red. It had stained her like ink, crusted her distorted face, and looped her body like ropes. The CSI people were trying to pull her out of there and it was like trying to yank ten pounds of hamburger out through a mail slot.

Good luck.

"Only Donny Cerrone now," Mann heard himself say.

"He won't cooperate, eh?" Perno said.

"No, not a guy like him. He's an old school hood . . . you can't shake those guys."

"Maybe we could charge him with something," Perno suggested. "Pull him in, rattle him about the murders, put him on the box maybe."

But Mann shook his head. "He'd never sit still for a lie detector and he can smell bullshit a mile off."

"What then?"

"We wait," Mann said. "We wait until it's time to bag him. Because it's going to happen and we both know it."

12

THEN ONE DAY, you just got sick of it.

You got sick and tired of the whole game you'd been playing day in and day out for so many years now. You got sick of fencing swag, moving hot securities and stolen stocks, running a sportsbook and squeezing gamblers and drug dealers for their shy money. You got sick of dealing with blowheads and lunatic mob enforcers, psychopaths like Jimmy Jack Furnari and Franky Geddaro, running scams and hijacking trucks and trying to stay out of prison, always looking for the angle, trying to see where they met and hoping they didn't come together and take your head off.

That was the life you led.

Always looking for the light at the end of the tunnel which you could never seem to find. And maybe more so, you got sick of parasitic cops and gamblers and thieves and racketeers and maybe the town itself . . . wall-to-wall crooks and petty criminals, grind joints and whores and hot slots, backroom monte games and paying street tax to the mob.

The day finally came like you knew it would, so you packed up what you could in your sky blue Crown Vic and got the fuck out of Dodge. And maybe it was all those things boiling in your brain and maybe it was something just a little bit worse. Regardless, you felt like you were zipped up in a body bag slowly suffocating, so you did what came natural to the beast: you ran.

And that's exactly how it was for Donny Cerrone.

The walls were closing in, it was coming from too many directions, and there was nothing left to do but flee. Archie Mann wanted to help him (he claimed) and Jimmy Jack Furnari was on his ass about the murders and then there was that other thing, that winged-nightmare right out of some evil fairy tale or a horror comic.

Cerrone had over a hundred grand in a hardshell case, some clothes and personals, a full tank of gas and two guns on the seat next to him: his .38 Smith Airweight and a sawed-off 12-gauge Marlin pump with a pistol grip. If that spook took him, then it was going to be war to the knife.

But the farther Cerrone got away from Atlantic City, the better he felt. And he started telling himself that maybe leaving would be enough and after awhile he honestly started believing it. By midnight, he'd crossed the state line into Maryland and he already had a motel picked out, was going to be coming up on it in the next ten or fifteen minutes.

It was going to work.

It was going to happen.

And then something hit the roof of the Crown Vic. Hit it and then hit it again. Cerrone cried out and tried to keep on the road because it wasn't much farther and he'd be on the turnpike and—

The roof was struck again and struck hard, so hard in fact that Cerrone saw the dents popping just above his head like a wrecking ball was dropping. *Bam, bam, bam.* The car swerved and Cerrone, just full of fire and ice, wasn't sure if it was him doing it or the impact of . . . whatever it was.

Oh, you know what it is, his screaming brain told him. *Don't play fucking games here, Donny. There's only one thing that could come out of the sky with that kind of force and it ain't Peter fucking Pan on dragonfly wings . . .*

But Cerrone was not giving into it. Not now, maybe not ever. He wasn't going out like Arroyo and Rice and Wade. He wasn't going to be put down like a tortured mouse a cat had grown tired of.

Bam, bam.

He kept the Vic on the road and was already cursing himself for taking this godforsaken shortcut through the country. Jesus, nothing but fields and trees and no other cars, no nothing but desolate-looking farmhouses now and again.

Something was on the roof, riding it like a gremlin on the wing of a plane even though Cerrone had the Crown Vic almost to ninety, barely making those turns and vaulting roughly over train tracks and bumps. He could hear it up there, making the roof creak and then something whipped down at the driver's side window, an impossibly long hand, bleached white and ending in black claws. It slapped against the window almost playfully, Cerrone thought, flattening out there like an albino spider soaking up the heat on a fence. The claws scraped against the glass. Then it disappeared . . . and came back, curled into a fist and smashing into the window. A webbing of cracks appeared. It smashed into it again and the entire window exploded into Cerrone's lap in a sheet of candy glass.

He screamed.

The Crown Vic jumped onto the shoulder, spitting up gravel and then Cerrone yanked the wheel and it was up on the pavement, tires squealing. That hand came in again and slashed against the side of his face, flaying it raw. Blood pooled in Cerrone's left eye, splattered over his face and there was pain, but he didn't have time for it. He took hold of the Marlin 12-gauge and stuck the barrel against the roof, pulled the trigger. The muzzle flash was blinding, the report almost blew out his eardrums.

But it bought him time.

For there was a wild, high shrieking from up there like a wounded cat and the creature was gone. Cerrone knew it. Just as he knew he was losing a lot of blood and the left side of his face was hanging low in a red flap.

He put the Marlin over his lap, held it between his knees and racked the pump.

Okay, you cocksucker, come and get it . . .

Then the thing landed on the hood.

Landed there on its feet, those immense bat wings spread out to either side. It just stood there, easy and confident like an acrobat on the high wire. Cerrone cried out and jerked the wheel this way and that and nearly lost control of the car, but his guest just stood there.

And then it leaped, crashing through the windshield, spraying more spiderwebbed glass into Cerrone, that horrid face sprouting teeth and one taloned hand slashing madly, taking off Cerrone's nose and ripping his left eye out of its socket. And Cerrone was screaming, hands not on the wheel . . . more out of reflex than anything, he had the Marlin up and he let go with a wild shot. It knocked the creature away.

But by then it didn't matter.

The Crown Vic fired off the road, leaped a culvert, sideswiped first one tree and then another, rocketed down a hill and flipped end over end.

And there came to rest.

13

CERRONE CAME TO maybe ten or twenty minutes later, upside down in the Vic. He was broken and bleeding, a knob of bone thrust from his left leg. The seatbelt had held him, but his right arm was shattered and numb. His jaw was broken and his mouth was full of blood.

The car rocked.

Then rocked again.

Something took hold of the banged-in driver's side door and ripped it free in a screech of metal. The dome light came on. Cerrone saw the creature standing there, breathing hard. It had taken a round of buckshot that had ripped its suit open so that you could now see its body. Although its wings were black, its skin seemed to be a mottled gray, completely hairless, and drawn so tight over the cage of its ribs that each time it drew one of those low, guttural breaths, the bones beneath stood out like iron rungs.

It had lost its hat.

Its chest was smeared with something brown and sticky that looked like tobacco juice or the blood of a spider. It reached in and yanked Cerrone free. The pain was so intense that Cerrone blacked out. Didn't come to until the wind was blasting him, cold and dark and forever. By moonlight, he could see the tops of trees flying by below, the frosted roofs of farmhouses as the creature flew with him, dipping and soaring and careening like it didn't have much control.

It went on for some time.

Cerrone kept swimming in and out of consciousness, knowing his guts were all busted up and he was bleeding internally. It felt like there was something hot and wet leaking out of his asshole.

And then they swooped down through the streets, cutting down alleys and then they disappeared into blackness and Cerrone could smell the sewers. Dankness. Musty channels of night.

When he opened his eyes, there was flickering candlelight.

He could hear water dripping, see with his good eye weird, phantasmal shadows jumping on the sweating brick walls. He didn't know where this place was, could remember something about a tunnel, an awful stink, then, then . . .

Then this place. A vault maybe.

The creature was there, as was its mate . . . if its pendulous breasts could be any indication. They were gnashing their long yellow teeth and glaring at him with those bulbous red eyes. They were making a squeaking, chittering sound that made him want to scream.

But they were just watching him, a noisome stench billowing off them that was rancid and dirty like they'd been chewing on dead things and sleeping in moldering graves.

Cerrone kept going in and out of consciousness.

He realized they had him in a box . . . a coffin . . . his fingers could feel the dirt beneath him, the things crawling in it.

"We have prepared a place for you, Mr. Cerrone," the male said, the female squealing in reply.

Then the lid came down and Cerrone could hear nails being driven into wood and the blackness was eternal, cloisterous, and smothering. He could hear their claws on the lid of his box and then, before long, something fleshy and moist squirming there in the dirt with him.

Something like a tongue, lapping at his wounds.

Then a mouth.

Biting.

DETAIL

Fred Venturini

THE VEHICLE WHISPERS about her, almost blushing, spilling all her secrets. May as well be her eyes, this interior. Truth splattered everywhere. Messy with truth. Truth needing the deft cleaning touch only I can provide.

The vanity plate on the vehicle says Taylor, so that's probably her interim last name. Yellow haze on the interior of the windshield on the passenger side, but not hers. So she's a non-smoker, but the passenger smokes frequently, who is either her husband or the guy she's banging on the side.

Autoglym glass polish does the job, dissolving the film and leaving streak-free, crystal clear glass. Windex? My ass. The ammonia in Windex is corrosive, damaging paint and rubber or plastic trim.

The driver's side door has some scuff marks, which isn't a shock. When exiting and entering a vehicle, a daily driver will often scuff the bottom section of the door panel. Sonus All-in-One Automotive cleanser, poof, they disappear.

She may be a non-smoker, but her eating habits are lax. The carpet has salt hiding in the shag, and there's French fries nestled between the console and the driver seat. The fries are like little pieces of petrified wood, so she's sloppy.

A Norah Jones CD is stuffed under the mechanics of the passenger seat. CD isn't scratched but the case is bashed to shit. Never looked for, never missed, never cared about. Probably a gift.

She drives a Hummer H3, which is supposed to mean money, but the high mileage tells me she's a commuter. She's probably still working a crap job and this baby isn't the more expensive H2, so they probably combine for a little over a hundred grand a year with two jobs. She likes the finer things, but can't have them. So she resents him a little bit.

On to the backseat.

Here is where you can see the footprint of infidelity, plain as day. This is why I can charge anything I want. Why there's no advertising, no invoices, cash only.

She brought it in because semen is a lot like bubble gum once it dries overnight, especially on synthetic leather.

Ms. Temporarily Taylor doesn't take care of her interior. The sun breaks down the factory's protective layer, making the surface porous. So when mystery man pulls out at the last second, his party streamers dry right into the material. You can't get them off unless you chisel the pieces away with a detailing spade.

Ms. Temporarily Taylor had her shoes on. Her legs were hiked up high and spread wide. It was a quickie. And I know it wasn't Mr. Taylor because rough sex in the backseat isn't the marital technique of choice.

Oh, and I found four hair colors. Long blonde, short gray, short black, short brown.

She doesn't have kids. Kids destroy interiors, like one big screaming orgasm.

After about three hours of meticulous interior work, my garage has microfiber detailing towels and applicators strewn about. The smell of cleaners mix in the air, and my hands are squeaky with the dried film of Stoner SPF 45 Cockpit Detailer Protectant and UV Defender. I can't find a dry spot on my shirt to soak up the perspiration on my face, and my right shoulder has the familiar ache of elbow greasing a detail job. But oh, that loving sense of done-ness.

I'm about to call her when the red light in my garage starts spinning and flashing—I fashioned it from a cop's dashboard berry. My old one. One of the few things they let me keep.

A quick look at the security monitor—fuckin' Vasper. I throw a cover over the Hummer and open the side door.

Frank Vasper was a rookie when I was a veteran, but ended up as my boss before I had my fall from grace. He went up, I went out—we're both no better for the move. He's younger than me but looks older. Tired.

"How you been?" he asks, because that's how all his conversations start. I act like I'm tidying up the products in my garage so I don't have to look him in the eyes—I was the one who taught him about eyes. When you ask a perp a question and his eyes flicker up and to the right, he's accessing the creative cortex of his brain. If they shoot down, he's recollecting something. So he's telling the truth.

"We could use a break in the Barnaby case," he says. "He hasn't been through, has he?"

I shake my head while I'm putting my Eagle One Stainless Wadding Polish neatly on the shelf.

"He's a clever one, and it's all conjecture. We got a warrant and his car looked clean. I'm not talking Johnny down the street, twenty dollar wash and wax clean either. I'm talking Jasper Franklin clean. So you sure you don't have a break?"

I look him down hard this time, shaking my head, noticing how heavy it feels on my neck.

"You know I'm not going to press you."

Fuck no he won't.

"I've got two-hundred here. Throw me a bone."

Now he's talking my language. Money's the only thing that has anything to say, nowadays. If honor had traction, if justice had teeth, I'd have a plastic badge with FBI on it by now.

"The money and the usual," he says. "You do your thing, keep it quiet, and you're good as gold with me and the boys. But I'm telling you—if Barnaby comes in, if I find out he came through this garage—"

He stops short, knowing that in my safe, I've got an envelope with his name on it.

"Look, I can probably give you a referral or two on top of it."

I grab the envelope of money.

"Wait outside," I tell him.

My safe is the size of a big screen TV, stuffed with envelopes, filed by date.

I pull one out marked "Danson." He called me after he saw my ad in the yellow pages—Prestige Automotive Restoration and Total Care. Discreet service available. He came in last month to have his front end repaired. Body work is extra, but the dent wasn't that large—the kid was only six, anyway. I used Klasse All-in-One to remove imperfections and seal with one step. Just to be sure, I cleaned the entire surface with Isopropyl Alcohol first.

Then, word gets around. Then, you have local cops knocking at your door like Frank, who remember your background. They remember your cool analysis of crime scenes, no matter how much gristle was around.

But Frank doesn't want to question you or shut you down or bring you downtown. He wants me to clean his cruiser. Turns out he's got a nasty case coming up. Guess he went a little overboard with the nightstick on some poor hooker's face.

So I file it all together, but while I'm at it, I find plenty of evidence that he's banging Tisdale, the only female on the force who works his shift. There was plenty of blood in his cruiser, but there were a few tiny spots in the front seat. The grease spot underneath the glove box was KY jelly, so I deduce that it's menstrual blood, document everything carefully, and make an envelope with his name on it. Sure, he denied it, but the eyes don't lie. We both knew I knew the truth.

"Here." I throw the envelope to Vasper. "The hit and run from last month."

He nods, then leaves.

With Frank gone, I make the call. Ms. Temporarily Taylor arrives, dropped off by a girlfriend who drives a Trailblazer, and not a new one. God, how she must hate Ms. Temporarily Taylor behind her back.

Taylor has an envelope with a "First State Bank" imprint clutched in her hand. Smiles. Fake-white teeth, bleach blonde hair, slender frame, a chest stretching her halter top to the limit. Legs are smooth and tan, leading up to aptly-named short shorts. No shit—she looks like a Barbie doll. And she got that figure eating McDonald's?

"Hi," she says.

My clothing looks like I just got out of pottery class, with polish and products spattered everywhere. Sandals don't cover my crooked toenails and I feel barren, a few rungs down her looks ladder.

I open the door to the Hummer and she peers inside. Smiles even bigger, because she's relieved.

"God, it looks like I just drove it off the lot!" She runs her hand over the backseat. Hands me the envelope.

"Thank you," she says. "This is just perfect. Perfect! Never had a spill dry up like that before."

She's looking at the only other man who knows her dirty secret, so she lies. Deflects the conversation to deflect her thoughts, which I don't blame her for. It's reflex, like when you're naked just out of the shower, you'll always walk on your toes.

She looks down, away from my eyes. I hand her the keys. I know the truth, and she does, so what's the point of arguing?

She fidgets, waiting.

Now, I feel like the naked guy. Her eyes flicker to the envelope. I follow hers, now peeling the envelope open, expecting to see five one-hundred dollar bills. A decent number for infidelity.

Instead, fifty bucks in crinkled ones and fives. I slide it out and gauge her face, her eyes. Her cheeks are red, eyes cast down. Nervous. Embarrassed. She waits.

"He'll know if I spend so much," she says. "He'll ask. There's no good reason to spend so much on cleaning a car."

"Fuck, I knew I should've gotten it upfront, like usual. I made an exception and this is what you pull?"

And now her life focuses in my mind, like a crime scene used to talk to me, breathing, spilling the secrets of the past. She doesn't work, but she drives daily. She eats. Shops. Fucks. She's a consumer. He makes six figures by himself. Probably works long hours, drives a coupe that gets solid fuel economy. Comes home and she models her sale items. But he's a suspicious guy and she doesn't want to choke the golden goose. He doesn't mind that she shops, but he checks her statements. Manages the money. Pays off Ms. Temporarily Taylor to look hot at a company party and fuck him once a week. But five-hundred for a car cleaning would look pretty suspect. He cleans the cars himself on weekends, shirtless, with a garden hose and Dawn detergent, judging by the dull finish on the exterior. Detergent soaps strip off wax and leave a dull finish. I personally use Sonus Gloss Shampoo. He pores through the interior with the same meticulous nature he pores through her credit card statements, her receipts.

"You know it's not a milkshake. Let's be serious."

She comes a little closer. Come hither, those eyes say. Let me pay for your services with my only commodity, they say.

To be honest, I'd rather have the five-hundred bucks. But when she gets closer, that old current runs through me. I've been so busy for so long, and I'm just a human. And the warmth runs through my crotch and up to my head. My hand reaches for the garage door button, and it closes, a long shadow swallowing her from the top of her head where the dark roots on down her legs, those long legs.

And it's sweet and passionate, gentle, like she really cares.

She tells me her boyfriend ran off with a younger girl, that she's not a bad person, it was the first time she'd ever cheated.

I ask her what she's doing for dinner this Thursday. She smiles at me, touches the side of my face and asks, "You cook?"

She leaves while I'm wondering about her name. I'm wondering just what the fuck I'm thinking, mixing up with Mrs. Temporarily Taylor.

HE'S A BALD GUY with a sleeveless denim shirt, frayed at the edges with a huge eagle on the back. Bald. A rough face, but a thin man.

Hands me the keys to a Subaru crossover SUV, but to me, these things are just cleverly marketed station wagons. Hands me an envelope.

"Here's your fee. I'm going to pay you twice. Double your usual amount. Just make sure that it's clean, top to bottom, inside out."

Before I even open the door, I know. You can almost smell them.

"Just in case, you know? Has to pass close inspection."

Leans in, his eyes unblinking. Serious. Not scared, which scares the shit out of me. The backseat is dotted with cumspots. The interior glass is a mess, ripe with handprints and smears. As I clean the carpet, there are hard spots from melted candy, short, pert hairs of a dozen colors and lengths. Underneath the passenger seat is a coloring book, and in the coloring book are a dozen different styles. Chet Barnaby has been through my service so many times, he doesn't even hide shit like this. He can afford this because his daddy is rich enough to own cops and loan him enough money to pay me.

After nine hours, the station wagon can pass a white glove inspection. Maybe even a UV light bar inspection. As promised, he pays me again, with actual money. And I've already got it spent in my head—I could use a decent set of fresh clothes for Thursday.

But before I clean up for our date tonight, I write down the bald guy's plate number. I've saved a few hairs and other samples in marked plastic bags. I log the date and description. I have enough to execute the prick. I put it into my safe.

The Barnaby envelope is thick—I may have to start a second one if he comes in again.

WE SIT AT DINNER, stuffed peppers with a mango salsa. I'm no cook, but

I cleared the docket today and my third attempt at the meal was perfect. She puts her hand on my wrist while we sip some wine. The tenderness shocks me.

"Can you believe this?" she asks, squeezing my wrist.

I can only shake my head slowly.

"I'm not who you think I am," she says.

I know already.

"I hope one day, you can forget the circumstances that brought us together."

What circumstances? All I did was clean her car. Our conversation is awkward. I'm clumsy with words, as usual. It was a total disaster.

She asks to see me again and kisses me goodbye on the mouth.

TWO WEEKS AGO, I was cleaning her Hummer. Now I'm driving her Hummer, getting a hummer. She tells me exactly where to go for her own discreet service, weaving through country roads until the city behind us is just a faint glow, a background to a perfect painting.

Two weeks ago, I was scraping semen off her backseat. She's wearing her dress as a waistband, top down and bottom up, her breasts heaving, her hair thrashing against my chest. Her heels clop against the window, then the headliner, then the door.

I'm making love to her, thinking, "I'm going to have to clean that later."

I push into her as she pulls me into her. The collision is violent, sexy, lovely, perfect.

But still my head is wondering who else was pumping her just like this, and what makes me different from them. We sit in the dark, cornstalks all around us, moonlight above us like teenagers. Mr. Marcus Xavier Taylor is like the dad we're getting away from. He's a tyrant, she says. I notice a bruise on her upper arm and don't ask about it. Just file away the detail.

I hear the stories of him screaming, berating her. His dinosaur walk that rattles the windows of the house. The way he cuts and carves companies apart, even his own employees.

"He's dangerous," she says. "He would hurt you if he knew."

This turns me on like you wouldn't believe, a feeling I haven't had since I could carry a gun.

THIS WEEK, regular business is slow. Folks don't want premium car cleaning. They think it's a waste of money. But one car a day is what a detailer shoots for. It's what I shot for when I was sixteen. One car a day at fifty bucks a pop.

Now, due to my exemplary product line, I charge a hundred per car for standard detailing. Not a whole lot of hundred dollar jobs in a week for me. They don't want the hassle of dropping off their car this far out in the country, where my garage is at the end of a long driveway, surrounded by woods, a kind of empty where no one could hear you scream.

This week, an alcoholic named Benny fell off the wagon and pissed his pants. He sobered up and needed his car cleaned quick. The yellow pages had an express detailer, but that word discreet got his attention. So I clean up the dried out whiskey and piss and save his marriage—for now. Wait until his wife sees that three hundred dollar dent in the old joint checking. But I tell him to make it out to Jasper Investments. He can explain it to the missus and even write it off on his taxes if he wants.

And I also get a ghost car this week.

The car is dropped off by a friend. The customer comes in a taxi.

She's young, probably mid-twenties. Hefty. Unhealthy. Her face could draw social security.

I don't think she can afford me.

"All I have is twenty bucks," she says. "Please. Make it go away."

A bit curious now, I open the door to the Grand Prix. Gray upholstery. Blood in the passenger seat. But a strong smell. Cologne. Not unpleasant.

"Not to forget him," she says. "But I can't afford a different car and I can't be reminded— "

Now she's right in my garage, crying. Breaking down. I fuckin' hate ghost cars.

She gathers up and pushes on. "I could've gotten to the hospital faster. He said to take the expressway and I didn't know that way. I just didn't want to get lost if he passed out."

She sits on her fat rump and cries, the twenty falling from her hand.

The twenty has tears on it. Sweat from her palms. All she can afford.

I clean the car while she sits in my kitchen drinking coffee. I don't know who he was, but he was important and now he's dead. So I make him go away and I leave the twenty in the center console so she can find it later.

The cologne is gone. The blood is gone. But he'll never be gone, not for her.

This is the first freebie I've done in about two years and I wonder if I can get Annie out of Mr. Marcus Xavier Taylor's clutches.

Weeks blow by in a fury. Annie and I see each other when we can. So far, we've covered religion, sports, hobbies, music, movies, pets, and how she likes to grind her pubic bone to achieve orgasm. That last part we experiment with a little, and lay together after, our sweat mixing, and the force seems a million light years away. New details are popping up. I notice that when a car's clean, it catches sunshine and eyeballs and this is basically art.

Summer shows up, sun and sweat and all that good crap. Annie comes by for dinner. I inspect her Hummer when I get the chance, and she's been true to me.

But I notice that her shirt is awfully concealing—for her, anyway. Tummy and cleavage are usually on full display.

Tonight, I'm going to tell her I love her. I'm going to ask her to leave him. But when she hugs me, I feel the bulge.

"I love you," she says. "And yes it's yours. You can tell, I know. I know you of all people, I can't hide anything from."

I ask her how she knows for sure.

"Because a woman knows, and I've fucked you more than Marcus."

This touches and disturbs me in unknown ways.

"Christ, he's got to be in a bad mood."

"The worst," she says. "I struggled with this for a while, but I can't hide it from him anymore. He's going to see this and beat the kid right out of me—our kid."

I take a deep breath.

"I only rent this place, and I've got a savings. We can scram."

It's automatic, right?

"Are you crazy?" she says. "He'll come after us."

That dazes me a little.

"I can't leave him," she says.

"I'll tell him the child is his," she says.

The haymakers just keep coming.

I ask her if this is the end.

"Things can stay the same, but I don't know what's going to happen. Especially with this baby. I just—I hope you'll trust me to make the right choice. Marcus . . . he'll . . ."

And she doesn't say anything, but cries and hugs me. We try out her little pubic bone game and I'm fascinated by her stomach, but queasy when the sex is over.

I tell her I love her before she leaves. She smiles and gets in her Hummer without looking back.

I'm so careful with it. I plan things out.

I read Mr. Taylor's tendencies. I take into account all I've learned, and all she's told me.

So I clean the few scuffs that are left. No semen spots. Not anymore. She doesn't waste one drop, not anymore.

But there's always enough evidence. Always enough for someone who's looking. I pull out the envelope dated about five months ago marked "Taylor." The hair in this envelope isn't mine, but it's enough for what I have planned. I'll leave the hair that isn't his, and I'll send him a little note. Let him know that she's foolin' around. He'll convince her to come with me; convince her with his fists.

I told the landlord I wouldn't be coming back, and he's free to sell off the furnishings. I've got a couple bags packed, enough to get to a fresh start without wearing the same shirt everyday. My bank accounts are liquefied and I'm ready to roll on a moment's notice.

I pray all night that when he hits her, he leaves her stomach alone.

The Hummer pulls up and my future flashes before my eyes. I hope she doesn't know that I was pulling these strings—and like a crime scene coming to life as the details fall into their little slots, I realize how wrong I was to try and manipulate her and how everything is over, dead, stillborn.

The first clue is that the license plates are missing, and before the door opens, I realize that she isn't going to jump out of the vehicle and run into my arms, beaten into sense, the final beating until she's in my arms where nothing can ever hurt her again.

The door pops open. Mr. Taylor gets out.

First time I've seen the guy, and he's what you would expect. Neat suit.

Stationary hair. No stubble. A watch that catches glimmers of daylight and throws them in your face.

He walks to me, a businessman walk full of purpose. This guy's finishing a deal.

"I hear you're a man who is discreet about things, eh?"

He reaches inside of his jacket and I close my eyes so he can't see the truth, and so I can't see the gun.

Mr. Taylor hands me an envelope instead of my demise.

"I don't know what your yellow pages ad means by discreet service, but if you can clean a car and shut the fuck up about it, I can make you rich. Here's five thousand dollars."

And before he says anything else, the details emerge.

"I'm gonna walk my ass to the payphone at the service station, snag a cab. A long walk, but this job will take a while, as you'll see. I'll be back tomorrow night. If it's done, I'll have another ten-grand. Cash."

What if I don't nod yes? So I do.

"Good. And just so you know, I'm not a bad person. She was cheating on me." Points to the Hummer. "In that very vehicle. Found hairs underneath the passenger seat. So if you're discreet, and you're as good as Frank says you are, do your job."

"Frank?" I say, because I can't think of shit to say.

"Seems to think you're quite a craftsman. But don't get the wrong idea—he doesn't know what's inside. I just wanted to bounce your name off someone. I like what I heard. I especially like what I heard between the lines."

Mr. Taylor walks away. I don't know if he knows. It would be ironic, or maybe just coincidental, if he did. But judging by the condition of the Hummer, I doubt he knows or I would've joined her instead of this punishment.

She didn't get out of the Hummer bruised and falling into my arms, begging me to take her away, be her savior forever.

By initial inspection, I believe he did most of this by hand, with a hatchet. The angles and pieces support my hypothesis.

Dried blood is actually easy to clean, emulsified by 303 Intense Stain Remover with a total stain shampoo applied by machine extractor. The secret? Mix in hydrogen peroxide, one part per two parts of cleaner.

Pieces of brain dry hard, like semen. Have to chisel them off with a detailing spade. Then you have to recondition the synthetic leather from scratch.

Disposal, I am prepared for. This wasn't my first client who requested special service. The best way to remove a body is to meticulously cut it into pieces, dissolve the pieces in acid, and bury the liquefied remains in a place that gets a lot of exposure to precipitation, say, the bottoms in the woods adjacent to my garage.

As for her . . . our . . . well I wonder if he was shocked when he chopped that particular part out of her. I prayed. I prayed for both of them over the makeshift grave.

Dark was creeping up, but I was done on time. I'm experienced. I'm always done on time.

Marcus Xavier Taylor shows up and I show off the Hummer.

"Un-fuckin-believable," he says. "I can't believe it. This—are you Moses? Is this some kind of miracle?"

I just stare at the guy. My psychological training makes me adept at anger control, and funneling it into productive tasks.

Initially, I wanted to kill him. That's easy enough. Bash him in the head, bury him with his wife and my kid and poof, he's gone like a scuff mark. But he deserves a special piece of hell before he goes.

So I plan things out.

He hands me an envelope with ten grand. Looks closer at the vehicle.

"What the fuck is this?" he says. "What's with the window back here—"

And before he can finish, I knock him out with the chloroform.

From my selection of envelopes, I can make a pretty compelling case. I don't use anything from Barnaby's envelope, though. Not yet.

I call up Frank and tell him that I'm moving on. He's kind of shocked that I called and listens without saying a word, just interjects some "yeahs" where they sound alright.

Marcus Taylor. You know him? I had him in. I had an attack of consciousness. You know that eight year old with the psychological trauma? The one who got raped and can't talk? Well Christ, it was this guy, and he brought in his Hummer for a second cleanup, a second victim. It's all here. And off the record, I knocked him out so you can catch him as he's driving out of my driveway.

I can hear Frank scribbling away, so I feed him details of Mr. Taylor's transgressions. The worst part of it all was milking Mr. Taylor—Jesus, giving a murderer a wet dream with my greased up hand isn't a party, but it'll be worth it.

I ask Frank what they do to child molestors in prison. We both know, so he doesn't answer, I just wanted that image in my head. Those hard cons don't like kiddie molestors—no sir. Lots of assault and rape and torture and violence in his future.

I'm still liquid, still out the door. I hang up with Frank so he can get busy and take one long, final look at my garage. Nothing speaks to me. The details are quiet.

Before I leave, I get the manilla envelope from the safe—the one with an instant case to destroy child molestor Chet Barnaby. I write his name on the front in big, red letters. With an asterisk and underlining to boot. I set it conspicuously right in the front section of the safe, face out, so no one could ever miss it, ever.

I drop off a number ten envelope with no return address, double postage, with Frank's address typed on the front. Nothing inside but a piece of paper with a typewritten series of numbers, and the words "Dear Frank. Combination to safe—this one's on me."

I HAVEN'T DETAILED a car in a long time, even my own daily driver. My apartment is small enough to cook, shit and watch TV at the same time. Ten grand has been commissioned to a variety of respected charities. I've worked the same factory job for about six months now. Keeps the mind quiet.

A girl named Rhonda likes me, but I wouldn't call it serious. She hates stuffed peppers and actually has the nerve to prefer Sprite over Seven-Up. I spend my spare time doing puzzles, and when I work midnights, I sleep on the couch all afternoon with a baseball game on the television.

The five grand left over made a pretty nice down payment on a new Hummer. A red one. I drive to work almost every day with the rear-view mirror turned down, afraid to look at myself sometimes. Afraid of which direction my eyes might flicker when I ask the really tough questions.

PARENTAL GUIDANCE
Simon Wood

PRESTON'S LONG, LOPING, rhythmic strides beat an impressive tattoo on the sidewalk. Each elegant footfall connected effortlessly with the concrete. Although he was tall and his gait was long, he floated a couple of feet beyond his stride. A sheen of sweat clung to his lean, black skin. He exuded strength, confidence and grace. He seemed to glide when he jogged, riding on a wave of self-belief. It was a sight to behold, unlike my lumbering attempts.

Preston and I were night and day. My footfalls slapped the sidewalk, sounding like wet meat tossed against a wall, sending lightning bolts of pain through my bones and into my groin. My corroded knees popped every other step and air struggled to make it into my lungs. Hell, Preston made me feel old.

The key to Preston's superior form had little to do with better diet, a good night's sleep, protein formulas or the elixir for eternal youth. No, he was riding a tidal wave of good fortune. Life, private and professional, was going his way. I don't begrudge him, though. If ever a guy deserved good luck and good fortune, it was Preston. He was a stand up guy and not many of those find themselves ahead of the game these days.

We used to be the perfect running partners, just two guys trying to fight off the effects of middle age, kidding ourselves that we could beat the effects of time. That was cool with me. I didn't run to keep in shape, to keep my wife interested or even to attract the eye of other women. I ran with Preston because he was my neighbor and my buddy. We were the same age, we liked the same things and it was a mark of our relationship—a guy thing, if you will. An unsaid bond between men.

But Preston and I hadn't been on the same page—hell, the same chapter—for quite some while. In the last eighteen months, I watched my friend grow in stature, leaving me behind to stagnate in my own pond. But the disparity in our performances hadn't all been one way. As Preston stretched out in front, I slid back. I'm definitely not the man I was six months ago or the six months before that, for that matter.

Time hasn't been the only thing that has caught up with me, even the general day-to-day has trampled over me. My checkbook doesn't balance. My expenses get higher as my income gets smaller. The kids demand more. My wife seeks and receives more gratification from television than she does from me. It's sad, but no different than many American lives, I'm sure. Preston has a secret to his success. I just wish I knew what it was.

"C'mon, Mike. Pick up the pace, I'm running at half speed."

I panted in apology.

"This isn't you. What's up?"

I tried to answer, but I couldn't. My response stalled in my chest, trapped in the syrupy air jellifying in my lungs. It was a particularly bad run for me. Current events were weighing me down more than most and my speed showed it. I shook my head, flicking sweat in all directions as my breath whistled in my throat.

Preston glowed. The lucky SOB.

"C'mon, spit it out."

He slowed his pace to allow me to catch my breath. I still seemed to be running full tilt, while Preston was doing the running equivalent of treading water.

"Kids, marriage, job, life, everything. Tell me, what isn't hitting the fan these days?"

"Me." He grinned. "Everything is cool in the house of Preston Barnes."

Preston couldn't have been more right. He was living the American dream. There wasn't a thing in his life out of place. If he fell, it would be into his wife's loving arms. If I fell, I'd crack the sidewalk and be sued for the privilege.

But it hadn't always been like that. About two years ago, Preston had trudged through the same quagmire the rest of the suburban world had and then some. His life was a blight no one in the neighborhood envied.

"I know," I wheezed. "You don't have to rub it in." Starbursts speckled my vision. "Well, we can't all be as lucky as you, Press."

Preston barked a short, sharp laugh. "Luck had nothing to do with it. I was losing the battle with life, so I took control. Now that I'm calling the shots, life couldn't be better."

"Easier said than done."

"I wouldn't say that. Once you make that first step towards resolving your problems, you'll be amazed at the results. Tell me what's up and I'll tell you what to do about it."

To be honest, I'd been hoping Preston would reveal his secret. He'd never offered before, even when others and I had asked. A feeling trickled over me that he was only telling me now because I was at rock bottom and I couldn't fall any lower. But I didn't care what he thought about my life. If he wanted to throw me a bone, I wasn't so proud that I wouldn't gobble it up with glee. Now, I would learn the Preston way and become a devout disciple.

"Jenny's been upset for days and dragging everyone down over her cat," I said. "It went missing last Thursday. The damn thing was probably hit by a car."

"Tragic, but that doesn't sound too disruptive."

True, it wasn't. My daughter's problems weren't the reason for my despair. They were just one in a never-ending laundry list of minor irritations that was draining my spirit. No, Jenny wasn't the problem—my son was.

"It's Kevin. He's going through the teenage thing. You know the drill. He goes out, but doesn't tell us where, then follows it up with the silent treatment. Lately, he's stepped up the pace. He's coming in after midnight on school nights and he's skipping classes. We've already met with the school principal, but it doesn't seem to have any effect. It's gone too far, but I don't know what to do about it. It scares me, Press. It really does. I have visions of where this is all going to end. Well, you know . . ."

"I know," he replied.

And Preston would know. He would understand my fears and problems. His son, Nathan, used to be every suburban neighborhood's nightmare, a black kid caught up in a street gang. No one dared give Nathan a sideways look when his gangbanger friends came visiting. Paranoia was a flag flown from every home's porch. Those were rough times for Preston and his wife. They felt the tension the neighborhood was feeling, but they turned that boy around. The kid was now a poster boy for everyone's child. At the moment, the nearest my Kevin would come to a poster boy would be on a milk carton.

"How far has he gone?" Preston asked.

"He was suspended last week for smacking a kid with his helmet during football practice and next week, he's got to answer to a petty shoplifting case. I'm hoping that I can get the store manager to drop the charges."

Preston nodded, assessing the information. "So it hasn't gone too far."

"Too far for me. Tracy's ready to wash her hands of the boy."

"You're a long way from bottom, my friend."

"It doesn't feel like it."

"Trust me, you are."

"So how did you sort things out with Nathan?"

"Parental guidance, pure and simple."

I snorted. "It's a bit too late for timeouts and spankings."

Preston laughed. "Ain't that the truth? Kids grow up so fast I wonder who the parent really is sometimes. No, you can't use the techniques our parents used on us. It's a new millennium and that calls for new millennium solutions."

We came to a major intersection. Jogging in place, Preston hit the pedestrian crossing button. I slumped forward, resting my weak arms on trembling knees. The specks of light in my vision were gone, replaced by a wave of nausea.

"It comes down to respect," Preston continued. I looked up at my friend. "We give them unconditional love. They give us unconditional respect. But as they start growing up and their little brains develop, we, as parents, are in trouble. It's inevitable that they're going to see chinks in our armor. They come to realize we aren't gods. We aren't perfect. You just have to reinforce their first impressions. They were right—we are gods."

The "Don't Walk" sign changed to "Walk" and Preston set the pace again with me trailing a stride and a half behind.

"So what did you do to teach Nathan that you and Amber are gods?"

"As soon as we saw the company he was keeping and respect they were getting from him . . . we took his CDs away."

That was it? I was disappointed, to say the least. I'd been hoping for more, a lot more. Up until then, Preston had impressed me. His approach sounded bang on, but the execution was weak.

"Did it work?"

"No. It pushed him further away from us and closer to his friends."

"So what did you do instead?"

"You have to understand, we were desperate and I did things that I wouldn't normally do, but we had to get through to Nathan. We had to leave a mark that he wouldn't forget. So I sat him down with his CDs and I told him that Amber and I loved him, but he had to be taught a lesson for his actions. Obviously, he went to smart-mouth me, but before he could, I smashed his CDs to pieces with a hammer."

Again, I wasn't impressed. I know what Kevin would have done if I'd done that to his music collection. Hell, I know how I would have reacted if Preston smashed up my music. I understood Preston's motivation. He was trying to strike at the kid's heart, to make him realize the effect he was having on his family, but it wouldn't have turned me around.

"Not surprisingly," Preston said, "that didn't work either. I was pushing Nath further away . . . any further and I'd lose him forever. I had to think, really think, about my next move."

Preston was reliving these moments, these trials, these decisions. His voice took on a reverential tone. He'd gone to the mountaintop to find his faith and had been rewarded. I stepped up my pace to catch sight of a side of my friend that I'd never seen.

"I knew I was losing Nathan. I could feel my son slipping through my fingers. Well, you know what they say about drastic times requiring drastic measures? I did what I had to do and it worked. I killed his dog in front of him."

Preston's last comment was a hammer blow, so much so that I stumbled and stutter-stepped a couple of times before I found my running rhythm again. He'd let his admission slip out so casually that I wasn't expecting it. My mind didn't have time to comprehend the viciousness of the act.

"How?" I asked. This wasn't what I'd meant to say, but Preston had knocked my brain out of gear and my mouth was freewheeling. I'd meant to say, "You killed your son's dog? Get away from me, you freak."

"Well, Nathan isn't so big that I couldn't pin him down and tie him to a chair in the kitchen. Then, we called in Hunter for his dinner as usual. Amber made the dog's dinner and I mixed in the rat poison."

"I thought you said the dog had died from a tumor," was all I could say. I pictured it all. Preston and Amber's immaculate custom kitchen with the beautiful tiled floor that I'd helped Press lay, and Nathan duct taped to an Ethan Allen chair as Preston, my friend, lowered the poison laced bowl to the retriever. I closed my eyes to blot out my vision, but only gave it greater clarity. I tasted bile.

"He thought we were bluffing, of course. He thought I was trying to scare him and all I was mixing into Hunter's food was crushed oatmeal. I told him, as parents, we were deadly serious about poisoning. This was a wake up call to the fact that there were consequences for his actions. And this was an indication of how serious we were. Thinking about it now, I saw a flicker in his eyes. He was taking me seriously. I could have stopped there, but I could see Nathan's resolve wasn't rock solid. A threat wasn't going to do it this time. So, I gagged Nathan, gave the dog the food, locked him in the kitchen with the dog and took Amber out for dinner. Do you know, it took that mutt over twenty-four hours to hemorrhage its last?"

"My God, I can't believe you did that!"

My horrified condemnation was misinterpreted. I could barely put into words my disgust for what Preston understood to be good parenting, but he took my remarks as a compliment. The son of a bitch actually smiled.

"Yeah, well, we had to do it. We were losing our son to a life of crime and eventual corruption. It had to be done. Obviously, we made our point to Nathan. Having been tied to a chair for twenty-four hours, he'd messed his pants, but we didn't let him clean himself up until he'd cleaned up the dog and its mess. You wouldn't believe the amount of blood and puke a poisoned dog will produce."

That was it. I couldn't run anymore. I was lightheaded to the point of unconsciousness. An ocean a time zone away sloshed in my ears and my vision dissolved to block shapes and primary colors. My response to Preston's parental guidance was to vomit. I yakked up a light breakfast into the gutter, much to the disgust of the coffeehouse's outdoor customers across the street. Splashing vomit speckled my ankles, but I didn't care. It took all my strength to prevent my feeble legs from collapsing.

Preston patted me on the back. "Steady on there, buddy. Drink too much water this morning? That stuff'll bite you in the ass. C'mon, let's run it off. It's the best cure."

I couldn't believe Preston. The man didn't have a clue what kind of monster he'd become. I wanted to rip him a new one, let him have it, but my stomach hadn't finished unloading its remaining contents. Mercifully, I stopped and I breathed like a bull ready to charge, with thick gobs of sputum trailing from my lips. I wiped a hand across my mouth before straightening. Preston called out. He was a hundred yards ahead. Although he'd taken a baseball bat to my emotions, I followed. I had to learn more.

"We pretty much cracked it," Preston said, when I'd caught up with him. "We did have a couple of setbacks but I took care of them."

I didn't know what Preston meant by "setbacks" and I wasn't sure I wanted to know. Not yet anyway.

"Yep, in a couple of weeks, Nathan was our son again. The respect was back. The bad influences were gone. You must have noticed the change?"

"And everyone lived happily ever after," I said.

Preston's smile slipped. A serious demeanor took over his features. Obviously, not all was perfect in Never-Never land.

"My tactics only work for so long before there is a call for further reinforcement."

I couldn't imagine Nathan slipping back after the trauma of Hunter. If it had been me, I'd never have put a foot out of line with Preston again. I couldn't help feeling sorry for the kid. His fear of screwing up must have been intense.

"Nathan's been slipping back. I've discovered that he's hooked up with some of his old associates. But I'm going to handle it."

Preston's words struck a chill in me. Never had I heard that simple promise sound so malicious.

He went to say something, but caught himself and a smile spread across his lips. "This might be good practice for you, Mike . . . to see how I handle matters. You never know, you may be able to use my tactics on Kevin. You up for it?"

I said yes. Yes, out of fear for what Preston would think if I said no. Yes, out of fear for Nathan. And yes, because let's face it, I was curious.

"Good. I'm pleased," Preston said. "I'll be 'round for you at nine."

THE KNOCK CAME right on the button. Preston was dressed casually in dark clothes, as was I, as instructed. We got into Preston's car, but not his Infiniti and not Amber's SUV. Preston had pulled up in an ancient Crown Victoria with a broken taillight. I had no idea where the car had come from. It was like nothing I'd seen him use before.

"Where are we going?" I asked once we were on the expressway. Funny really, I didn't want to know what we were up to while we were in our neighborhood. Subconsciously, I didn't want my home tarnished by what Preston had planned. Although Preston hadn't made any disclosure, I knew, just knew, it wasn't going to be good.

"We're heading over to the warehouse district. A couple of Nathan's friends deal out there."

Deal what? I thought. I didn't think it was cards.

"How did you find out?" I asked.

"I followed Nath. He'd been late home from football practice a few times and from a study session once. We have ground rules in our house. He's allowed to stay out to a prearranged time. When he stopped obeying that rule, it was time to investigate. Parenting isn't like having a Chia Pet. You can't just feed it once and leave it to do its thing. Parenting requires constant diligence. Tonight will be a good example." Press turned to smile at me. "Trust me, follow my lead and Kevin will be snapping to attention before the month is out. And once that happens, you'll see your world following suit."

I didn't smile back. I couldn't. Fear coursed through my veins like a virus. The best I could do was nod in agreement and wait for the heat of Preston's gaze to leave me.

We entered the decaying warehouse district. The properties became seedier the further we were from the expressway. Ripe for redevelopment, it was ignored by the city and left to descend into a haven for every kind of criminal activity available on the books. At least crime was contained in a confined space making it easy for the cops to mop up after the event.

Driving through the decaying streets, my heart raced. Although he had the air going, I was sweating. He was determined—the focus apparent on his face. He didn't plan on taking prisoners tonight. I knew this and I could have avoided the event, but I still came along for the ride. I had to see.

Preston parked a car length from a four-way stop with weather-beaten striping. The street was deserted, except for a couple of junkers skulking on the cross street. Interrupted streetlight peppered the neighborhood thanks to burned or shot out bulbs. I didn't feel safe, even with the Crown Victoria's engine still running.

"This is it," Preston said, gazing at a three-story, graffiti-scarred warehouse with most of its windows missing. "This is where I followed Nath to. Let's hustle."

Preston switched off the engine, but left the Ford unlocked. He strode across the four-way without heed to any possible oncoming traffic. Not so bold, I followed in his footsteps, keeping an eye out for traffic or anybody else.

Preston stopped by a side door, which looked secure until he put his shoulder to it and it caved in with little resistance. From the silent street, the sound of the fracturing lock was deafening. I expected that we'd disturbed every dealer and chop shop in the district, but my fears were unfounded. Preston's never-ending stream of good luck knew no bounds.

We stepped inside. Shattered glass crunched under foot. Sinuous electrical wires hung from the ceiling like exposed veins. A muffled baseline throbbed in the distance.

"They hang out on the floor above," Preston said.

He led the way to an emergency access stairwell and a flight of steel stairs. Our footfalls clanged on the metallic surface, but the music masked our intrusion. I eased back the second floor door. A jerry-rigged light feebly lit an area. Three figures shifted in the shadows at the center of the warehouse floor. I went to ask Preston our tactics but he brushed by me.

He walked towards the group of three. His cool was astonishing. There was no haste or excitement to his pace. Fear was not an emotion that existed inside him. Being spotted was not an issue. As observer to this demonstration of parental guidance, I followed.

"I know we don't have a sign posted, but no trespassers," a shadow said before we were halfway across the floor. Laughter followed the quip.

"I'm here for Nathan," Preston commanded.

"Dad?" Nathan managed.

"Dad?" the comedic shadow echoed. "Is it your curfew, Dog?"

More laughter followed. Nathan mumbled a curse.

When we reached them, the light exposed Nathan's bad influences as being not much older than Nathan, just a couple of punk kids. One wore a Raider Nation sweatshirt and the other was a walking advertisement for FUBU. What elevated them from punk kids were the bags of dope, pills and weed sitting on top of a wooden, upturned packing case. None of the three made any move to hide their stash. The dealers flopped into a couple of worse for wear loungers. Nathan remained standing, rigid in his fear.

"Nathan, I thought we had an agreement," Preston said.

FUBU cranked the volume on the boom box. He swapped a mischievous glance with Raider Nation. Preston wasn't to be trifled with and kicked the boom box clear across the room. The CD player skittered across the floor, pieces breaking off as it disappeared into the gloom. With the boom box dead, an oppressive silence squeezed the standoff.

"Hey, man," FUBU said, jumping to his feet.

Preston thrust him back down into the lounger. FUBU didn't get up again. He swapped another glance with Raider Nation. This time, there was no mischievousness present, only shock.

"Is this what you want, huh?" Preston demanded, ignoring the dealers.

Nathan said nothing.

"We had a deal. You don't associate with drug dealers."

"Hey, we ain't no drug dealers. We're businessmen," FUBU said, but not with the conviction I'd seen when we'd first arrived. He sounded more like a whining child.

"Did you think for one minute I wasn't going to find out? Was what I did to Hunter not example enough to show you how far I will go to keep you on the straight and narrow?"

Fire burned in Nathan's eyes. I felt the pain of that event. I'd only heard the tale second hand and it was a raw wound to me. God knows what it was like for Nathan who'd lived through it.

"Do you think being a drug dealer makes you special, huh?" Preston flung his arms wide before stuffing them in his jacket again. "Do you think it's cool or something?"

Nathan still said nothing. I felt the escalation in the air. Preston was building to something. I willed Nathan to say something to calm his father down.

"I want an answer."

Nathan mumbled something inconsequential.

"Do you know what happens to drug dealers, Nathan?"

Before Nathan could answer or FUBU and Raider Nation could mouth off, Preston jerked out a small revolver and shot the two dealers. FUBU took one in the forehead, killing him instantly and Raider Nation took one in the throat, mortally wounding him as blood geysered from the wound. He clutched at his neck. Pleas for help were reduced to gurgles, but they didn't last long. He was dead within a few seconds.

I hadn't been prepared for what Preston had done—none of us had, least of all FUBU and Raider Nation. The look of shock and stunned amazement on Nathan's face mimicked my own. Preston had crossed a line, but it was obvious by the way he talked and acted he didn't believe he had. To him, this was parenting plain and simple—just good old-fashioned methods to keep a kid on the right track.

Preston turned to me, the gun still in his hand. For a glimmer, I thought I'd been brought there to create a scenario—drug deal gone bad—but the gun wasn't aimed at me.

"You see, Mike," Preston said. "There are no limits. You have to do what you have to do. If not, you'll always be at someone else's mercy."

"You killed them, Press."

Preston smiled the kind of smile intended for dense children. "No, these boys were on a slippery slope to this end. If anyone is responsible, then Nathan is."

"No," Nathan protested.

Preston grabbed his son by the shoulders, the gun still in hand, muzzle inches from Nathan's head. "Yes. You are responsible for what happened here tonight. You were told what would happen if you didn't keep your end of the bargain."

Nathan tried to interrupt, but Preston shut him down.

"Nathan, listen," Preston commanded. "You promised to stay in school, not to smart mouth your mom and me, stay away from bad influences, not to drink or do drugs and I promised not to take action. I've been true to my word. Haven't I?"

Nathan couldn't look at his father when he replied. "Yes."

This was tough love at its harshest. Preston, whether you agreed with his methods or not, was a devoted father. I am too, but my devotion has never caused me to go this far. He was certainly a father among fathers.

"Let's get out of here," Preston announced. "C'mon, Nath." He rested a hand on his son's shoulder and escorted him out of the building.

As I hit the street, the cool night air struck me. I'd hoped it would refresh me and clear my head of what I'd just witnessed, but it didn't. Instead, nausea overwhelmed me. But I wasn't the only one suffering ill effects. As I helped Nathan into the back of the Crown Victoria, he was shaking. I wanted to tell him it was okay and not to worry, but I knew Preston would negate that. Tonight was a demonstration that things weren't okay if Nathan carried on this way.

On the drive home, Preston got me to ditch the gun down a storm drain and told me to dispose of the clothes I was wearing. He detailed other measures I should take to ensure that nothing came back to connect us to the killings. I listened and took it all in.

As Preston parked up, I glanced back at Nathan. The kid was broken. He was clay to be molded into whatever shape Preston desired. I couldn't see Nathan breaking the rules again. If he did, then he deserved Preston's special form of parental guidance.

"You go on in and apologize to your mother," Preston instructed as we got out from the car.

Nathan said nothing and traipsed inside.

"Good kid, really," Preston said, as Nath closed the door. "Just needs a few taps in the right direction. Know what I mean?"

I nodded. I did.

"Thanks for tonight," he said. "I really appreciate the support. I hope you learned something."

I nodded. I had.

"I just need your help with one more thing."

"Sure."

"I have to dump the car. Can you pick me up from this address in an hour?"

He handed me a scrap of paper and I read the address. "I'll be there."

"Good." My friend smiled at me. The smile scared me, but I welcomed it. Things had been leading up to this point. This had been what I'd been waiting to hear. "We should talk about how we're going to solve your problems."

"I'd like that," I said.

"I'm glad. Did you know these skills can be adapted to suit any problem? It's totally universal." Preston sidled up to me conspiratorially. "My boss kept taking credit for my ideas but since I cut the brake lines on his car, he gives credit where credit is due and now I have his job. My father-in-law said I was a good for nothing. It's not a tune he likes to sing since his house burned down."

Once Preston started he didn't stop. He proceeded to catalog his triumphant successes, describing in minute detail how he'd won battles with his church pastor, store clerks, car mechanics and a bank manager. As wrong as it sounded, I took it all in, never once questioning his ethics.

"Like I was saying, it comes down to respect. Once you have respect the world is a much finer place. I think if you take my approach, you'll see a marked improvement in your quality of life." Preston spread his arms wide. "Aren't I proof enough?"

Yes, he was, but I didn't respond. I still wasn't sure I wanted to follow my neighbor's path, irrespective of its successes. For all Preston's stories and his demonstration, I couldn't decide whether I was that kind of a man. Could I inflict the same ruthless love on Kevin? I needed something to push me.

"Fall is certainly upon us now," Preston said.

"Er, yeah." Preston knocked me off guard by the observation. I was still preoccupied with his teachings. My mind was thick with the visions of Hunter writhing on the kitchen floor and Nathan's face when Preston had killed the two drug dealers.

"Leaves are getting everywhere. Sidewalks are covered in the things. I'd hate to see my gutters right now."

Preston was right. Drifts of leaves were everywhere and who didn't have a lawn hidden under a blanket of nature's castoffs?

"The problem is I don't have a leaf blower."

"Yes, you do."

"Oh, I know I do, but I don't have it." Preston turned to face me. "You do."

"Sorry, about—"

"I lent that blower to you last winter and you still haven't returned it."

"I'll get it back to you," I promised.

"Mike, would you like to know what happened to Jenny's cat?" Preston's eyes were hard. "I can tell you, you know, but it won't be good news I'm sorry to say."

"That's okay. I understand."

I returned home full of Preston's teachings. Things were going to change around here—and for the better. Preston had shown me the way.

RINDELSTEIN'S MONSTERS

David Tallerman

"THE COMMON TERM is lycanthropy; or, if you really want to descend to the level of the pitch-fork-wielding masses, werewolfism. But this clinic, this sanatorium for the therianthropically impaired, is a *scientific* establishment."

I stare at him, trying vaguely to hide my contempt. Is he joking? Since Rapture, saying you believe in science is like saying you believe in vampires, except that since the attack on 'Frisco pretty much everyone believes in vampires, and knows to be scared shitless of them. "That's not how I understand it. The Order put you in charge of this place to keep your residents under wraps. Where does science fit in to that exactly?"

Dr. Rindelstein looks up at me across the rim of his pince-nez. "Mr. Fièvre, science fits in to *everything*. Unlike many of my colleagues, I don't choose to abandon centuries of learning because certain unfortunate events fail to correspond exactly with my worldview. I choose instead to study, to learn, to *understand*. I believe that science has not abandoned us, only we it."

I'd call the apocalypse something more than an "unfortunate event." Still, I'm not here to argue the point. On the contrary, I'm here to investigate a murder. Granted at this point it's still death under mysterious circumstances, but I have a nose for these things, and most deaths I investigate turn out to be murders of one sort or another. "Let's see the body," I say, "you can give me the theory lesson later."

The doctor harrumphs through his nostrils, as if one dead body doesn't amount to much when science is at stake. It only reinforces what I've thought about him since the moment we met, that he isn't so much a human being as a set of outdated principles wrapped in a dingy lab coat. At least he has the sense to do as he's told. "This way," he says. "We left everything as we found it, just as instructed."

Rindelstein's so-called clinic, like many similar institutions, was founded as a panicked response to the Rapture crisis. Through five hundred years the building has been a manor house, a prison, and for the last hundred or so an asylum, which is basically what it looks like now. It's obviously never been rebuilt, just reconditioned for each new phase of life. Ancient walls have been whitewashed over in layer upon layer; lamp brackets have been clumsily torn out and replaced with strip lights; fixtures and fittings are a random mix of antique and modern, with here a yellowed porcelain sink and there a cheap plastic table.

The ground floor, where I met Rindelstein, has suffered more modernisation than the lower level he's leading me into. A narrow stone staircase takes us down to an even narrower corridor, where paint's been allowed to chip and stain and the ceiling light looks as if it might fail at any minute.

The corridor twists and turns before opening finally onto a wider passage, which is just as dilapidated but straight at least. It seems to run close to the edge of the house. Every so often doors are spaced on either side, and from them come noises: Snoring, whispers, the occasional shout or groan.

At one point a low voice calls, "Rindelstein . . . Rindelstein, you smug bastard, I know it's you. You can't expect me to eat this shit!" The doctor only tuts to himself and keeps walking.

Most of the doors aren't locked. Some don't even have locks on them. The one the voice came from was, and reinforced as well, with clumsily-nailed bands of metal.

A minute after we come to another sealed door. This one's only secured with a padlock, and the bracket is shiny and new. A sheet of old cloth has been gaffer-taped over the small window.

"I didn't want our other residents to wander in and be . . . *disturbed*," says Rindelstein, fumbling with the key. As the door swings inward he adds, "Mr. Price was our, and perhaps the world's, only known kuknothrope—if you'll forgive the neologism."

I'm not about to pretend I know what he means. Instead I glare at him until he continues. "That is, Mr. Price was a were-swan. Was . . . until his accident."

I glance over his shoulder at the broken, bloody thing on the floor. "That doesn't look like any accident."

"Surely you don't think anyone would do such a thing deliberately?"

There doesn't seem much point answering that one. Rindelstein reported a suspicious death and I'm here to investigate. Still, if I had to answer I'd say that in my experience people will do pretty much anything if the urge takes them. "You must have some idea how he ended up like that?"

"I'm afraid my background is in clinical psychology rather than biology. Truth be told I'm a little out of my depth. What I *can* tell you—well, therianthropy isn't an exact science. A sufferer may exhibit symptoms, physical or mental, related to his animal half, which in turn may or may not relate to the lunar phases. Actual physical translation into another species is quite rare, even in these times."

"And Price? What were his symptoms?"

"For an average of three nights a month, Mr. Price was—by every definition known to science—a swan." Rindelstein sounds pleased with himself saying it, as if he expects me to be impressed. Which is funny, because I'm a firm believer in what I see, whether it makes any damn sense or not, whereas he's the one going on about science. "Yesterday was the first night of the full moon, and it's clear that Mr. Price began his transformation. You can see from the elongation of the neck, the distortion of the arms—and of course, from the feathers. But something interrupted the process."

"Something or someone?"

"*Something*, Mr. Fièvre. He died from massive organ failure. There isn't anything in there that could possibly function in its current state. Even if it weren't for that, his heart has—well, exploded isn't too strong a word, as you can see. I'm willing to accept that it was some unprecedented side-effect of his condition, certainly, but if you want me to believe it was murder . . ."

I bend over the body, cupping a hand over my nose and mouth. "I don't much give a damn what you believe, doctor." Unfortunately, anatomy is hardly my strong point either. Still, as up close as I can manage without my stomach turning over, I do notice something of interest. "This coarse hair?"

Rindelstein kneels beside me. "Well, it looks human. It's certainly odd though."

"Why odd?"

"Because Mr. Price was blonde, and this hair isn't."

He looks suddenly nervous, and I can't blame him. Though it would be easy to press him, I like the idea of letting him stew even better. "Maybe it's time I met some of your patients," I say conversationally.

By "patients" I mean "suspects," but I figure he already knows that.

AN HOUR LATER and I've met enough were-people to last me a lifetime. They're a sorry bunch, and some of them I doubt are even cursed at all. A bit of facial fuzz doesn't make you a were-badger as far as I'm concerned.

As suspects they're even worse. For a start they don't mingle. As Rindelstein explains it, their condition leaves them with feelings of guilt and a need for punishment. Whether that's true or psychobabble, if they're to be believed then none of them leave their rooms if they can help it. And even if they'd had the means to kill Price, I can't find much sign of a motive. Most claim they've never said two words to him.

"Is that it? Is that everyone?"

"Ah, well." Rindelstein's looking uncomfortable again. "No, not quite everyone."

"Go on."

"Well, there's Mr. McKennan. But look, you shouldn't believe everything he tells you. He'll say just about anything to be provocative."

I like the sound of that. Provocative suspects are my favourite kind, because half the time they're the guilty ones.

Rindelstein leads me back down the corridor, round a couple of corners, and stops in front of a door. Lo and behold it's the same locked and barred room we passed earlier, whose occupant expressed such vehement dissatisfaction with his diet.

Rindelstein slides back a hatch two-thirds of the way up, revealing a small barred window. When I stick my face up close to look inside I hear a growl from somewhere back in the corner—not animal, not exactly human either. The light is out. Maybe it's some kind of punishment, maybe he broke it himself to make a point. The only illumination comes from the window in the door and a slit of grey at the top of the back wall. I can't make out much beyond a silhouette. That's enough to tell me he's big: broad and well over six feet, big in every direction.

He can see me a lot better than I can him, which I don't much like. When he speaks his voice is like the growl, not all human, not quite animal. "You want to know who killed Price? You're looking at him. I ripped his lily-white throat out with my bare teeth. Man's got no business turning into a swan; it's an embarrassment to all of us."

"Yeah? You want to tell me how you got out of this cosy cell?"

He shifts into the light, just enough for me to see better how god-damn big he really is. "I'm a werewolf, man. I got means. Ain't no cell can hold a werewolf."

"Sure. Why don't you give us an example of these amazing abilities of escapology then? Why don't you come out here and rip *my* throat out?"

"Maybe I will, man. Not right now, not when you're expecting it. Sure, maybe sometime soon I'll come out and show you what's what."

"In the meantime, enjoy your shit food," I say, and slam the hatch shut.

When I turn around, Rindelstein is trying his best to glare at me through those ridiculous glasses of his. "You shouldn't encourage him. Mr. McKennan is a difficult enough patient at the best of times."

"You don't think he killed Price?"

"Oh no, how could he? He's kept locked up night and day. Most of our patients choose to stay in their rooms, as I said. Mr. McKennan *likes* what he's become. He's far too dangerous to be allowed to roam freely."

"He knew Price was dead."

"Well, it's not something we've particularly tried to keep a secret."

"Great," I say, "that helps. Now every nut in here has a head start on the case."

"We don't have 'nuts' here, Mr. Fièvre, only patients with a tendency to transform into animals. And if I may remind you, there's still no proof this was anything other than an unfortunate aberration of biology."

"Where there's a body, there's a crime. Something did something to somebody."

Rindelstein sighs. "What will be the next step in your fallacious investigation, detective?"

"What about other staff? I'm guessing you don't look after this nut-house on your own."

This time he doesn't try to argue. "There's only myself and Miss

Trimbault. I'd ask that you don't draw her into this. The poor girl hasn't been herself since we discovered the body."

"Sure, you can ask. It'll give us something to talk about on the way to her room."

MISS TRIMBAULT, who tells me to call her Mary, certainly does look traumatised. It suits her. Most women can't pull off the crying thing but on Nurse Trimbault it's oddly charming. Her make-up isn't so streaky that you can't tell she spent time putting it on, or see how pretty she is beneath the panda eyes.

It's hard to look bad in a nurse's uniform and Mary isn't even trying to. They also don't leave a lot to the imagination, and she isn't trying so hard to do that either. From a professional point of view, that suggests she's either genuinely upset, or that she's playing me. From an unprofessional point of view it doesn't stop me looking. One other thing I can't help noticing through that cotton blouse is that she's not as soft as those pretty blue eyes would suggest. There's a set of weights in the corner, probably a sensible hobby given some of the inmates she has to take care of.

On the whole I like her a hell of a lot more than Rindelstein. Still, there are questions to be asked, and I figure I might as well start with the obvious. "You seem pretty torn up, Mary. Did you know the deceased well?"

She sobs at the word "deceased," a small noise caught in the back of her throat. "I hardly knew him at all. I took him his meals and changed his bedding once a week. I know I shouldn't be so upset. It must sound ridiculous to you, but in all the time I've been a nurse I've never known a patient to die before."

The way she says it, it sounds plausible, and I'd like to believe her. "How long is that?"

"Oh, just over two years, I suppose. I did some care work in Africa when I finished studying, and then came here about three months ago. What I mean is—well, I've seen dead bodies, of course, just not like that. When I found him . . ." Another sob snarls in her throat, and she breaks off. She has a point. I've seen more than my share of bodies and the thought of the mess that used to be Price is still making it difficult to keep my lunch in place.

"It was you that found him? Not Rindelstein?"

"It was me. I try to check in on the patients that turn fully—it's painful for them, traumatic. I calm them down afterwards, if I can."

"Does that include McKennan?"

Nurse Mary blanches. "I don't think Mr. McKennan would accept any help from me."

Again, she's probably right. He didn't look the type to be put off by a little pain; hell, he'd probably enjoy it. Since there are no obvious holes in her story, and the whole questioning thing has never been my strong point, I decide to call it quits for the moment. "Thank you, Mary, you've been a big help. I'll look you up if there's anything else."

RINDELSTEIN TAKES ME to a room on the second floor and scurries away before I can interrogate him any more. I've had enough anyway. I've always preferred open-and-shut cases to mysteries and this is looking too much like the latter.

The room isn't bad. In fact it's more of an apartment. There's a shower and a sink, fresh linen on the bed, even a kitchenette. It suddenly occurs to me that this must be Rindelstein's pad. The poor guy's given it up to try and make a good impression. Well, his personality has already screwed that up but I'm still more than happy to abuse his hospitality. A hunt through the fridge reveals a microwave casserole. It's only a shame there's no beer to go with it, but beggars can't be choosers.

As I chew my way through the doctor's chicken dinner, my brain struggles half-heartedly for a handle on the case. The fact is I've got nothing, and as much as I hate to admit it Rindelstein's diagnosis of bizarre accidental death might even be on the money.

It doesn't sit well with me, though. I'm not a believer in crimeless victims. Still, I figure I might as well sleep on it. A lot of my best deduction happens when I'm asleep, and there's nothing more I can do tonight.

Rindelstein's bed is pretty comfortable, and as much as I think the case spiralling around my brain is going to keep me awake, it doesn't. After five minutes all I can think about is how much better this is than my bunk back at the station. After ten I'm fast asleep and not thinking about anything at all.

WHEN I WAKE it's still dark. There's no clock, but my mental chronometer tells me it's nowhere near morning. That means something woke me.

At first I'm not sure what. Then I hear it again—the creak of wooden floorboards, right outside my door.

My first thought is that it's McKennan, come to make good on his promise. Common sense points out that if it was I'd be dead by now, and probably in small pieces too. In any case the steps are receding. Whoever it was, they're going past, not coming in.

It could be nothing. It could be that Rindelstein's got a weak bladder and no toilet in his new lodgings. But my case is at a dead end, and suddenly I'm wide awake, so I pull on my trousers and shirt. I manage to make it across the room and through the door with barely a sound.

By the time I'm into the corridor I can't make out the footsteps anymore. If I remember rightly they passed from the right, so I take a gamble and go left. At the end of the passage I can hear them again. Whoever it is, they're not trying to be so quiet now that they're past my room, and that's suspicious in itself.

I hang back as much as I can, relying as much on guesswork as the mysterious tip-tap ahead of me. I don't exactly know my way around, it's dark, and the building design doesn't make much sense in the first place. After a couple of turns we take the stairs down to the first floor, and after that I'm surer of where I am. I'm retracing my route from earlier, the one Rindelstein led me by when I first arrived.

Sure enough the footsteps change to the dull slap of skin against stone. We're heading down into the basement, and I'm not too pleased about that. It might be a trap. Even if it isn't I haven't forgotten that Rindelstein likes to leave the doors of his menagerie open. Maybe McKennan is the only really dangerous patient and maybe the good doctor just told me that to keep me off the trail. Either way I don't want to be stuck in a dark corridor with a guy whose idea of fun is turning into a stoat once a month.

Still, the case is down those stairs, so I guess that's where I'm going too. It's actually not so dark after all—Rindelstein's left the strip lights on along the main corridor, which is good for my nerves but lousy for my investigation. I peek out round the corner, just in time to see my new-found suspect disappear around the next bend. They've got a good lead, my eyesight's lousy, and they could be just about anybody.

I pick up my pace, trying to close the gap a little. I'm so absorbed I don't realise where I am, so that when I hear a voice from off to my right I nearly trip over my own feet.

"I can smell you, Mr. Detective. Cheap cologne and bad attitude, I could smell you a mile off."

I freeze. I could care less about McKennan, he's safe behind a reinforced door, but the creep's not exactly whispering and I *am* trying to tail someone. But when I listen hard I can hear the footsteps: still steady, still receding. "Better that than wet dog," I mutter, and keep moving.

Round this corner and the next, I realise I've come to the end of the parts of the basement I've seen before. The strip lights cut out after the last of the cells, and the next corridor is steeped in half-darkness. I'm thinking about how this could still be an ambush. Then I hear a door opening somewhere up ahead, and a moment later the sound of it easing shut.

The door turns out to be at the end of the next passage. It's a recent addition, unlike those on the cells, white laminate plastic with a frosted glass window. Up close I can hear sounds from the other side; at first just the shuffle of feet, then the clank of something metallic being moved around. Finally there's another noise that I can't quite place, a low electric hum.

I decide to wait and see what happens.

After ten minutes leaning against one wall, listening to the mysterious noise, I'm starting to get bored. After what seems like half an hour my eyelids are becoming heavy. I'd shuffle about, but I don't want to make too much noise, so I try to think awake thoughts. I guess there's a hot water pipe running through the wall, it's nice and warm, and that and the dark aren't helping. Whatever the hum from the other side of the door is, it's soothing, like the tinkle of a stream or wind in leaves.

I hear a loud thud, and suddenly my head is sore. Where am I? The last I remember, giant plants had taken over the world, only one of them was my mother and she was telling me I had to get up for school.

I have a moment to realise this was a dream, that I'm lying in the corridor on my back and the thud that woke me was me falling over, and then the door swings open and I barely have time to scrunch up and get my arms over my face before it crashes into my shins. That hurts more than my head does. By the time I even think to look who's run past me they're around the corner, and I realise I don't have a chance of catching them.

I get to my feet, massage my bruised knees, and swear loudly. After all, there's no reason to keep quiet anymore. Through the door I can see what looks like a laboratory or a surgery. There's a padded trolley in the centre of the floor, and work benches ranged along two sides, with glass cabinets full of what I assume to be medical equipment. Sadly we're not exactly in mad scientist territory here. It makes sense that Rindelstein would keep a lab, and it's clean and orderly, no severed heads in jars or pools of blood on the tiles.

Inside I notice a table on the left, and this one catches my interest. On top is a large metal box with knobs and dials spread over its face, with something like a soldering iron hanging from it by a lead. Beside that is an electric shaver, a handful of BIC razors, two cans of shaving cream and a tub of aftershave gel. The cans and tub are open and the lights on the box are on. When I step closer, I can read "Holier 0911 Electrolysis" in black type across its top.

There are globs of shaving cream everywhere, and careful inspection reveals dark stubs of hair scattered over the floor and the edge of the table. Somebody has an exfoliation problem, and this looks a lot like the hair growing all over Price. Of course there's no shortage of people here with body-fuzz issues. But how many have a reason to sneak around to treat themselves in the middle of the night?

Now all I need is a motive, and some proper evidence.

I'm not feeling much like sleep anymore. I'd wake Rindelstein for another bout of interrogation, but I don't know where to find him, and the thought of searching the entire building in the dark doesn't appeal. I do know where his office is, we passed it yesterday. I figure even in the dark I can find it pretty easily.

In fact it takes me half an hour of dead ends and aimless wandering, aggravated by a limp from the soreness in my knee and a buzzing in my head from the knock I took. In the end, though, it's hard to miss. Rindelstein has his name stencilled across the glass pane like in those old detective movies. I'm pleased to discover that the door's not locked.

Rindelstein's office is the opposite of his lab. At first I think someone's already searched it, but careful inspection reveals that he's just ridiculously untidy. Books and papers and bric-a-brac are scattered everywhere, including the floor, and his desk looks like some homeless guy made a house out of it. While searching it isn't going to be easy or fun, I'm still far too wired to sleep, and I've nothing better to do.

On the plus side, my initial root around reveals a half-full bottle of scotch and an almost-clean glass, so at least I'll have some company while I search.

When two hours have gone by and most of the scotch is gone, I'm starting to wish I had some idea what I was looking for. I could just wait and talk to Rindelstein in the morning, perhaps ask him to explain his filing system to me. Maybe going back to bed wouldn't have been such a bad idea; maybe the third of a bottle of whisky wasn't such a good one. I decide to make a start on one last pile and one last slug of booze, and if neither offers any answers I'll call it quits.

Then, finally, there it is—crammed between medical notes and pages torn from magazines, half a dozen sheets, and maybe I didn't know what I was looking for but I know when I've found it. The top two pages are a job application, the next two an employer reference, and behind that is a copy of Rindelstein's reply. There's an address and phone number at the top of the reference. I still don't know what any of it means, or exactly why it's important, but there's a feeling in my gut that isn't just the alcohol.

Now all I have to do is work out where the hell Rindelstein's hidden his phone.

AN HOUR LATER and the case is pretty much closed. I don't know all the facts, I don't have a motive, but those are things a good detective can work out as and when he needs them. The devil isn't in the details—he's holding court in the south of France the last I heard—and as far as I'm concerned the hard work is done.

I push back in Rindelstein's chair, a vast construction of padded leather that's surprisingly comfortable now that I've cleared away the books and half-eaten food. Suddenly I'm desperately tired. There's something almost post-coital about the adrenaline rush I get from breaking a tough case. And of course there's the whisky, which has gone right to my head, and to everywhere else as well.

I figure it's okay to catch up on a little sleep. If my suspect was going to make a break for it they'd have done it by now.

This time when I dream, it's about angels—a sky thick with them, swarming like fireflies, fearsomely beautiful. So when I open my eyes and

Nurse Mary is leaning over me it doesn't come as so much of a surprise. It's still dark, and I guess she's just got up because her hair is attractively tousled, her uniform crisp with starch, her expression one of drowsy concern. She's so close I could kiss her. If my mouth didn't taste like a hamster cage I might be tempted.

Rindelstein spoils the moment by pushing into her place, pointing a bony finger at my forehead, and exclaiming, "What on earth do you think you're doing in my chair?"

I brush the finger aside. "I'm solving a murder, doctor, what else?"

"Mr. Fièvre, your persistence in pursuing a non-existent crime is simply flabbergasting. I'm almost impressed by your determination in the face of overwhelming evidence."

"Yeah? I'm glad that impresses you, doctor, because I'm about to go one better." When I stand up my hangover punches me in the brain. Fortunately the desk is close at hand. I manage to turn falling over into what I hope is a suavely casual stance. I notice the clock above the door says ten to five; I guess the working day starts early when your tenants aren't all housetrained. Rindelstein is still hovering over me, but Nurse Trimbault has backed away toward the door.

"It was good of you both to come here."

"You're in my office," Rindelstein points out sulkily.

"I'm not going to bore you with my long and complex process of deduction. I'll skip right to the important bit. A couple of hours ago I managed to get a call through to Lisala in the Democratic Republic of the Congo; which took some doing I can tell you. I had a chat with a Doctor Lavander. It was a lousy line, but I did pick up a few pertinent facts."

Nurse Mary's whole body stiffens when I mention her former employer. If I didn't already, I now have her full attention.

"He told me about an incident with one of his employees. The young lady in question was attacked by something, some kind of monkey, he thought. It bit her pretty badly before they managed to put a bullet in it.

"After that she was sick for about a week, nobody was quite sure what with. Then suddenly she got better, and she went back to work. But, he said, she kept acting strangely after that. She stopped going out, stopped mingling with the other staff. Less than a month later she asked for a reference and left, just like that."

Nurse Mary's glare could strip paint. "Yes, I worked for Lavander. I told you that. It hardly makes me a murderer." The way she says it, you'd think I had my hands around her throat.

"So here's what I think happened. I think that after you got bitten, you started noticing hair sprouting in unusual places. Like *everywhere*. Maybe you weren't swinging from trees and craving bananas once a month, but you weren't one hundred percent human any more either. Still, you figured you could keep it under control, it just meant spending all of your free time shaving. Then you read about this place . . ."

This time her voice has gone very small. "Just say you're right. It doesn't make me a killer."

". . . maybe you can find a treatment. Maybe you can find a cure. Either way, Rindelstein's been struggling to run this place on his own, and he's not about to say no when a qualified nurse writes asking for a job. It turns out Rindelstein probably couldn't cure hiccups, but he minds his own business, and at least he has plenty of equipment you can use to keep things under control. For a couple of months everything's okay—until it all goes bad."

"You couldn't know . . ."

"Know what? That one night you were visiting Price, you were comforting him after he'd changed back. He's sitting naked in a pile of feathers and you're trying to calm him down, warm him up, make him feel better—"

"Shut up!"

"Then things got a bit out of hand? Suddenly you're caught up in the moment, suddenly you're carried away with—" I can tell from the look on her face that I'm steering away from the facts. She doesn't look guilty or scared, just annoyed.

"That's not what happened!"

"Oh." Damn it. "Then why don't you tell us what *did* happen?"

It takes her a while to reply. When she does, she sounds pretty calm. Maybe she's actually glad to be getting this off her chest. "He tried to—I don't know what he was trying to do, but he wouldn't stop, I told him to stop and he wouldn't. He had my arms trapped, he had them pinned to my side. I didn't mean to hurt him. There was just nothing I could do, nothing except—"

"Except bite him."

"I didn't mean to hurt him." I know she means it. Nobody could look that shattered and be lying.

"Only you did. Oh, not at first, not for a month—not until the next full moon. One body trying to turn into a swan and a monkey at the same time, one body pulled in two different directions. I guess he just sort of popped."

"My god." Rindelstein looks genuinely appalled. I was wondering if he'd known, or even suspected. I can tell from his expression that this is all news to him. I brush him gently out of the way, take a step towards Nurse Trimbault and say, "Mary, we need to talk about what happens . . ."

She looks so completely broken that her fist intersecting with my nose is the last thing I expect. I was right about those muscles of hers, even if the weights were only a ruse. The woman punches like a freight train. As I tumble backwards and floorwards I can see her feet disappearing out the door. It just didn't occur to me that she'd run. I know I should get up and give chase, but there's a storm cloud descending, and it's hard to concentrate on anything else.

A second or an hour later, Rindelstein is calling my name and shaking me enthusiastically by the shoulders. "Fièvre? Fièvre, don't you think we should—"

I lurch to my feet, more to get him off me than because it seems like a good idea, and the world turns upside-down. It's sheer luck that I succeed in grabbing the door frame before I fall over again. My jaw feels like it's been surgically removed, then stuck back together with staples and chewing gum. "Where'd she go?" is all I can manage through gritted teeth.

Rindelstein just points, out the door and to the left.

Once I start moving it's not so bad, momentum kicks in and I find I can run okay so long as I don't have to stop or change direction. After I've bounced off a couple of walls my head's cleared some, enough for me to wonder what I'm doing. I don't know what kind of lead Nurse Mary has. I don't know where she's going. On the plus side, we're in the middle of nowhere; there isn't so much as a bicycle within ten miles. If she's running blind then maybe I have a chance of catching her before she gets into any more trouble.

I'm half way down the stairs to the first floor when I hear the crash. It sounds like someone dropped a hippo on an outhouse. When it's followed by a scream I know I'm already too late.

Still, at least I have a direction.

Somehow it doesn't come as a surprise to find myself running towards the ground floor. Mary isn't screaming anymore. That's either a good or a bad sign, I don't know which. There's nothing but silence as I barrel down stone stairs three at a time, but when I turn into the first passage I can hear breathing, heavy breathing, like some big animal hyperventilating. My head hurts like all hell. I feel like I'm running though glue.

Finally I make it to the main corridor. McKennan is standing there, like I thought he might be. At least I'm pretty sure it's McKennan. He's bigger than I remember, a lot hairier, and his muzzle size has gone up some. What's left of the door would make a good bonfire but not much else. Nurse Mary is curled around his feet; as far as I can tell she's still breathing.

When he speaks, it's barely English. It's like someone trained their dog to talk. "I told you, man. Ain't no cell can hold a werewolf." But he's not looking so good; he's wavering back and forth like a ship in a gale. However tough he is in his werewolf form, going through that door has taken its toll, there are cuts and splinters of wood all down his right arm, and Nurse Mary running into him at high speed probably hasn't helped.

I reach for my gun, and almost freeze up altogether when my hand comes back empty. Where the hell did I leave it? Probably in Rindelstein's apartment, when I gave chase last night. Rather than die from absent-mindedness I decide to chance it with a right hook, before McKennan has time to come around. It's like punching a brick wall. Only a brick wall wouldn't look quite so pissed off. "What the hell, man?"

Considering he's broken out expressly to kick my ass, I'm not convinced he has any right to look offended. Still, he staggers about an inch, which is more than I was hoping for. I decide to go in low with my left.

I'm just as surprised as he is when this time he falls over backwards and doesn't get back up.

"Glass jaw," I explain to no-one in particular, while I nurse my hand and wonder just how badly I've broken it.

TO BE FAIR TO HIM, Rindelstein does a pretty good job of strapping my hand. After that I suggest that we make a start on waking Nurse Mary up. Rindelstein tells me he's got some smelling salts somewhere, but she's not in my good books, what with her fleeing arrest and the fact that we've just had to drag her up two flights of stairs to her room, so I veto his suggestion and ask for a glass of water instead. The doctor dutifully brings one over, and I throw it in Mary's face.

Though she twitches her nose a bit, her eyes stay closed.

I hand the glass back. "Another."

"I hardly think—" My look shuts him up; the bruises over half my face probably help. The second glass does the trick. Mary splutters, makes a complaining sound, and finally her eyes flick open.

She doesn't look pleased to see me.

"You could probably break those ropes," I tell her, "and you could probably deck me again if you wanted to. How about instead you sit quietly for five minutes and listen to what I have to say?"

Instead of answering directly, she says, "Mr. McKennan?" It's amazing that she can still feel professional concern, even after everything.

"He's okay. We got him locked away again. Once the sun came up he was easier to deal with." I don't mention that the only other lockable room was Price's old pad. She probably doesn't need to hear that.

Nurse Mary nods, as if somehow that means everything's all right. "I'll listen."

"Good. Because what I was trying to tell you, Mary, before you went all crazy ape-lady; since everything went to Hell the rules have changed. The Order isn't a police force. It's about making the best of what's left. We're not interested in right and wrong, because let's face it, all the good folks got out on the Rapture train and those of us left are pretty much damned already." Rindelstein tuts at that. Well, he's entitled to his idiot opinions just like everybody else. "So here's the thing: I could have you locked up, you could be another addition to Doctor Rindelstein's freak show. Somehow, though, I don't think that you're going to make the same mistake twice. You're a good nurse. You do good work here. If I put you behind bars that job doesn't get done."

"You're saying you're letting me go?"

"I'm saying I'm committing you to the care of the good doctor over there. He has strict orders to keep you on the grounds, and to call us if you do anything even remotely suspicious. If you leave we'll track you down and lock you in a deep dark hole somewhere. Because, Nurse Trimbault, you *did* nearly break my jaw. But yeah, basically, I'm saying I'm letting you go."

Perhaps it would be kinder to punish her. Perhaps that would make it easier. It's hard to read the look on her face. There's relief in there, sure, but there's something else too, and I think maybe it's disappointment. For the last two days she's had to deal with the fact that she killed a man, however indirectly. Something tells me that knowledge will be keeping her awake for a long time to come.

Nurse Mary starts crying, very quietly and softly.

I'm prepared to leave her to it.

THE HOOKER IN THE BACKSEAT

Erik Williams

THE MORNING THE STATE released me from prison, cold air, gray sky, and my no good, piece of shit father waited for me outside the concrete walls.

Before I stepped through the doors to freedom, I opened the manila envelope holding my personal possessions. The guards had confiscated them right before they handed me my prison uniform the day I arrived. Now I had them back and couldn't remember what they'd taken.

I looked inside. One cheap wrist watch with dead battery: trash. A picture of my now dead Bull Terrier Brutal: trash. Three sticks of petrified chewing gum: trash. One Swiss Army knife: a reminder of my childhood before life sucked. Dad gave it to me when I was five. He started running drugs two years later.

I pocketed the knife and tossed everything else. Tossed it away with the rest of my past and took my first step into a new existence.

The door behind me shut, the guard on the other side twisted the lock home, leaving me and my father alone for the first time in five years. He leaned against the hood of his cherry '65 Chevelle, cocked his head to a forty-five, and took a deep drag on a Marlboro. Five years and forty feet stood between us but the son of a bitch looked and smelled the same.

"Hello, son."

A thick cloud of smoke rode his words and drifted up around his leathery face.

Only one response found a way out of my throat.

"What the fuck are you doing here?"

I had a pretty good idea why but figured playing dumb might work long enough for me to get out of town.

"Now what kind of way is that to greet your old man?"

"I don't pay politeness to pieces of shit."

I unstuck my feet from the position they seemed glued to and walked toward the bus stop. Just wanted to catch the bus and make arrangements for my trip west. I had enough money for the fare. Didn't know where I'd go and didn't care. But I did know west was far away from all this shit. Far away from Dad.

As I neared the Chevelle, he pushed off the hood and blocked my path. I figured Dad knew I had more than enough money for bus fare. That or he wanted me to work for him again, which was just his way of keeping me under his thumb.

"What's that supposed to mean?" Dad said.

"You know exactly what that means." He looked the way he did the last night I saw him, the night he plowed a Ford pick-up through Walter, right down to the same damn smirk. "Look behind me. See that large structure? I spent five years there for you."

"No you didn't."

"Fuck you. Hit the road, Pop."

"I got work for you."

"I don't want anything to do with your work or you."

"I got a place for you to stay. Don't reject me without hearing what I have to offer."

"I'm done with you. I said my goodbye the day they sent me here."

"This work is legit. I don't run powder anymore."

"Am I supposed to respect you now? You don't run powder. Great. You probably cook meth instead."

"I'm offering you an honest job, good pay, and a bed. Why not get in the car and hear me out?"

"You know why. You know exactly why."

"Call it a peace offering. You helped me out. Now I help you. Square the house."

"You don't know when to quit."

"Look, get in the car and hear me out. If you like what you hear, then you get a place to stay tonight. If you don't you get a free ride into town and I leave you alone."

"Consider this a formal rejection. I'm not getting in your car."

I tried to step by him but his hand clenched me by the bicep. Still had the iron grip.

"Yes, you are."

Dad's face had tightened, his lips curled into a sneer. His tone lost its diplomatic cut.

"No, I'm not."

"Yes, you are."

"What makes you think I will? Peace offerings? False promises? I've heard this bullshit before."

Dad cocked his head toward the back seat of the Chevelle. A woman, bound and gagged, lay in the back. Her wide eyes stared at me. Blood had colored the white rag with red blotches. Her skirt had been hiked up over her hips, revealing what God gave her. Maybe she'd pushed it up involuntarily by squirming around on the seat. Maybe Dad had raped her while waiting for me to walk out. The latter probably more likely than the former.

"You know what I'll do to her if you don't."

"What do I care about a two dollar whore? Your business with her doesn't have anything to do with me."

"You skipped your parole boards and did your full five years. Why? Were you afraid they'd let you out?"

I didn't say anything.

"Or was it because you didn't want to be on a parole officer's leash?"

Dad was a step ahead of me but I stayed silent.

"You see, I think you did your full sentence so you'd be free and clear the day you got out. That way you could walk right over to that bus stop and leave town for good without fear of being chased by the Feds. But if you did that, you'd leave without seeing me and I'm not ready to let you go yet. You see, son, I don't want you to leave. I want you to get in the car so you and I can have a nice little talk about your future."

I should have seen this coming. Should have known Dad wouldn't let me leave town easily, whether he knew about my stash of money or not. He wanted to keep me close but beating up or killing some whore wasn't enough to keep me around.

"I've got a bus to catch," I said.

"You'd turn a blind eye to that poor girl and let her wind up dead just so you can be free of me and this town? The joint didn't soften your heart, huh?"

"That's right."

"Well, then I guess I need to remind you I've got other negotiating tools on me."

He didn't need to say anymore. Dad carried a .357 and a switchblade all the time. The gun didn't scare me because Dad wasn't dumb enough to pull it in front of a prison. But I knew he wouldn't hesitate to gut me and leave me to die where I stood.

"Why all the talk of going legit?" I said. "Why not threaten me right off the bat?"

"Because I wanted to get you in the car nicely. Wanted to maintain a civil tone out in front of this nice prison."

"God damn you."

"Get in the car."

"You mother fucker."

"Get in."

My fists clenched, ready to fight. But I knew my dad. Nothing had changed about him. Which meant he had the switchblade ready. Knew he'd split me from my belly to my dick if I made one ill move. Then he'd kill the whore for good measure.

I looked at her, saw the panic in her eyes, and then thought of his knife and accepted the son of a bitch had me cornered.

"Get in."

DAD DROVE at a safe speed down wooded Country Road 9. I tapped my thigh and tried to figure a way out of this mess. The whore moaned in the back. Needed to get out of this without getting any blood on my hands. Couldn't risk another stint in the joint.

Not once had Dad made reference to the money. Maybe he didn't know. After all, he never reached out while inside. But then why use the whore to get to me? He knew I didn't give a shit about her or anyone else. The only person I had connections to was him and I wanted those severed as soon as possible.

"Who's the whore?" I said, probing for any hint.

"Hooker, son. Whores do it for free."

"And what does she have to do with whatever you're doing?"

"It's a simple matter of trust. I don't trust you."

"I did five years in prison. Isn't that enough assurance?"

"No."

"God damn it, I took the rap for you. Five fucking years for what you did. That should be enough proof I want this dead and buried with that poor bastard you ran down."

"I need to keep you close, son. You doing time in the joint ain't got nothing to do with me."

"I was there for you."

"You were there for you. You didn't rat me out because you felt guilty. Because you didn't stop me. You believed you deserved punishment for letting me drive my truck through Walter's chest."

"I didn't let you do anything. Walter was all you."

Dad chuckled. "Yeah, you did. You knew god damn well why I was going to see Walter. And you knew damn well what I'd do to him. It wasn't the first time you'd seen me take it out on someone who couldn't pay."

"I knew you'd be dead the moment they put you in the pen. All the enemies you've got almost got me killed just for sharing the same name. I saved your life."

"I know what you did and it didn't have anything to do with me. Doing time was your penitence. Doing your full sentence was your ticket to freedom but I can't let you go."

"Fuck you." And your mind games. Dad kept his cards close to his chest and spun webs like a bullshit spider.

"If you did it for me, if you did it to protect me, then you shouldn't feel any ill will toward your dear old dad or mind sticking around and hanging out with him. After all, it was such a selfless act. Yet you're ready to jump on the first bus out of town. Can you say you feel no ill will toward me? Can you say you love me?"

"No." Whatever game he decided to play, he'd decided to string it out rather than cut to the chase.

"You see, you went to prison a guilty wreck, sorry for what you did. Took the rap. Vehicular manslaughter. Dark foggy night and Walter high out of his mind. Your baby face sold that bullshit to the jury. But you thought you deserved more, not less. In the joint, you found God, Buddha, or maybe learned to love a man in a spiritual way. Now you're a changed man. You did your time and made peace with yourself and decided when you got out you'd leave for good. But you still know stuff about me."

"What do I have on you, Pop? Not a fucking thing. All that time in the joint, I didn't say one thing. And trust me, the opportunity was there. But my knowledge of your life died five years ago. And that's the way I want to keep it. There's nothing I can pin on you."

"You know shit you couldn't possibly forget. More than I'm comfortable with. I know all about the deals the DA offered you. I kept tabs with people inside still friendly. But guilt is strong and it did a good job keeping you quiet. Now you're out and I need to see for myself what kind of man you've become."

Maybe he actually believed the shit he spouted. Yeah, I felt a little guilty about letting him kill Walter but I took the rap because it got me away from him. Prison was the first freedom I'd ever enjoyed.

"And her?" I said. "Threatening her is useless. Gonna kill her now since she serves no purpose?"

"Something like that."

The hooker screamed around her gag.

"Let her go. You've got my word. Everything I could ever use against you is now forgotten. But I won't work for you and I won't stick around to be your puppet. You'll have to kill me first."

"I guess we'll see then."

"How does this play out? Huh? Spell it out!"

"I will soon."

"Now."

"Soon."

I punched the dashboard a couple of times and yelled a bunch of shit but all of it bounced right off him. His game, his rules. Dad kept driving and I looked out the window at the woods passing by.

"Where are we going?"

"We'll be there soon enough."

THIRTY MINUTES of silence passed. Well, not silence, just no talking. Dad hummed. I tapped my thigh and the hooker moaned weakly around her gag.

I'd failed to talk my way out of this, whatever this was. Dad had planned something to ensure my trust to keep me local. I didn't care about her anymore than an ant. But I didn't want to watch him kill another person. Did I have a choice?

We arrived at a beat-up old cabin in the middle of Blackwater Forest. I'd never been there before but had a sickening feeling Dad had many times. The cabin had only one purpose and vacationing wasn't it. He used to have a beat up trailer near the beach for this type of work. Apparently, he'd gone rustic since I'd gone into the joint.

"Let's go in." Dad killed the engine. "I'll grab the hooker."

He did, dragging her kicking and whimpering body inside.

The cabin smelled of fresh animal piss and death. Dull sunlight spilled through grime-covered windows. Mold had spread across most of the ceiling and down the knotty-pine walls. Blood stains covered the floor. As soon as I took in my surroundings, I understood how dad planned to gain my loyalty. I don't know why it hadn't occurred to me before.

"I'm not going to kill her," I said as Dad dropped the hooker between us.

"What?"

"You want her blood on my hands but I won't kill her."

"Is that a fact?"

"I know that's what you want. I kill her and then you've got one thing you can always hold over me. That's the loyalty you want, right?"

Dad chuckled. "No."

"Then what, you piece of shit?"

He reached behind him and pulled out the .357 which he'd had tucked in the back of his pants. Dad pointed the gun at the hooker's head and cocked the hammer.

"I'm gonna kill her. Not you."

"What?"

I stepped forward, a foot away from him.

"I kill her in front of you. If you decide to rat me out, you'll be a murderer."

"Bullshit."

Then I noticed Dad had gloves on. He must have pulled them on before bringing in the hooker.

"The piece look familiar?" Dad said.

The .357 looked no different than—

Mine. The one Dad gave me when I turned eighteen. Just like his but my initials on the grip.

"You kept it in your car," Dad said. "I got it before the cops came. I made sure not to touch it with bare hands."

Which meant it still had my prints on it.

"Still has the last three rounds you had in it last time you shot it."

He'd preserved it the last five years. If he shot her . . .

"Testify, point the finger, drop a dime on any of my activities, tell a DA about some other bodies I dropped in the past, I take you with me. Run, walk, or even crawl out of town, this gun ends up on a cop's front door with directions to the body."

The hooker screamed around the gag.

"You work for me, son. You're mine."

"You've got me. I swear it. I'll do whatever you want. Run powder, meth, anything. Just don't kill her."

"Your word means shit to me. Knowing you hold murders and drugs over my head, knowing you can run at any moment, is unacceptable. I need to stamp you with blood, son. Her blood."

"Why not just kill me? Huh? If you're so concerned about me, ensure I'll never talk."

"You're worth more to me alive."

"The money, okay. I'll give you Walter's money."

Dad tilted his head. "What money?"

"Walter's money. I have it. I took it the night before you killed him. He was too high to remember."

"You set Walter up?"

"Yeah, and I'll give you the money if you let me walk."

"You let me kill Walter to keep the money. You did your time to pay off the guilt. And you have the nerve to judge me you little shit. Let me do your dirty work for you."

"I paid what I owed with time. I took the rap to get away from you. And I'll give you the money to square us and her."

"The hundred thousand." Dad chuckled. "I make that in a month running meth. Keeping you under my thumb is worth more than that, especially now that I know what a slimy piece of shit you truly are."

Panic flooded me. Dad turned and looked down the barrel of the .357 into the hooker's brown eyes. Only a few moments until he squeezed that trigger. The crazy bastard would kill her just to keep me in line, keep me close.

"Sorry, honey."

I glanced around me for a weapon within arm's reach. Found nothing. Then I remembered the Swiss Army knife.

I pulled the knife out of my jeans pocket, flipped the blade, and stepped forward. Dad caught me out of his peripheral, though, and twisted toward me, the switchblade springing to life in his other hand.

Closing the distance before he could bring the blade up into my guts, I shuttled forward fast and thrust the tip of the Swiss Army knife into the side of my father's neck as he caught me in the love handle with the switchblade.

He screamed and tried to wheel around with the gun. I slapped his hand with my left, knocking the .357 to the floor. The gun erupted, shooting the round through one of the windows.

I kicked him in the back of the knee and took him to the floor. Dad tried to fight me off but I dropped all my weight on his sternum. His smoky breath hit me in the face and sent me into a stabbing rage. His hand let go of the switchblade, leaving it sunk into the soft flesh of my side.

Over and over I thrust the knife into his neck. His warm blood soaked my hand so much I lost my grip on the knife, leaving three quarters of it in the soft tissue under his jaw.

Dad's breaths grew short then stopped. His eyes rolled up and looked toward the now shattered window. The hooker continued to belt her muffled wail.

I looked at my hand. The bloody sight would have repulsed me if I didn't know it was my father's blood. That bit of knowledge filled me with a sense of warmth and confidence. It was over. Finally, it was over. I should have known I could never run away from him. It was always going to come down to him or me and he had to die for me to be free.

The howling of the hooker snapped me back to the now. I pulled the switchblade from my side. The wound bled like a sonofabitch but I'd live. I wiped my hand on Dad's chest, and then went to remove the gag from her mouth.

I stopped short. She'd heard and seen everything. She could tell her story about how dad had planned to kill her. How I'd killed him to save her. But the damn whore could also say how I'd confessed to setting Walter up. How I'd stolen money and let the bastard die for it. How I'd killed Dad to save myself and couldn't give two shits about her.

My hands started to shake. I looked at my father's corpse and imagined landing back in prison. I was thinking like him and hated myself for it. Dad wins.

I pushed up to my feet and grabbed the .357. I looked at it in the dull light. All those years just to go back? This time for life? I couldn't do it. I knew I wouldn't make it. No way would I go back.

Only one solution. Only one way out of this trap.

I cocked the hammer.

Only one exit. Only one way to finally be free.

Then I heard Dad's voice in my head say, "Why leave a living witness?"

I leveled the gun and put two rounds through the hooker's head. Her blood mixed with dad's in a pool engulfing their bodies.

"God damn you both."

I left them to rot in the cabin and took dad's Chevelle. Thirty minutes away from the cabin, I dumped the car with the gun and the knives in a lake in the middle of the night.

Now I head west, Walter's money in hand. Now I leave this shit behind me, left dead on the floor of an abandoned cabin in the middle of nowhere.

THE MOUTH

John Everson

THRUST.

    Pull back.

    Buck, fist, pound.

    Thrust.

    Pull back.

The heart speeds up, briefly, adrenaline pumping in crazed waves.

The mouth opens and shuts, gasps for air. Moans fill the air like rain, musk melds with the stench of sweat. And then it's over, and the attack diminishes, the cries taper, the galloping heart slows.

The defining evidence that separates sex and murder is really only the amount of blood left behind on the bed. The amount of heartache afterwards separates lust from love.

I'VE BEEN A SLAVE to these passions for so long, the gaping mouths and gasping wounds have all blurred together in my head. There are memories of thrusting—hands, knives, cock—inside the mouths, mammaries and musk of blondes and brunettes, fat girls and thin, ugly trash and haute delicate skinned models. In the end they're all sloppily the same and yet beautifully different. The tenor of their cries, the strange tics and angular movements that separate one girl from the next are delicious to watch, to feel. Some bleed heavy and thrash like mad. Others go wide-eyed in shock and disbelief. But in the end, sex or murder, fat or thin, it all comes down to moans and thrusting, hard nipples and harder cocks.

And the challenge of distancing yourself after. Both in heart and body. I've never had much of a problem managing either, and I didn't expect to today.

Kyla, a D.C. hooker who's played with me in my sex-death revolving roulette often over the years, told me the story that set me packing instantly. She knew I'd never resist the temptation. Her acne-pocked cheeks crinkled in a lopsided grin as she measured my interest and excitement.

"They call her 'The Mouth,' " she whispered, and then ran a thin tongue tip across her lower lip. She knew I could rarely tear my eyes (or cock) away from an eager oral slave. That's why so often I had her videotape our little explorations with our chosen slaves. Or, as the case may be, victims. Later I could pick up the other details missed during my initial fixation. And rerun them, again and again.

"She's all fucked up," Kyla explained, leaning in to nip my ear. A light chocolate breast slid out of the silk entrapment of her slip, and my hand didn't hold back from trapping its eager nipple. She hissed and pulled away as I squeezed hard.

"Tell me," I demanded.

Her fist pounded at my shoulder, but I didn't ease my grip. Kyla would try to make me fuck her for the information, but I wasn't trading.

"Later," she moaned, nails now in action across my chest and back.

"Now."

AND SO, A FEW HOURS and a diseased fuck from Kyla later (sometimes I'm generous), and I'm in backwoods Virginia. "The Mouth" is apparently an Appalachia throwaway. A backwoods freak. Genetic disaster.

And the thought of it has me harder than nails. Kyla has her ways and her contacts and she owes me more than I owe her. Her fascination with dismemberment in the midst of orgies has been a logistical nightmare for me on many an occasion. And there's something highly unarousing about hosing the splatter of another man's sperm and bile off the dead girl beneath you so that you can finish your own fuck.

I hate it when Kyla cums before me.

The houses had thinned to one per mile, and for most, the only evidence that there was a dwelling behind the tangle of lush forest and vine was the rutted track that broke the barrier of heavy hedge along the gravel road. I couldn't go above 30 mph without fearing a hernia. This was not well-travelled country.

But every time I felt lost, I'd spot one of Kyla's landmarks passing by.

A rusting John Deere overturned in a ditch. A wooden sign declaring "Keep Out. Property of O'Clannahan. Trespassers Shot First, Questioned Later."

I stuck to the road, such as it was, and watched for the only clue I had remaining on my list of landmarks. An outhouse.

Why anyone would put an outhouse at the edge of the road out here was beyond my guessing, and why anyone would be brave enough to step inside such a structure in the midst of snake and spider and hornet country was a better question. An outhouse on an unused road would likely harbor more critters than shit, and I wouldn't dare consider contributing to the latter given the threat of the former. Then again, many of the property warning signs might leave one a bit shy of pissing on a local bush. You might end up without privates.

The outhouse jolted out of the brambles like a belltower, and the car jerked and slid as I slammed on the brakes. A lurch, a shuddering slide, and I was skating down the rocky hillside drive that the outhouse had marked. A canopy of fern and leaf left me with the impression of driving through a poorly lit tunnel. Just as my eyes accustomed to the shade however, the forest roof broke to a clearing and in the white shine of a sweaty noon, I caught my first glimpse of The Mouth's house.

Correction: shack.

It looked to be four or five rooms, a rotting testament to lazy carpentry. A series of mismatched gray boards jutted from the roof eaves and only a door cut through the warped boards of the front wall. I could see one window on the side of the structure, a four-paned bit of relief that threatened to disappear inside a nest of leaves. The hum of bees filled the air and as I stared at the decaying structure I saw why. A stream of fat, slow flying insects traded flightpaths from the nearby woods to a dark fissure in the roof above the window. *Precisely why I avoid outhouses in the woods*, I thought.

Shrugging to myself, I trampled through the kneehigh scrubgrass and tentatively knocked on the peeling white paint of the front door. Could anybody really still be living here?

From inside I heard the squeak of old floorboards and the murmur of voices. And then the door opened a crack. No more than four inches. I could see the glint of a dark eye and the grey of gray curls.

"Yeh?" came a suspicious, guttural question.

"Kyla said you'd expect me."

The door opened wider and a wrinkled short woman inspected me, hands on hips, not moving aside to let me pass 'til her consideration was finished.

"You been fixed?"

"Not broken," I said.

She shook a heavy head.

"Fixed. You had a va-sex-tommy?" Her accent was heavy with the hills, and I stifled a smile.

Once her meaning sank in, I shook my head. "No."

"Then no oral for you."

I looked at her and thought that I didn't want oral, anal or anything else from her. She was a potato sack of a woman, and long beyond child-bearing years. I started to back away but she grabbed my arm and dragged me inside the dark house.

"She likes the oral, but no fixed, no oral. Deal?"

I said okay and she slapped my face, lightly. "Promise. You like her, you get it fixed. Then you kin fuck her mouth. Only then."

Again I agreed, and she led me past a brown couch, stuffing leaking from its belly and into a brighter kitchen. She pointed to an old white wooden chair and I sat, noting that the drone of bees was louder here. I thought the window over the sink must have been the one I'd seen from the drive.

What the fuck had Kyla sent me into? Was this a punishment for something?

The inside of the house was no more kept up than the out. And in the heat of summer, with no air conditioning and no open windows, the air was stifling. And sour. Flies bumped heads against a grease-blurred window, and on the table a handful of mugs and glasses remained full of recent leavings. A glass of tomato juice, another of some light golden juice, maybe apple. A mug of coffee was in front of me, and I pushed away its curdled contents in disgust. Something with a lot of legs ran across the broken tile at my feet.

The old woman came back then, this time with a younger woman. At first glance, she was a beaut. Long raven black hair flowed over her shoulders, and a thin, ratty tank clung tightly to her and did nothing to hide the fullness of her breasts. The dark point of her left nipple pressed tightly through the fabric. A wide trail of sweat ran from the hollow of her neck to the point just above the deep pock of her bellybutton. The shirt ended there, and so did her clothing.

I didn't disguise my stare.

Her hips were wide and full, her flesh cooly pale as winter. The V of her groin was hairless, and the distended, pink lips of a human face parted there. A cunt that truly smiled. It looked utterly bizarre, unreal. The twisted product of a demented artist who tortured his sexy models by distorting them on-canvas. And as I expected, it turned me on instantly.

My gaze returned to her face, and then I saw the sleek aquiline nose and intensely blue eyes rested above what some men crudely call a "gash." Even when I'm going to kill a girl I generally have more respect for her than to call it that. I stared forever at her face, taking her in pore by pore. The lips of her mouth were thin petals of pale pink flesh. Not firm at all, but rippled and wavy.

The lips of a pussy.

"Take off your clothes," the old woman directed, and before I could start myself she was reaching up and unbuttoning my shirt.

I brushed her away and finished the job myself. For a moment I worried that she'd kill my fledgling hard-on; maybe this freakishness wouldn't turn me on as much as I'd thought. But before I'd even slid down my jockeys I felt a stirring again; it flopped out awkwardly and in seconds was pointing across the room at her.

The old woman was reaching into a cabinet as I kicked off the pants and the buzz in the kitchen grew louder. I looked up and almost screamed. Her hand was buried in the thick waxy comb of a bee's nest! We were only separated from being stung to death by the uneasy kiss of a cabinet door!

She pulled her hand back dripping with golden sugar and shut the cabinet door again, somehow not letting a single bee into the room. Then without a word she coated my cock and lips with the warm, sticky sweet liquid and nodded towards the back room.

"Go on then. Her pussy likes the taste."

I followed the silent girl to the back of the house. She reached out, almost shyly, and took my hand as we walked. The older woman stayed behind.

Her bedroom was unlike the rest of the house. It was tiny, but neat.

The walls gleamed a fresh coat of lilac, and the mattress on the floor was covered in a light linen to match. There was one dresser in the room, a man's highboy, but aside from the dents and scars of probably 50 or more years, it was clean and uncluttered. She turned to me and made a grunting noise.

"What?" I asked.

Her eyes looked pained for a moment, and then her hands touched my chest.

Lightly. A feather's exploration.

The sweat was rolling down my back and forehead but her fingers felt cool as they traced the line of my sternum and then followed the faint hollows between my ribs. She grunted deep in her throat again, and then nodded.

I guess I'd "do."

I reached out to lift her shirt but she shrunk back.

What the fuck? She had her pants off already, and then I thought about it again. Of course she had her pants off. Her fucking mouth was in her crotch. She probably never wore pants. And if her pussy was in her head . . . shit. When the older woman said no oral sex, which hole did she mean? An abortion through your face would be a bitch! But maybe her ovaries remained where they belonged, in which case, no fucking with her "mouth."

I suddenly didn't know what to do. Did I go back and ask the old woman? My cock started flagging at that, and I laughed at myself. If this freak couldn't tell me which way or the other it was her own problem. I reached out and pulled her towards me, and kissed her on the mouth.

On the pussy, rather. Whatever. I kissed the lips in her head. What a fucked up feeling. My tongue was buried in her cunt, but my eyes looked straight into hers. And she looked scared.

Of what??

She tasted salty, heavy. Not the sort of taste you expect from a first kiss. More like the taste of a woman after she's fucked your two best friends and then wrapped her legs around your face.

But usually it wasn't her nose that was in your face for that one.

I frenched her quickly, and the flower of her mouth seemed to expand around my lips. She grew wet; her eyes opening and then rolling back in pleasure. My tongue is legendary in some circles.

My hands caressed the rolling mounds of her buttocks, and slid upwards, dragging the dirty cotton rag she wore with them. She broke our kiss and shook her head no again, but I didn't listen. With a yank I pulled it up and over her head, and then she was naked in front of me, her breasts drooping with a heavy fullness, slicked with sweat, and covered with scars. I saw now why she was reticent. Why her eyes looked scared. Someone had used her poorly.

Circles of scarred buttmarks littered her chest, and one of those abused mounds had lost its nipple. Bitten off? Cut off? She wasn't telling. She crossed her arms quickly across her middle and lowered her gaze. But I would have none of it. Gently I massaged her shoulders, and then tipped her chin up to look at me. Her eyes were pools of tortured darkness, and I bent to kiss them, each eyelid. Then I tasted her forehead, her neck, and the bloom of her lips. Soon her arms slid around my back and we collapsed to her bed. The 69 position took a whole new meaning with her. In minutes we were slick with sweat, and her pussy lips were hungrily sucking my cock into her throat. Meanwhile, her thighs held my head like a vise as her tongue matched the timing of my thrusts. She stabbed me in the head with her tongue and I stabbed her in the head with my cock.

How fucked up is that?

It was heaven, and I wanted more. By the time I stopped slipping around on her bed, I had decided I might actually *get* a vasectomy so that I could get between her legs and fuck her mouth. I wasn't looking for kids in this lifetime anyway.

WHEN I PULLED MYSELF together and got dressed, I went back to the kitchen in search of the old woman. She was washing dishes in a faded manila plastic washbasin.

"She everything you dreamed of?" she said and then cackled as she rinsed a mug with water from a tall pitcher.

"She was wonderful," I admitted.

"You like fucking freaks, then?"

"Never have before, but seeing as I've fucked just about everything else . . ."

"Well, that pays my debt to Kyla," she announced. "So next time, it'll cost ya."

"You her pimp or her mom?"

"Both."

"Nice."

"What do you expect me to do with a freak like that? She's good for fuckin', and not much else. And then only by perverts like you."

"Sweet attitude."

"You paying for sugar?"

"Naw."

"Then fuck off."

Nice.

"You got a bathroom here?"

"Nah. That's what we use The Mouth for."

"You're a sick old bitch, aren't you?"

She looked me over silently for a moment. Then she reached up and put one large ham of a hand on my shoulder. I hate to admit it, but I flinched.

"Listen. We live out here in nowhere. The Mouth's a retarded freak. She got no teeth up top so she cain't eat nothing but sauce and syrups. I got no money. Given where her taste buds are, she likes the taste of piss and shit. Hell, she tastes her own every day. So I saves up what I can."

She nodded over at the glass of pale liquid on the table that I'd taken for apple juice earlier.

"You wanna drink, or donate?"

She laughed long and loud as I left.

Fast.

BUT I COULDN'T STOP thinking of her. Every night, I dreamed of eyes staring back at me as I kissed the rippled flower of a pussy. And scat fantasies. I'd never been into it before, but suddenly I imagined myself pissing between her open lips, that mouth hungrily slurping up my waste.

She was suddenly all I could think of. Mostly though, I imagined plunging my cock into the pussy of her head. Fucking that mouth 'til she was choking. It was very disconcerting, this obsession. I'd had women live with me, naked on their knees for me whenever I called, and had them dispatched and forgotten quicker than most men can cum. Why did I keep going back to this freak in my head?

I was making a pickup near the Areland Costume shop when I hatched the idea.

I bought a scar kit. Fuck if I was going to pay for a vasectomy. But I was going to fuck that girl's pussy mouth.

The bees were buzzing warm and loud as I pulled up the decrepit backwoods drive to The Mouth's house. I had a roll of $20s in my pocket for the old bitch pimp. The lust rolled off me in waves on the drive down. I could smell it. My cock got hard and long thinking of those pocked breasts in my mouth, that warped mouth going up and down on my pole. And afterwards, I'd stand up and piss right down her pussy mouth.

I was ready.

THE OLD BITCH answered the door, slate grey hair matted to her forehead, a stain of sweat revealing the fat floppiness of her breasts. What a turnoff.

"You!" she snapped. "Lotta nerve, you!"

"The Mouth at home today?" I asked sweetly.

She didn't answer, only glared at me. Then with a shrug of her head she motioned me inside.

"I take that as a yes," I answered myself. Still she didn't reply, only walked through the stink and hum of the kitchen and back towards the room of The Mouth. I followed.

"You gonna take care of this?" the old woman asked as we entered The Mouth's room.

She was lying on the bed, sweat from the heat of the summer day rolling off her forehead in lazy beads. Her eyes were large as cows', that same deep brown look of open innocence that a bovine faced with a shotgun to the ear has. Her fingers toyed gently with the pussy lips of her face, teasing and stroking it in a masturbatory fugue.

"This is all your fault," her mother announced. "What are we gonna do?"

That, was a very good question.

Apparently, I'd chosen the wrong mouth. The Mouth's neck was swollen to the size of a small melon, that delicate white skin stretched and almost translucent. Spider veins snaked around and up from her bare chest to meet in a web of blood pulsing right where her Adam's Apple would have been, had The Mouth been a man.

I'd chosen wrong. If her pussy was in her head, and she pissed from those same lips, naturally her uterus was in the wrong spot as well. Or unnaturally.

Which would make her about two months pregnant. And she was gasping for breath already. Three months would kill her.

Abortion through the head? Could they do that?

I went to her. Put my hands on her face and kissed her forehead. There was a sick pain in my heart that I thought had grown impervious to stabs of guilt. Not so.

Those brown cow eyes looked up at me in trust. In fear.

And the hands of an old bitch began pounding on my back.

"You did this. You did THIS!" she shrieked. "You gotta fix it. You got money. Take her. Fix her."

I stepped back, took the old woman by the shoulders and shook.

"I'll take care of it," I whispered. Sharply. "Go. Leave us alone for a bit."

She squinted at me then, as if not trusting my motives. But what else could I do to her freak of a daughter at this point? I'd already fatally knocked her up.

When the door closed behind her, I dropped my pants to the floor and pulled the shirt over my head. Naked, I joined The Mouth in bed and kissed her swollen neck, her musky lips. Her eyes rolled back with each thrust as I lay my cock between her teeth, between her legs, and fucked her the way I should have the first time. I wondered as she swallowed my cum in the mouth between her thighs if she could taste it there.

Afterwards, when the sweat had dried on her chest and my hardon had diminished, I asked her if she was thirsty. She nodded vigorously and I let her drink from me. I coated my finger with some honey from a discarded comb lying half eaten on the floor by her bed, and tenderly fed her glistening lips the sweetness. They slurped together like an infant's, hungrily sucking at the teat. Then I stroked her hair softly, until her lids closed and a steamy slumber overtook her.

She didn't stir when I put the cold steel next to her ear. But I kissed her lips before it went further. Once more for dreams. Her eyes opened then; confused but happy, they stared into mine.

And then with a small but thunderous pop, her brains were against the wall and The Mouth kissed no more.

I was crying when the door slammed open and the old bitch screamed. But I had another bullet and wasn't nearly as careful about where I placed it. The result was that I had to pull the trigger twice more to still the woman's wailing, choking cries. Those didn't phase me. All I could see were the deep brown eyes and trembling, half opened pussy lips of The Mouth as I gave her the abortion she—and our baby—both deserved.

Fuck.

NINE COPS KILLED FOR A GOLDFISH CRACKER

David James Keaton

> *"I asked her for water. She brought me gasoline."*
> —Howlin' Wolf

THE JUNKIE FOLDS the thousand dollar bill in half nine times, swearing it's a new world's record. Jack watches the money transform to a tiny green cube, disgusted that everything he owned, every record, movie, and dirty magazine, even his best platform shoes, could be reduced to a piece of paper so small it couldn't even effectively wipe a spider's ass.

"I said, 'no,'" Jack mutters.

Ignoring him, the junkie shuffles over to a huge aquarium along the wall, an endless green coffin so thick with green muck and stink that during previous visits Jack never imagined anything alive in there among the empty beer cans, dirty dishes, and long-forgotten plastic scuba divers.

The junkie giggles at him, dangling his idiot's origami out into the smoky space between them. Then he tosses it into the tank. Equally confused and insulted, Jack watches the green cube swell and soak up the stagnant water, and it's just starting to unfold when a streak of copper pushes through a puff of fish shit and algae to gulp the money down. Jack stands up so fast that the card table flips off his knees. Three coffee cans blow soggy cigarette butts into his face, reminding him of his woman's last kiss.

"Why the fuck did you do that?" Jack shouts, running to the tank while shaking ash and filters out of his greasy curls.

"Because it meant more to me than it did to you," the junkie laughs. "I mean, more to you than it did to me? Whatever. What do you care! My money now."

Jack shakes his head. This prick had insisted on a $1,000 bill to pay the debt. Not just the amount, but *that* particular bill. Last circulated in 1969. Series of 1934. "Not that rare," someone shrugged. It took a little time, but Jack did find one. And when he first saw it framed behind his parole officer's desk, Jack couldn't believe his luck. Then he couldn't believe that this one slip of paper would solve all his problems. But when his asshole P.O. turned around to yell at another ex-con on the phone and Jack had time to slide the frame a little closer and read the inscription . . .

"Legal tender for all debts, public and private."

. . . he started to believe it might after all.

IT LOOKED LIKE SOMETHING you'd see in a cartoon with all those extra zeros, and he broke in and stole it the same night. A $1,000 bill was not that rare but still rare enough to be worth almost twice as much as the numbers in its corners, so Jack knew the junkie would erase his woman's debt the instant he held it under a streetlight and first noticed Grover Cleveland staring up at him with his big, Nieszchian, toilet-brush mustache, something that most junkies, usually slick and hairless as grubs, could never grown themselves.

When he first walked in and looked around the apartment, Jack noticed that the junkie had a telephone shaped like a football. Scrawny as he was, the junkie did claim to be a football fan, Cleveland Browns of course, when the Browns still had a team. Maybe that's why he wanted Grover's tiny portrait so bad. Then there was that goddamn cookie jar . . .

He remembered his daddy slapping a football out of his hand once and telling him, "No self-respecting thug has any love for sports."

"You dial where the stitches would be," the junkie had told him when he first saw him staring at the phone. "Too bad it's not real pigskin though, huh?"

Jack didn't get the joke, but he knew he'd remember it forever because it was the first time he ever saw a junkie smile.

And now he knew the junkie would never smile again.

Jack thought about calling his woman to yell at her about what he was enduring to settle her debt. But he knew he would have looked stupid arguing into a football.

"Can you even spend it?" he asked when he first handed the bill over, right before the junkie made the mistake of folding it up and feeding it to his fish.

"Didn't you read it? 'Redeemable in lawful money at the United States Treasury or any federal reserve bank.' "

"Yeah. I read everything on it."

"How long before your parole officer knows you took it?"

"Hell if I know. I swapped it out with some Monopoly money so maybe he won't notice for a little while."

"Wait. What Monopoly money?"

"Well, they don't make a $1,000 bill for that game, so I put two $500s instead."

"Good job, dumb ass. He'll never notice with them being bright orange and all."

"Who cares. He sees 20 ex-cons a day, maybe more."

"Hey, you want to see a magic trick?"

Five minutes after Jack said, "No," the junkie was folding up the money. Ten minutes after that, Jack was still punching a purple stain on the floor where the junkie's head used to be.

He calls his woman on the football and tells her that the junkie let him keep the money, says he put her on a payment plan, says maybe they're gonna be okay. She tells him that if he can pay the landlord by 7:00, they won't have to move out, says maybe he better hurry since it's 6:00 right now, says they'll never be okay.

Jack's trying to listen, but he can't stop staring into the green water, trying to figure out which one swallowed the money. The tank that had seemed empty before now has a swarm of goldfish nipping at each other, apparently waiting for another thousand-dollar snack. Then he hears a distant siren and knows he doesn't have time to perform half-ass surgery on a dozen fish bellies to find that bill. His eyes dart around the room, panic setting in. The voice in his ear is squawking louder. Now his woman wants to know why he wasted a quarter in a pay phone when she's only a block away.

"If you hang up right now, can you get your quarter back?" she whines.

Probably not, he thinks, hanging up anyway. *Wait, did she just say, "quarterback?"*

He suddenly remembers something and runs through the bloody junkie pile toward the kitchen. Something crunches under his shoes, and he almost trips.

That's the thing about junkies, he thinks. *Celery where their bones used to be.*

He sweeps a year of empty cereal boxes off the counter to reveal the prize. A goddamn glass cookie jar, shaped like a football, of course, full of rolling papers and fortune cookie fortunes. He feels the weight, tries it out under an arm. It was made to carry fish. All of them.

He grabs a coffee can off the floor and empties the butts. Scooping and splashing green water like a baby's first bath, he manages to wrangle all the goldfish into the cookie jar. At the last second, he snatches a glass starfish ashtray from the bottom of the tank and shakes it dry, just in case he needs it. He screws the lid back on the cookie jar football, the tiny handle where the stitches would have been, and he holds it up to the light to watch them swim around. He's wondering if he can see the money cube through their stomachs when he hears a car door slam out the window. Tucking the glass football under his arm and the starfish ashtray in his pocket, he bolts for the stairwell.

It's three hundred yards to the slumlord, he thinks. *That's only like three touchdowns.*

At the end of the hall, he sets down the football in a pile of pizza boxes, pulls out the ashtray, and stands where the door from the stairs will swing. He glances into the cookie jar again, glad he doesn't have to kill all the fish right now. Why bother? That money's not going anywhere. But he doesn't think twice about killing this cop.

The door swings opens, and when it creaks back to reveal Jack, he buries the ashtray in the cop's face, right around the bridge of his nose. It goes in so deep that the lenses of the cop's sunglasses snap shut around Jack's fist like a Venus flytrap. Snorting blood. Sinuses collapsing. The weight of the cop's utility belt, along with a typical lack of physical fitness, drags him down the stairs so fast that Jack has to chase him.

High-stepping after the rolling cop all the way to the basement, he starts realizing that cops are much easier to kill than you think. He stuffs the body out of sight behind the last row of steps and takes his gun. .357 Magnum. He thinks that's a good trade for the ashtray.

"All you need is something to protect," he tells the starfish as he wipes his hand. "That's the key. You can drop any cop if you're protecting something, anything at all. A woman, a dog, even a goldfish. Hell, if you don't have an actual goldfish, even a goldfish cracker would do. Empty a bag, eat all but one. The one you save, give it a name. Then ask some pig to fucking try to take it from you. Wish him luck."

He spits, retrieves his football, and counts the fish. Nine. All still swimming.

"But don't try this with animal crackers, boys," he tells them. "You'll get so attached to the gorilla cookie you won't eat, the killing might never stop."

Outside, he squints down the street, mapping out his path to the goal line. All he has to do is run across the parking lot where the car wash used to be, through the alley where the baseball card shop used to be, up the steps where his mother used to be, then give the money to the slumlord. Never talk about the stain where the junkie's head used to be.

But running with anything under your arm looks suspicious, especially something shiny. He's rounding the corner where the miniature golf course used to be when he's arrested.

"IT'S IMPOSSIBLE, ASSHOLE. Don't you know there's no way to fold any piece of paper in half more than eight times?"

"Bullshit. Nine. It's a new record. I saw him do it."

Jack is talking through the cage to the cop in the front seat. The football full of fish is sitting on the dashboard while he waits for Jack's name to come back from dispatch. The cop turns the football around and around, looking for any sign that Jack's story is true.

"No way. Can't be done."

"I saw it."

"You *thought* you saw it."

"What are you, a magician?"

"Used to be."

"Let me guess," Jacks snickers. "The Amazing Andy."

"Fuck you. So, where were you running again?"

"You know, like Andy Griffith? Get it?"

"Yeah, I got it. I'm telling you, he palmed it. You can't fold any bill more than eight times. After that, the area can no longer be manipulated by human hands. The force required is 256 times more than when you started."

"I know what I saw."

"You don't know what you saw. That's my point."

"A magic cop, huh, Andy? Can you get out of a coffin underwater? Can you get out of the belly of a fucking whale? Because that's what I need."

"I can slip handcuffs."

"So what."

"It's easy. If you have long fingers like me, you just put your middle one down so the cuffs click on it, then slip it out. Leaves enough of a gap to get loose. A similar technique can help you pick pockets, too. Even take a slow cowboy's gun. But I can't tell you *all* the tricks."

Jack notices him fiddling with the snap on his holster, something he recognizes as a "tell" in poker. And if there was one thing Jack hated more than cops, it was poker players. Mostly because they dressed like magicians.

"I can't wait to kill you," Jack mutters.

"What?"

"Nothing." Jack figures he doesn't have long before they find that dead cop with a starfish where his face used to be crammed under those steps. He's kicking himself for even telling The Amazing Andy about the $1,000 bill, but there was no story he could come up with that made any sense for why he was running down the street with a cookie jar. He's glad he tossed the starfish cop's .357 into a random mailbox before he got picked up. He put the flag up.

"He fed the fish something else," Amazing Andy said. "You should go back and make that man give it back. Your money's still in that apartment. Not that you'll ever see it again. Hey, which apartment did you say it was?" Jack ignores the question.

"Did you know it's also impossible to eat more than nine crackers," the cop goes on. "Six in sixty seconds is the limit. Your mouth won't make enough spit to keep getting them down."

"What kind of crackers?"

"Regular crackers. Cracker."

"What about goldfish crackers?"

"Something like twenty. The same age I was when I first shot somebody." He leans down to mumble to the radio on his shoulder then turns around to Jack.

"Tell you what, why don't you stop talking awhile? Looks like I'm handing you off to someone else. Unpaid speeding ticket in another county, eh? You didn't look that fast to me."

"Hey! What the fuck are you doing?!"

The cop has his hand in the cookie jar. He catches a fish and lays it down on the dash while Jack punches the door. And before Jack can blink, the fish is ripped in half. Andy shakes the end with the tail, showing Jack it's empty. Then he reaches in and grabs another fish. Rips it in half. Jack grinds his teeth so hard one cracks. He wants to know if the junkie really fed a fish the money, but he can't stand to watch this cop shred another fish. Now he knows he won't do it.

Can't do it, he thinks. *It would be kinda like playing Russian Roulette. Except that you'd want the bullet. And, of course, it would be with fish . . .*

ANOTHER COP CAR is approaching, and Amazing Andy quickly drops the third fish back in the bowl, tucking the glass football down by his feet and out of sight. Fake yawn and stretch to cover the movements. Right then, Jack knows he wants the money. Not because he killed the fish, but because when the cop yawned Jack swears he saw his tongue curl like a cat's.

JACK WAS BORN with long fingers. "Piano playing fingers," his daddy once laughed. "But that's not what the girls will love them for, better save 'em." Then he bent Jack's fingers back with his own, short as sausages, black as crickets, to drop Jack to his knees. It was the day he found out Jack had tried out for football.

But tonight, Jack uses those fingers to cut half moons into his palms until his hand are red. And when the third cop spins him around to switch handcuffs, he noticed Jack's wrists and stands him up straight, turning to Andy.

"Uh . . . what's wrong with . . ." the third cop starts to ask right when Jack slips a hand free and unsnaps the cop's holster. Glock in his fist, Jack spins and pumps three shots in Andy's chest, aiming for the badge, a target over their hearts that Jack always thought was a great idea. Then he drops and puts a bullet in the third cop's back as he's running for the car. The way he falls under his wheel, no hands to stop his mouth from cracking the curb first, Jack knows he's dead. So he concentrates on Andy.

His face is so blue, he seems like an empty uniform, and for a mad minute Jack thinks his clothes deflated like a balloon. Then Jack sees his eyes open, aware, a glare of black and red.

"Are you dead or just angry?" Jack shrugs. "'Cause either one will do."

He claims Andy's .38 Special. Old-school. Feels good.

In the glare of the cruiser's headlights, Jack quickly gets the keys from the third cop's belt to take off his other cuff. Then he starts thinking about the money that might not be in the fish after all, and he glances at the third cop's ear against his hubcap. Time for an experiment.

It turns out you can fold a cop in half only once, no matter how hard you try. Even if you jump up and down with both feet.

But if you use the wheel of their car, you can get at least three.

WITH A FOOTBALL FULL of fish back comfortably under his arm, Jack is running again. He has a Glock in one pocket, a .38 in the other, and a stomach full of more excitement than fear. He looks for some landmarks. The Amazing Andy drove them about three blocks in the wrong direction, putting him back on his own goal line.

Kind of like a penalty, he thinks. *Loss of down.*

So he moves faster, trying to avoid a delay-of-game, too.

When he's gained back all the ground he lost from the arrest, he notices a fish floating in the cookie jar. He stops to catch his breath, holding it up under a streetlight. He remembers this streetlight. It's where him and his woman had their first kiss. Then their first fight. It's brighter than the rest, never goes out, and it's the only streetlight harsh enough to see through anything, your hand, even someone's head. He holds the fish high, looking through its red belly like the webs between his fingers. There's nothing in it. Nothing at all. He starts to raise the bowl over his head to check them all.

Nothing in their guts, he thinks. *Maybe I should feed them . . .*

But he's interrupted before he can remember where a pet store used to be. It's cop number four, walking the beat, twirling a whistle like a lifeguard. And it's the easiest one to kill yet, still trying to sneer while the slugs stretch his lips into a smirk. He watches the Fourth Cop's shoes wiggle as he shoots him one last time to make sure. It's the same thing his toes do every time he jerks off.

See, he thinks, firing again. *How can you feel bad when they clearly fuckin' love it?*

JACK'S ABOUT FIFTY YARDS from where the pet store used to be when the Fifth Cop gets the drop on him, quick-draw squeezing his 9-millimeter Parabellum fast enough to send a spray across his scissoring legs. Jack takes two bullets to the meat of his thigh. The blood that fills his shoe is cold. But the Fifth Cop expects him to fall, and Jack lights him up when he goes for another clip.

But the shoot-out costs more than he thought. Another fish is float-ing in the football, and he's surprised how upsetting this is. He plucks it out, looking crazily for a bullet hole before he feels for the $1,000 bill. It's empty, but he's got to be on the 60-yard line by now. He's running again, faster than he has in twenty years, feet slapping from the effort, the cookie jar splashing, spilling, water level getting low.

"Why are you running?" his daddy scoffed once. "Only suckers run."

Now Jack knows he was wrong. Sucker makers run. Widow makers, too, it seems.

He's actually smiling to himself when the Taser darts hook his neck. He expects the same surge of electricity he felt last time he got in a fight on Spring Break, but the jolt never comes. He runs out the wire and the darts rips free. Then another dart catches him in the lip. He slows, again ready for the jolt. Nothing. He decides the cop's Taser must be broken because he doesn't feel shit. Then remembering the way the walleye played dead until you reeled them close to your boat only to snap back to life and stab hapless hands with those spines, Jack falls to a knee, setting his glass football down like an egg. He shivers, giving the worst performance in the history of fake electrocutions. And when the Sixth Cop is close, right before his head vanishes under his hat in a supernova of pink, black, and powder flash, his black cop eyes go big like a man who just realized he hooked a sperm whale instead of a bluegill.

"Fuck that," Jack tells him. "More like you hooked a submarine."

Curious, he tests the Taser barbs on the water in the football. There's sparks, but the fish don't seem to care. He thinks maybe they have the same small heart he does, and he's really starting to love the little bastards.

OKAY, PET STORE, *slumlord, home. 6:35.*

He's got time to stop where the pet store used to be for fish food and fresh water. It's been out of business for years, but he knows there's still plenty of tanks inside with shit swimming around. He's seen them through the window when his P.O. forces him to drop off job applications.

He pries the wood loose around the lock with the barrel of the .38 and slips through. Inside, the place smells like a slaughterhouse. The tanks are still there, and the water in every one is green as grass. But he starts scooping it into his football anyway. Jack doesn't notice the extra fish he's splashing in with his goldfish, and he's retrieving some off the floor when someone pumps a shotgun. The fish tanks light up, now purple instead of green, and Jack sees a black man with an explosion of white hair creeping by the wall. He reminds Jack of a '50s blues man gone to seed. Except for the shotgun.

"*Blues Man With A Shotgun,*" he thinks. *I always knew those songs were easy to write . . .*

As he gets closer, Jacks sees that the Blues Man is covered with every hair, feather, and scale known to science. He's 6'5", about 300 pounds, same dimensions of Howlin' Wolf, of course. And he knows this judging by the song Jack hears crackling on a turntable upstairs. Like the Wolf is singing, he looks like he "eats more chicken than any man seen."

"You went for the right tank, boy," the Blues Man whispers. "Goldfish are the only things left alive in here. How'd you know that?"

"I was just looking for some water for my own."

"I see." He steps closer to get a look in his bowl. He makes a quick diagnosis.

"Goldfish are the cockroaches of the fish tank. They don't need much of anything. Barely even need you at all."

"Is this your pet store?"

"Ain't no pet store!" The Blues Man levels the shotgun at Jack's face.

"This was an 'aquarium.' Too bad black people don't buy fish tanks. Don't commit suicide neither."

"Do you have any . . ."

"No reported black suicides since the 1800s. True story. No black serial killers neither."

"Is that true?"

"Which part? About the fish? Sure is. That's why you've gotten as far as you have. No cop thinks a black boy like yourself would be running with a fish bowl. Football in one hand maybe, with a scholarship in the other. But not a fish bowl. They think you're white. That's why you continue to get the drop on 'em."

"How did you know I was . . . I mean, even my own daddy thought I was white. Called me his 'little cracker' more than once."

"Oh, I can tell. I'll bet you've even been known to eat mayonnaise from time to time, trying to hide that shit. Don't worry though. One more generation and we'll all look the same."

"Can you lower that thing a bit?" Jacks says, pointing up toward the shotgun.

"What, this? My baby Remington 187? Sure won't."

"Actually, I think it's called a 1187."

"Sure ain't."

"You know, there's new music out now," Jack says, pointing up toward the music.

"At some point, a man has to stop and make do with the music he's got. New music is just someone's old music. You take the music you been given and stick with it. It's all you get."

"What the fuck does that mean?"

"No idea. Remember, there's worse things to be called than 'cracker,' son."

"I'll remember that. So, do you have any fish food? You know, those little pellets?"

"Try these." He smiles and hands him the shotgun.

When Jack leaves, he's covered with every hair, feather and scale known to science, too. But it's invisible to the naked eye, not enough of a disguise to fool the animals waiting outside.

Didn't Odysseus try clinging to the bottom of a pig to escape? No, that was cousin Odell.

He looks into the cookie jar. The water's still low, but there's a gas station on the way. Gas station, slumlord, home. Reaching behind his back to secure the shotgun, his jeans stretch and he suddenly realizes he's got about five more fish jammed in his front pockets. He stares at them twitching in his palms, not remembering how he gathered them up like loose change. They've been without water for a half hour, almost as long as he's been without killing a cop. He sees pennies in the bottom of his football. Oops. Back in the water, the two fish do a lap and then start floating.

ANOTHER ONE on the corner. Cop number seven? He's a big buck though, worth about three of the regular ones. He sees what's under Jack's arm and laughs.

"I used to play football," the Seventh Cop says, holstering his Ruger but forgetting the snap like they always do. "Try to get by me."

"I used to play football, too," Jack says. "Until I realized the ball wasn't made of real pigskin."

At this, the cop looks furious and gives away the pivot foot he's going to use. Another tell. Jack runs, jukes, spins, skips, even jumps over a candlestick, and in the end, just like magic, he slips the tackle and he comes up with the cop's gun. He'll use his Ruger on him, of course, saving the shotgun shells, but he won't keep his weapon. He's still digging the .38. Police-issue since the '20s. They never should have stopped.

"Hell, how much shit can one man carry?" he asks the Seventh Cop who is crawling toward a drain as if it's the answer. "Sometimes you got to make a choice. Fish or guns."

At some point, the Seventh Cop is saying he doesn't deserve to die. Saying that he was only working tonight to do seatbelt checks at the corner. The shotgun shuts him up, and this murder feels like a crossroads. Only because Jack's on the 50-yard line now, and there's finally less field in front of him than behind.

DEEP INTO THE RAMPAGE, tiny dorsal fins are breaking the surface. He can smell them drying out, too. After hitting that pet store, there's now more fish than water. He needs to fill it back up. He crashes through the door chimes at a gas station, tracking blue blood and feathers in across the tile. At the counter, he asks a jaded clerk for the key to the toilet. Without looking up, the clerk grumbles "employees only." Shotgun behind his back, cookie jar in both hands, he clears his throat and sets it down next to the animal shelter donations and beef jerky.

"Listen, here's the thing. A goldfish swallowed all my money. And I need to pay the rent in about ten minutes to keep a roof over some miserable pregnant bitch's head. But tonight I've done so many things I never thought I would do just to keep these fish alive, and I'm not sure why. And for some ridiculous goddamn reason, I feel the need to protect them no matter what. So, if you could just let us all swim in your toilet a little while, you'd really be helping me out."

Jack counts to eleven as the clerk looks up, chews some gum, and soaks in the story.

"Go ahead," the clerk finally says, as if his story made perfect sense. "Back through the cooler past the power drinks."

It's the most compassion Jack has ever felt for another human being. But not fish, of course. He splashes water in the bowl, on his face, and the cold water revives the goldfish just as much as the clerk revived him. Tonight he feels like he can kill every cop on the planet. Then fold them in half nine times.

Outside the gas station, he kills his Eighth Cop, a woman of all things. He was starting to forget they existed. He has no guilt as he empties his Glock for good, the rest of the clip overwhelming a carefully placed shot from her SigP229 meant to stop his heart but having no discernible effect. No guilt at all as he thinks back to all the role-playing porn he snuck into the bathroom in school and how women in any position of authority, teacher, doctor, librarian, hell, even a four-star general, were his favorites. With one exception. A ragged mag he stole from his daddy, one with an especially baffling title that should have reduced any chance of intimidation, *Busty Cops III: Calling All Eunuchs!*

But when he opened it up . . . nothing. It was only the spreads where a woman dressed as a cop that killed his erections. Now he was paying them back for every one.

HE'S IN FIELD GOAL range, but he chooses to run. He stiff-arms a pimp, stiff-arms a bum, stiff-arms a crazy cat lady that stinks like piss who makes a grab for the ball. Breathing hard through a hole in his chest, he takes a time-out at an open-all-night drive-thru where the miniature golf course used to be. There's a girl at the window he's been eyeing, and he thinks tonight's the night to take his imaginary relationship to the next level. When he first saw her, she just said "hello," all formal. Then it was "hi." Last time it was "oh, hey." All the encouragement he needs.

He's sure he senses recognition when she sees him. And she does. But only because she can see him on the camera before he gets to the window. It's recognition from twenty yards back that he mistakes for encouragement.

"Oh, hey."

"Can I get some water?"

"No walk-ups, sir," she says as a full minute ticks by. Then, "Get the fuck out of here."

"Um . . . I'll take a bag of goldfish crackers, please."

"We only sell those with our chicken soup."

"If you give me a bag of goldfish crackers, you'll never see me again, I promise."

"Coming right up!"

She throws a handful of bags at him and slams the window shut. Running again, he's thinking he can swap the crackers out with the goldfish. But the crackers don't look anything like he remembers. Way too small. And there's too many flavors to choose from.

He drops a couple into the football anyway, but the experiment's a failure. They stain the water like piss and blood as he watches them dissolve. Bad idea, sure. But nowhere near his worst.

Still almost as much fish as water. Always almost as much fish as water.

RUNNING HARD. Running hard. Inside the 15-yard line. Goalposts in sight.

The slumlord.

The only person on the block who can afford a satellite antenna that big.

He passes a priest locking up a church. Sunday morning already? He punches him in the face on the way by, a tenderizer right hook where his smile used to be.

"Why?!" the priest wails from the sidewalk.

"Because it's the nicest thing I've done all night, daddy, I mean, father."

Over his shoulder, he sees the priest slump and vanish under his long black coat, and Jack can't resist a joke his daddy told him after he punched his first nun on a Sunday.

"I thought you'd be tougher than that, Batman!"

RUNNING. RUNNING. RUNNING. Two bullets made his leg faster. One bullet made his heart stronger. He asks the next cop what the fuck a seatbelt check is.

"That's like saying it's a 'smile check' or something," Jack laughs. "I mean, I would just make sure I'm not smiling by the time you got to my car."

"What are you talking about?" the Ninth Cop asks, hand hovering over his holster.

"How could you prove I wasn't wearing it?" Jack asks, scratching and stretching hard to reach the spot on his back where the shotgun is nested. "Unless you roll some obstacle out into the path of the car to make me wreck. So, is *that* what a seatbelt check is? Never mind."

The shotgun comes over his head as the Ninth Cop draws his Springfield XD. A small gun. Something the new kids are packing. It's no match. He wonders if the Blues Man was right. Do they think he's just white enough to hesitate? Does it give him the edge? Now he remembers the story. His cousin Odell didn't hide under a pig to sneak out of that cave.

He hid under a sheep.

Boom.

Daddy always called cops "Lloyds," and Jack thought that was their real name until he turned 18. Turned out it was short for "mongoloids," which seemed harsh for a whole hour after he first deciphered it.

Another dead fish in the football. Only three left swimming. He cuts it open with a thumbnail to see that it's empty. Is he crying? No, just blood. He needs to kill another cop to even the score. Will that make ten? He needs the same number of fish to keep track easier. That shouldn't be too hard.

The Tenth Cop dies screaming, so Jack decides to gut him this time. When he runs out of thumbnails, he uses the edge of a handcuff. Turns out they look just like us on the inside. The fish, not the cops. But he swears their hearts might be a little smaller. The cops. Not the fish.

SLUMLORD THEN HOME. No. Home then slumlord. He's got five minutes. He needs to see his woman. Needs to see if it was all worth it. He paid her debt with the junkie, gonna pay the rent next. He even paid for her teeth once, even though she only used the appointment to get pain killers, and she didn't thank him then either.

He calls her on a pay phone to put a toe in the water, and she's yelling already. Never any good news with her.

"Why the fuck are you calling me? I can see you from here!"

He runs up the steps of their building, the burning smell he recognizes immediately as home. The smell of smoke and ash used to tell a cavemen to run. Now it meant dinner. Or her kiss. She turns the corner, a cigarette in each corner of her mouth. Yep, it's just her. Arms crossed and a gas can balanced on eight months of stomach. Maybe it's not dinner after all.

"Where's the fucking rent?"

She's threatened to burn down the building before. Every time they fight. He's even woken up soaked in it, the smell so thick it cured him of his boyhood love of huffing the stuff.

He shows her his .38, pleased with the way her cigarettes sag in shock.

"Hold on, baby, that's what I'm trying to tell you," he sighs. "It's not this gun that makes me a man. It's how many fish I got in my football."

"Huh?"

"Do you have any idea how hard it was to get them here?"

She starts to notice the blood and slowly sets down the gas can. He starts to notice her noticing the blood and slowly sets down his cookie jar. Then he's suddenly rabbit-fucking her against their cleanest wall, and for a couple seconds loves her. When he's done, his toes wiggle so hard he fears they'll finally bust through his shoes. Then they both stare over each other's shoulders as the feeling fades from love, to like, to hate, to indifference.

At least I can't get her any more pregnant, he thinks. *Once they're knocked up, it doesn't have any effect anymore. Maybe each time we fuck, I change the baby's eye color or something.*

"Go on," she sighs. He looks at the clock. The craziest hour he's ever had in his life.

"Baby, you ever been on the toilet and all the sounds and sensations coming from your body seem to indicate that you're taking a shit but then you look into the bowl and don't see anything at all?"

"No."

"Well, that's our relationship."

"Out!" she screams, gas can back up and ready.

"Wait! You misunderstand! You're not listening, bitch! I'm saying that we're 'magic'!"

His woman is flipping out, saying if his bullshit story is true, the money might dissolve, and she's reaching for his fish. Again, he worries the $1,000 bill has never been in any of them.

"Which one is it?!" she screams, splashing around the cookie jar with her yellow claw.

When you get too many fish in your football, he thinks, *you just have to pick one and stick with it. Now that's something daddy should have said.*

"You know what?" he scoffs, moving for the door, pride wounded. "I take back every goddamn romantic thing I just said."

"Good!"

Pick one and stick with it, he thinks. *Maybe that's what makes you a man. At least more man than cop. But not more man than goldfish.*

He takes one random fish and puts it in his pocket. He's still got a minute left on the clock. So he runs across the hall to his other woman's apartment, the one that's less pregnant.

HE TELLS HIS OTHER woman to stash one of his goldfish. She stands in the doorway, fish swimming around in the coffee cup propped on her belly. She hugs it tight. She's stashed guns and drugs for Jack before, but this fish feels more important than them all. She puts it on top of her television, hoping he'll pay her rent tonight so they won't be evicted.

Then he runs back across the hall to kill his first woman. His *first* woman, not his first *woman*. The first woman was cop number eight.

He doesn't take this lightly. He knows it would be wrong to compare it to the killing he's already done. Sure, he's learned many new ways to do it, but that was practice on one particular species. Woman is a whole 'nother animal.

When he kicks open the door and sees what she's doing, he knows he can do it.

She has a pile of flopping goldfish on her ironing board, knife coming down when he hits her like a linebacker.

"You can't kill 'em! I already named 'em!" he pleads from the floor.

"What fucking names?!" she hisses.

"Cheddar, pretzel, corn, ranch, cinnamon, pizza, graham, parmesan, chocolate, baby . . ."

She stabs him instead, stabs him again. He changes his mind about the fight real fast and decides to save as many fish as he can.

Crawling for the bathroom, fish in his fists, pockets, and mouth, he hopes the last person in there remembered to flush. On his hands and knees, he realizes that he'd try to keep them all alive forever if he could and never look inside, just so he'd never know they were empty all along. But none of them are moving when she sticks him in the back where his spine used to be. Before his last breath, he attempts to give them a proper burial.

He drops as many as he can in the bowl and pulls the lever as he falls. But they're too big to go down. His head cracks the rim and the lights go out.

HE'S AS SURPRISED as anyone when he starts breathing again. He opens his eyes to see one fish in the bowl under his chin. It's still swimming in circles.

"Too big to flush, huh?" he asks it. "So am I."

He struggles to his feet, grabs the fish, snatches the glass football from his woman's hands. As he's running down the steps, he sees more goldfish in the corner of his eye still in the cookie jar. Jesus Christ, how many fish are there in the world?

Outside in the intersection, the Amazing Andy is standing in the way no matter which way he chooses. He's seen better days. Blue uniform now purple, black tie wrapped around his head covering the hole where an eye used to be. He holds his other .38 Special, of course, the grip wrapped in rubber bands so it can hide under a shirt against skin without slipping.

"Back to nine." Jack sighs, cocking the shotgun.

During the fight, Jack soaks up three more bullets. Andy loses an ear and at least half his piano lessons along with the side of his head. When Andy's gun starts clicking, Jack snaps as many fingers as he can so there's no more tricks. Then he handcuffs him. Still struggling, Andy babbles about metal rings and handkerchiefs, and Jack spins one of his hands completely around, snapping it free from the burden of a wrist forever. It's past 7:00. It's overtime. It's sudden death.

"Bad move. The only thing I hate more than cops are magicians."

His own gun against the burger where his nose used to be, Jack pulls a tiny bag of goldfish crackers from his back pocket. Dangles them in Andy's face.

"Bet you can't eat a hundred."

"Never said I could."

"Check out these flavors," Jack says, reading the back of the bag. "Cheddar, pretzel, corn, ranch, cinnamon, pizza, graham, parmesan, chocolate, baby, and original. Makes your tongue curl, don't it? Whoa, does that say, 'baby' flavor?"

Forcing Andy's mouth open with the barrel, he pours the bag into his maw. Only they're not crackers. They're goldfish. Real ones. He ran out of pockets a long time ago. He taps his temple with the gun to keep the bloody mouthful crunching and munching and crunching away.

"Of all those flavors," Jack muses, "It's weird there's no seafood. No actual 'goldfish' goldfish crackers. You know what other flavor they need?"

"Murfg," Andy bleats around a mouthful of fins.

"Sweet Fucking Revenge."

Andy spits the pulp and scales to the street, trying to wipe his mouth with his shoulder.

"I'm the one out for revenge, motherfucker!" he shouts. "You shot *me*. I'm the unstoppable revenge machine in this equation!"

"Consider yourself stopped," Jack says, trying to curl his tongue to taste it.

He pulls the trigger and really isn't that surprised when it clicks. But he's surprised when the clicks keep on coming from all directions.

Jack turns around and around the four-way stop and sees the circle of blue and red, guns cocking, car doors popping. There's .38 Specials and Remington 187s for everybody. He counts cop number 10, 11, 12, 13, 14, 15, 16, 17, 18, 19, 20, and 21. And 22.

Jesus Christ, he laughs. *How many cops are there in the world? And unless someone's packing three hands, that's two more hiding behind that car door. Penalty. One too many players on the field . . .*

He can't believe no one blows a whistle.

Standing in the intersection, black tar cooking his bare feet, he remembers how he used to play "connect the dots" with the white lines on the road, dragging a brush load of white paint (once a jar of mayonnaise) past any intersection where the lines stopped. He connected every road he could find, knowing that the black void was the only thing that made people stop, the sense of a drop-off into darkness. It was the void that made a normal person stop, not the red sign at all. He looks up, squinting as a streetlight flickers on bright as the sun, burning through every cop like an X-ray. Jack sees that they aren't blue inside after all. Just gutless. He stands up taller than he thought possible, tucks the football under an arm, and lights a last cigarette. He wishes he could see this during a game. Last cigarettes, not the cops.

Then his nostrils flare as he realizes his woman switched the water with gasoline.

The fish are cooked white, no more gold, but he swears they're still swimming, taking fuel into their gills and open mouths like sweet nectar.

Touchdown. He spits his cigarette as he spikes the ball.

Fire and fish fry everywhere.

THE NEXT DAY, a newspaper screamed "Fish Bites Cop!"

After the autopsy, the blood and tangles of animal hairs on Jack's shoes were used to connect him to every unsolved murder in the city. Apparently, the last serial killer on the East Coast (and the first black one) still operated unchecked among those green fish tanks. Jack's body was buried, but they kept his feet in a box. And in secret, the worst cops called those rotten feet their "Rosetta Bones" (sometimes "The Fastest White Boy We Ever Saw") and used them to make sure no crime went unsolved in their state for at least a decade. Just like those same cops used to keep some poor bastard's hand in a locker to fingerprint every Saturday Night Special they needed for an unlawful shooting, whenever a case got "cold feet" as they now said instead of "cold case," they would walk Jack's feet across a corpse when no one was looking. Bam. Case closed.

But some cops would creep in to cradle those feet like puppies, remembering in awe how quick they moved that night.

And that last fish Jack stashed at his other woman's apartment was taken home by one strangely compassionate cop balancing on crutches and slings when she was finally detained and questioned. This cop wanted the fish as a birthday present for his son once enough publicity pictures were taken with it.

His son overfed it to death within a week. Then finding it too big to flush, he buried the goldfish under an exhaust-stained apple tree too close to the road, refusing to tell his dad where it was no matter how hard he shook him by the shoulders or how many nasty black apples he rattled loose over his head.

So, a year later, the boy snuck out of bed to dig up the grave and see the bones, only to end up slowly unfolding a thousand dollar bill in the glare of a street light instead, a particularly incompetent counterfeit, one of hundreds collected and framed for laughs by a local parole officer who also happened to be a recently downsized Secret Service agent.

His daddy tried to take it away.

And the cop ended up on the ground, curling like a bug, protecting his head from a flash of fists and hate where his son used to be.

BOARD THE HOUSE UP

Zach Sherwood

THE DOOR WAS WIDE OPEN. Garrett had one earbud dangling, the other still had Mick whispering to him something about wild horses. He thought he had heard a scream. He tried to sing along about the wild horses to try and get that wild idea out of his head. His blast furnace of a brain smelted all solid rational thought into his own cast of soupy logic, which in turn, allowed him to do these wild things with a clear mind. That's what his brain was working hard to do right now, so "wild horses couldn't drag me away" came out as "wild horses couldn't snag any hay." He never could get it right. Garrett was a wild horse. He couldn't snag any hay either. Hay was reserved for domesticated horses, who were tamed and cared for, and Garrett was neither of these things. He still felt he had an obligation to protect this block as it used to be on his patrol route, which was now his jogging route. Deputy Sheriff Garrett Gittes was on call (or at least in his mind) as he proceeded to march up to the house—this was just the thing to shorten that suspension of his (or at least in his mind).

459, he thought, which was ten-code for burglary. It was a conventional 2-story home, much like all the others on the block, sky blue in color with white accents around everything else. He suspected it housed a father, a mother, and 2.47 kids (or whatever was the national average at the time). The neighborhood was one of those that had that same uniform shade of green grass lying in front of each picture perfect suburban home. At 6:33 AM this door shouldn't be wide open, and Garrett shouldn't be thinking about what he thought of doing. He crept up to the door and inspected the frame for signs of forced entry before he poked his head through it without bringing his feet across the plane. He reached at his shoulder for a radio that wasn't there. Embarrassed at this reflexive response he bobbled inside and closed the door behind him.

Garrett processed his surroundings. It was just as lovely inside as it was outside, but one minor hindrance called attention to itself. Lying straight ahead of him in the kitchen was an overturned chair—that shouldn't be like that, thought Garrett. Garrett decided he could: A) walk straight past the foyer into the kitchen, B) walk right into the living room and circle around, C) walk left into the dining room and circle around, D) walk up the stairs, or E) leave. Garrett chose C; he was surprisingly hesitant to go into the kitchen head first. The dining room had an enormous rug which was covered with floral patterns and intertwining geometric choreographies. Upon it was a dark wooden table with 6 chairs, 6 plates, and 6 sets of silverware; it appeared as if dinner was about to be served. All these peculiar little alloy bits were being compiled by Garrett's blast furnace. He certainly did not belong in this house, especially in his jogging outfit, but Garrett imagined himself cloaked in the black of his police uniform with his badge gleaming, gun unholstered, and helpful hand extended. He thought he was going to find Jimmy Hoffa's body or the Hope Diamond in the next room. His brain produced an image of tomorrow's *Pittsburgh Post* with the headline reading "SUSPENDED DEPUTY HERO REINSTATED!" Garrett smirked. He was absolutely delirious. However, in the kitchen wasn't Jimmy Hoffa's body or the Hope Diamond. Instead there was a scattered mess of utensils which extended from the stainless steel fridge around the island to a drawer that had been ripped off its rails, which then met up with some red smears and smudges near the overturned chair leading toward the den. 10-42, he thought. Garrett stalwartly moved across the spattered black and white tile of the kitchen until he reached the dark den.

The only light was muddied through the thick grey curtains over the doors leading outside. It had a leather couch across from the television set, a body near the flipped over table, and a well-beaten recliner next to the fireplace; of these items Garrett seemed most concerned about the body. Garrett fumbled for the light switch with both hands and flicked it on. The body slowly, but jerkily, rose to the introduction of this bothersome bright light. He looked like death, but the red stitching on his light blue work shirt said his name was "Walter." Garrett lost his focus and took a step back horrified, then took another step forward cautiously to try and help him over onto the couch. Walter's frail skin was too tight for his face, especially for a man that was seemingly only in his thirties, thought Garrett. Walter had a hollowed look to him, his head looked like it had been pumped full of battery acid that was slowly eating him from the inside out. Garrett noticed Walter's neck. It was shredded into red licorice ribbons and was slowly leaking out the little of the remaining blood he had left in his body since most of his blood was carpeting the den's floor.

"Walter? Is there an intruder in the household?" inquired Garrett. Garrett didn't even think to ask if Walter was alright or not; justice was the first thing on his mind. Walter stood there in the middle of the room as if it were the first time using his legs. He looked vacantly at Garrett with this same type of bewildered wonder. This man was not all there. Garrett went to repeat his question, but Walter's gaze caught him, which went past his skin to stare at his heart beat and the blood that travelled through it.

"Sir, I'm going to phone for backup," nervously assured Garrett. He tried his best policeman voice to emanate a sense of comfort through his stern authoritative tone, but it came out sounding like how he had when responding to the chief that told him of his suspension. He slowly backed out of the room, keeping his body square to Walter until the last second possible. Much like everything else in this house, the phone wasn't how it was supposed to be. It laid on the ground ripped off from the wall. It seemed Garrett wasn't the first person today to try and make an urgent phone call. He reached at his pockets, but remembered that he had left his cell phone with the empty inbox in the car before jogging. The man who was not all there was now there in the doorway of the kitchen.

"Walter, can you speak?" No response. "My name is Gary, I need to know what happened." No response. Garrett disliked his name, people close to him called him Gary. Garrett didn't have anyone close to him. He did not know what to do, his primordial urge to help his fellow man was tugging at his sleeve, but obviously something was not right. 9560, he thought. Garrett always thought in this automated fashion, referring to police codes to himself. Walter began to bobble over towards Garrett, who put his hands in front of him as if to make a force field to keep the man back.

"Sit down, you shouldn't be walking around." No response, he made his way past the knocked over stool. "You need medical attention." No response, he made his way past the broken phone. "Sir, stop where you are." No response, he made his way past the drawer. "I can help you."

No response, he made his way past the island. With limited options, he could: A) destroy Walter, or B) hide in the bathroom to the left of him. Walter looked human enough for Garrett to reconsider using force, as last time he did it cost him his job. Garrett chose B. He dashed for the door and slammed it behind him.

His back slid against the door as he lowered himself to the floor while turning the light on then reaching up again to lock the door. The bathroom was very colorful. Pastel stripes ran laps around the tiny bathroom while a nautical net with seashells and starfish served as a finish line on the adjacent wall. This cheerful setting was a welcome change compared to everything outside of the room. A rumble behind him disrupted this string of thought. Walter was banging against the door. Garrett glued his feet to the ground and tried to combat the attempt to bring the door down. Someone screamed upstairs, a girl, followed by a storm of heavy footsteps swooping in from above him. He wasn't the only one to take notice, as the banging stopped on the door.

Garrett, relieved and huddled on the floor, could see the top of his short blonde hair peeking from above the sink in the mirror as he slowly began to rise to look at his reflection. Garrett's square and narrow head, which also mirrored his overall body type, appeared to have been crushed by a trash compactor at some point of his life. The soft glaze of his beard was there to tell the few that knew of his situation that he wasn't taking care of himself as much as he used to. The tiny slits of his eyes could hardly show his emotions, they were simply there to feed Garrett's brain information to make more ill-advised decisions about. He splashed his face with some water and took a good hard stare at himself. Someone needed help upstairs, but there wasn't much to arm himself with: a curling iron, a plunger, a hairdryer, or a picture frame. "Cancun 2002" was written underneath the rainbow frame. There was a man (which wasn't Walter), there was a woman, and there were 2 kids, a boy and a girl; they looked happy. Garrett studied the picture; he wanted more out of his life besides just his job. He only was on the force for three years before this lofty suspension and he wondered if he had really forgotten how to live his life outside of this. Garrett then took notice of the thick wrought iron towel bar, which at each end had a spiraling metallic pine cone shape. Garrett gripped it with both hands as he gave it a few wiggles to loosen the screws out of the drywall before he gave it a hard tug tearing the bar out along with a good amount of the wall; the house winced. He picked the pieces of drywall off it and gave it a little practice swing.

The door slowly creaked open as Garrett poked his head out and looked both ways before crossing through the kitchen and into the hallway towards the stairs. Walter was nowhere to be found, perhaps he returned back to his dark den since dawn was just beginning to tear through the windows of the house. Along the wall against the stairs were pictures of the family: family portraits, school photographs of the kids, birthday pictures, etc. He was jealous of the life this family had, even with Walter roaming around being a nuisance. An unrecognizable form at the top step was contoured by a flashing white light somewhere behind it. A crimson puddle slinkyed down the stairs in an array of canals and ravines. Garrett's eyes sailed up the bloody tributary to the mouth of the ruddy river, which was also accompanied by a full set of teeth, a nose, and two eyes looking toward the heavens. Garrett lurched up the stairs and got down on his knees to the fallen woman. He held his fingers against her throat desperately scanning for a pulse. No response.

Flustered, he stood himself up and peered down the hall. A ceiling fan produced a dreary drone, which was quite unsettling to Garrett. The door at the end was wide open with a flickering glow strobing outward. The walls were covered with more family pictures. Garrett tried to focus on the sickening pulsing of the white light and tried to ignore the smiles teasing him from his peripherals. He gripped the pipe tighter. Garrett's heart was skipping at irregular beats and felt as if it would break through his chest at any second only to run down the stairs and out the door to find someone who would put it to better use. He was at the door, he extended his weapon into it to open it. Inside it looked as if Jackson Pollock had been here painting with a bucket of human entrails. Something, a boy, perhaps the son from the photograph, thought Garrett, was all over the place. A knocked over television set had wild black ants attacking the white screen sending a dizzying static spectrum of flashes across the already morbid scene. At the foot of the bed, the father was knelt over the central hub of his son's extremities as his head bobbed up and down with each snarling bite.

This man is a monster, thought Garrett. "Hey," yelled Garrett, not knowing what else to say, as he stood tall with his makeshift club at his side. No response. Garrett was fed up with getting no responses today.

The figure levitated up to turn around. He wore a crown of blood, a bib of human tissue, and the gaze of the devil. His face looked like it had been gnarled by the tip of a jackhammer only to be illicitly repaired with clay to make him appear somewhat human again. Garrett thought he deserved a response. He made a lunge forward and frantically slammed the bar against the side of the father's head. The bar flew back from the impact and the vibrations resonated through Garrett's arm, but he pulled back again and sent another crushing blow that sent half of the father's face to join part of his son on the dresser. The father tumbled backwards as his calves caught the bottom of the bed frame. Garrett moved to the edge of the bed and delivered another whack that sent his nose into his head. The father's arms began to reach upward for his throat as Garrett held him down with his free hand. That gaze was still there, but one of his eyes wasn't. Garrett pulled back and dropped another blow that bent the bar at nearly a right angle. He flung it aside and grabbed the father's shirt and began to wallop away with his fists; not even wild horses could drag him away. Garrett's shoes struggled for grip in the swamp of the son's intestines and accompanying bodily fluids; he was putting his whole body into every passionate strike. His body was pumping loads of adrenaline through his body while he did his own Jackson Pollack impression, using the ivory satin sheets as a canvas. Soon enough the father's arms and legs had stopped struggling as Garrett's fists were getting closer and closer to the bed itself. Garrett would have kept punching until his fist met the bed and he wasn't punching the father's head anymore, but just the space where the molecules that once made up the father's head were; matter cannot be created nor destroyed—Garrett was about to try and detest the second part. Garrett's mind was yelling at him to keep hitting, but his knuckles were screaming not to. He wildly took a step back from the bed. Off balance, swaying on one foot with his chest held out, he nearly fell down as he slipped on what could have been a pancreas and stared at his masterpiece. Who was the monster now.

Garrett fell to the floor in pain and stared at his mauled hands that looked like the terrain of a ballooning desert due to the abhorrent amount of swelling and cuts. Something was obviously broken inside him. He didn't want to look up. The television kept spewing its seizure of monochromatic madness into the room. He had to get out. Garrett clumsily swung himself off the floor and drunkenly stumbled into the hallway, when the soft sound of sobbing swiftly sobered him up. It was coming from a door down the hall.

"Hello?" asked Garrett, shaken.

There was a whimper, a girl's whimper. "Who's there? I'm not opening this door, get away," yelled the voice, also shaken.

"I'm a police officer, I'm here to help you," replied Garrett erratically. He heard the lock click and the door swung opened to a frightened girl. Startled, she took a step backward awkwardly yielding a butcher knife with both hands. She looked like she was made of porcelain. Garrett was afraid if he touched her she'd break into a million pieces as she already had a crude bandage around a crack in the ankle hinting red.

"Why are you covered in blood? You're not a cop! Where's your uniform? Get away from me," screeched the daughter.

Garrett was choking for words. "I heard a scream," leveled Garrett.

"Get out," fired back the daughter before he could finish explaining himself.

"Calm down, what's your name? Are you okay? I see your ankle is hurt. I am a cop," pleaded Garrett.

"What did you do to my family?"

"Nothing! I heard a scream, I'm a cop." He was beginning to sound like a broken record, and this teenage girl did not know how to deal with broken records as she grew up on CDs and .MP3s. He was leisurely getting closer, hoping she'd recognize him as human. She got frightened when he got within arm's reach and she stuck the knife into his stomach. He stumbled backwards, crashing into the hallway, sending a shockwave through the wall that knocked down most of the pictures. The door slammed shut with a click. The only human that was seemingly all human hurt him more than the other beasts lurking around the house. He slid down the wall clutching the open wound while staring at the empty puddle of blood that was still waterfalling down the steps.

This house was not what it seemed, it had all the makings of a typical house: doors, windows, walls, floors; but this house was not like any other house he'd ever been to. Garrett was a horrible house guest here and there was no way he'd get all that father out of the sheets no matter how hard he scrubbed. He struggled getting up, clutching at his wound. Garrett was on his feet and began to head over to the stairs where the lone blood pool was serving as a welcome mat to this scene of horror. The glow of the flashing television seemed to subside. He stopped to turn around.

A woman appeared from the room to the right of where the son and father were laid to rest. The television's glow behind her casted a long distorted shadow from her silhouette that seemed to claw at Garrett's feet; he moved his feet as if to get out of her grasp. It was the mother that he had seen staring up at the heavens only moments before.

"I'm sorry. I really am, but I couldn't watch him do that," whimpered Garrett. No response; the motorized drone of the ceiling fan seemed to mock the emotionality of Garrett's plea. She started to shuffle down the hall.

"I'm a deputy sheriff and I had to intervene. He was eating him. Him. Your son," cried Garrett. No response; the fan was still laughing and she was still shambling. This phantom of a woman was surrounded by shades of her former self glaring at her from the walls as she hobbled down the hall, arms stretched out. His shoes were soaking in her blood from the puddle he'd seen her lying in not too long ago when she looked very much dead. She still looked very much dead, yet was on her feet now.

"I just needed to be a hero," said Garrett softly, as she extended her icy grasp around him. Garrett tried prying her snarling mouth away from him. His hand against her forehead was ineptly tilting her head back as the other tried peeling her hand off his shoulder. She sunk her teeth into his swollen broken hand. Garrett cried out in pain as she took a part of him away as he tossed all of her away down the staircase. The first step her neck met created a boom that sent her body cart wheeling like a rag doll. The second step she met tossed her laterally and changed her cart wheel into a barrel roll with her arms flailing. The third step her neck met nearly spun her head completely around as her body slowed to a dead stop.

Garrett peered down from the top step and waited for a new puddle of blood to form at the base of the stairs. His hand pulsated with pain. A pain different than the one in his stomach. Pins and needles. This house was evil, he thought, but he belonged here. Razorblades and tent spikes. Garrett wanted to grab a hammer and some nails to put boards across every window and door of the house. Screwdrivers and daggers. He wanted to board the house up. He didn't want anyone to come inside to witness what took place in here. Rebar and shiskabob skewers. He thought he could save the world, but he couldn't even save Pittsburgh as a deputy sheriff, let alone save this one family. How was I capable of doing any of this, he pondered sourly, what happened to me. Harpoons and javelins. All these prickly items were flowing up his arm and dissipating through the rest of his body—he was losing it, thoughts scattering, vision blurring, heartbeat slowing, hunger growing. He was no hero and this house proved it. Garrett entered the castle, foiled the guards, slayed the dragon, but the princess foiled his plans for heroism. He didn't want a badge anymore as much as he wanted blood now. Everyone was dead, thought Garrett, well, besides the daughter and himself (in a sense). Garrett haggardly marched down the stairs—he needed to find a hammer. He was going to board the house up, his house. After all, he did have his own daughter now.

ABOUT THE AUTHORS

RANDY CHANDLER is the author of two novels, *Bad Juju* and *Hellz Bellz*, and is the co-author (with the late t. Winter-Damon) of *Duet for the Devil*. He has written numerous short stories, including those in the new Twilight Detective series, the first of which appears online at thuglit.com.

TIM CURRAN lives in Michigan and is the author of the novels *Skin Medicine, Hive*, and *Dead Sea*. Upcoming projects include the novels *Resurrection* and *The Devil Next Door*. His short stories have appeared in such magazines as *City Slab, Flesh&Blood, Book of Dark Wisdom*, and *Inhuman*, as well as anthologies such as *Flesh Feast, Shivers IV*, and *Vile Things*. Find him on the web at: www.corpseking.com.

JOHN EVERSON is the Bram Stoker Award-winning author of the novels *Covenant, Sacrifice* and *The 13th*. John shares a deep purple den in Naperville, Illinois with a cockatoo and cockatiel, a disparate collection of fake skulls, twisted skeletal fairies and a large stuffed Eeyore. In order to avoid the onerous task of writing, he records pop-rock songs in a hidden home studio, experiments with the insatiable culinary joys of the jalapeno, designs photo collage art bookcovers and chases frequent excursions into the bizarre visual headspace of '70s euro-horror DVDs with a shot of Makers Mark and a tall glass of Newcastle. Visit him at www.johneverson.com.

BRANDON FORD has written 3 novels; *Crystal Bay, Splattered Beauty*, and the soon to be released *Pay Phone*. He has also contributed to the anthologies *Abaculus 2007, Abaculus III, Sinister Landscapes, Raw: Brutality as Art*, and *Creeping Shadows*, a collection of 3 short novels. He currently resides in Philadelphia.

KELLY M. HUDSON grew up in the wilds of Kentucky and currently resides in California. He has a deep and abiding love for all things horror and rock n' roll, and if you wish to contact Kelly or find links to other stories, please visit www.kellymhudson.com for further details. Kelly thanks you for reading his dumb old story and wishes you and yours a very happy day!

DAVID JAMES KEATON's fiction has recently appeared in *Big Pulp, Six Sentences, Pulp Pusher, Espresso Stories* and *Crooked*. He is a contributor to *The College Rag* and the University of Pittsburgh's online journal *Hot Metal Bridge*. He is also a part-time graduate student at Pitt and a full-time closed captioner. He is constantly rewriting three screenplays; a prison movie, a thriller, and a western. And although he should be working on a fifth novel, he continues to unwisely cram more material into his first, a book which can, at this point, land comfortably on one of six sides if dropped from chest level. Usually this happens when someone checks the page count. Find him occasionally at buglove.blogspot.com.

SCOTT NICHOLSON is the author of seven novels, including *They Hunger* and *The Skull Ring*. He's published more than 60 stories, six comic books, five screenplays, and two collections. A freelance editor and journalist, Nicholson's website is www.hauntedcomputer.com.

TOM PICCIRILLI is the author of twenty novels including *The Cold Spot, The Coldest Mile, A Choir of Ill Children*, and the forthcoming *Shadow Season*. He's won the International Thriller Award and four Bram Stoker Awards, as well as having been nominated for the Edgar, the World Fantasy Award, the Macavity, and Le Grand Prix de L'imagination. Learn more at his blog at www.thecoldspot.blogspot.com.

ZACH SHERWOOD lives between homes in Chicago at the University of Illinois at Chicago, and back with his family in the south suburbs. Things like zombies, cowboys, and grizzly bears frequent his mind as he aspires to create dark witty works of fiction.

DAVID TALLERMAN spent four years at York University studying English Literature, specializing in the literary history of witchcraft—a specialization he totally failed to capitalize on by becoming an IT Technician. Over the last couple of years, he's had published reviews, poetry, a comic strip, and numerous stories across a variety of genres. Highlights include appearances in *Chiaroscuro, Pseudopod* and *Flash Fiction Online*, and having a zombie story printed alongside the work of genre luminaries like Neil Gaiman and Stephen King in Night Shade Books' *The Living Dead anthology*. Find him on the web at www.davidtallerman.net and davidtallerman.blogspot.com

FRED VENTURINI has written in exchange for various treasures, including an MFA from Lindenwood University, contributer's copies, token payments, checks that sometimes do not bounce, and most of all, for the love of the act. His fiction, most of it horrific in nature, has recently appeared or is forthcoming in *River Styx, Polluto, Underground Voices, Necrotic Tissue, Twisted Dreams*, and others.

ERIK WILLIAMS lives in Southern California with his wife and daughter. His stories have appeared in *Greatest Uncommon Denominator, Apex Digest, Necrotic Tissue* and other small press venues. His novellas *Blood Spring* and *The Reverend's Powder*, as well as his novel *Demon*, have all recently been sold and will be published in the near future.

SIMON WOOD is an ex-racecar driver, a licensed pilot and an occasional private investigator. His short fiction has appeared in a variety of magazines anthologies, such as *Seattle Noir, Thriller 2* and *Woman's World*. He's a frequent contributor to *Writer's Digest*. He's the Anthony Award winning author of *Working Stiffs, Accidents Waiting to Happen, Paying the Piper* and *We All Fall Down*. As Simon Janus, he's the author of *The Scrubs* and *Road Rash*. His next thriller, *Terminated*, will be out next June. Curious people can learn more at www.simonwood.net.

LaVergne, TN USA
09 September 2010
196491LV00009B/66/P